SECRET ORIGINS

STORY THIEVES

SECRET ORIGINS

JAMES RILEY

ALADDIN

NEW YORK   LONDON   TORONTO   SYDNEY   NEW DELHI

ALADDIN

An imprint of Simon & Schuster Children's Publishing Division

1230 Avenue of the Americas, New York, New York 10020

First Aladdin hardcover edition January 2017

Text copyright © 2017 by James Riley

Jacket illustrations copyright © 2017 by Vivienne To

Interior illustrations by Patrick Spaziante copyright © 2017 by Simon & Schuster, Inc.

For information about special discounts for bulk purchases, please contact Simon & Schuster Special Sales at 1-866-506-1949 or business@simonandschuster.com.

The Simon & Schuster Speakers Bureau can bring authors to your live event. For more information or to book an event contact the Simon & Schuster Speakers Bureau at 1-866-248-3049 or visit our website at www.simonspeakers.com.

Jacket designed by Laura DiSiena

Interior designed by Tom Daly

The text of this book was set in Adobe Garamond.

Manufactured in the United States of America 1216 FFG

2 4 6 8 10 9 7 5 3 1

This book has been cataloged with the Library of Congress.

ISBN 978-1-4814-6125-2 (hc)

ISBN 978-1-4814-6127-6 (eBook)

Dedicated to authors, the true villains of every book.

Change is coming.

CHAPTER 1

The evil King of All Stories held his enormous eraser to Bethany's head as she tried to escape.

"It's too late, heroes!" the king told Owen, Kiel, and Charm. "There's nothing you can do! Now I'll erase the parts of Bethany's life story that make her a good person, thereby turning her into my evil minion. Then, together, we'll invade the nonfictional world and rule everything!"

"Let her go!" Owen shouted. "Or you won't like what comes next."

The evil King of All Stories sneered. "You? The nonfictional hero who's saved the fictional world more times than I can count? You have no power here, boy."

"Don't I?" Owen took out paper and a pencil and began writing.

The King of All Stories drops his eraser.

The king's eraser immediately dropped out of his hand. "What?" the king shouted in amazement. "But *how?*"

"Through the power of *words!*" Owen shouted. "Books are magical, and so is writing!" He wrote something else on the paper.

The King of All Stories lets Bethany go, then trips on his own feet.

The king let go of Bethany, then spectacularly wiped out on his next step, doing a front flip before landing hard on his back. The Crown of Stories fell off his head and rolled a few feet away.

The Crown of Stories appears on Owen's head, Owen wrote.

Immediately, the crown disappeared from the ground, then reappeared on Owen's head. It was exactly the right size, as if it were made for him all along.

"No!" the former king shouted from the ground. "You can't do this to me. This is all I had!"

"*Not true,*" Owen said, turning to his former

archenemy. "This isn't you, Your Majesty. You're not meant to be evil. Someone's rewritten *your* story, just as you tried to do for Bethany."

"I'm not?" the former king said. "Then what *was* I meant to be?"

"A father," Owen said quietly, then wrote something on his paper.

The former King of All Stories turns back into his real self.

Instantly a bright light filled the room, then spread out over the entire Kingdom of Stories, blinding anyone who happened to be looking at the castle at that moment. The light enveloped the former king, raising him into the air in a completely awesome way.

The light became too bright to look at, and they all covered their eyes except Owen, who wrote himself sunglasses that made him look even cooler. Then abruptly, the light disappeared and everything went dark.

"Looks like this story," Owen said, pulling off his sunglasses, "just started a new chapter."

Bethany slowly stepped past Owen, her eyes on

3

the figure on the ground. The former king was no longer dressed in royal robes. Now he wore normal clothes, and his hair had turned the same shade as Bethany's, a bronzish red.

The man shook his head, then slowly pushed to his feet, his mouth hanging open.

"... Bethany?" he said, his eyes widening.

"Dad?" she said, not believing it.

"It's me, Beth," her dad said, holding out his arms. "You've saved me! I never thought I'd be able to turn back to my true self, but you've done it!"

Bethany ran forward and jumped into her dad's arms, knocking them both to the ground. "Dad!" she shouted. "I can't believe it's you! Owen, you *did* it!"

"I've never seen anything so sweet," Kiel said from Owen's side, rubbing his eyes.

"I have," Charm said, looking at Owen as her hand slipped into his.

The white paw of a black cat touched Owen's hand, and he stopped writing. Spike, Owen's fictional self's former cat, glanced up at Owen from his desk with a look that said, *Really?*

"Too much?" Owen asked his fictional cat.

Spike just blinked his eyes slowly, leaving his paw on Owen's hand.

"I have," Charm said, looking at Owen with affection.

Spike dug his claws into Owen's hand, and Owen sighed. "Fine."

"Really?" Charm said, stepping away from the other two. "No one else thinks this is a trap? I'm the only one?"

Spike took his paw off of Owen's hand and began to purr contentedly as he closed his eyes to nap again.

"You know, *I'm* the one who's writing this," Owen said. "And it's not exactly easy. Maybe at least hold your judgment until it's done?"

Spike briefly opened his eyes, then closed them again, completely unmoved.

Owen absently scratched his cat's stomach, reading over what he had written. *Ugh.* Why was it all so bad? Did every writer have this problem? Everything just seemed so . . . obvious. Make the villain Bethany's dad? It'd been done a thousand times.

He began to idly tap the keys without pressing them while

he stared off into space. When he glanced back at the computer, though, there were new words. Apparently he'd been typing without realizing it?

"Owen," said a man who appeared out of nowhere, with no features or details anywhere on his body. The mannequin-looking man had his back to the Owen in the story as he spoke to the real Owen. "Stop this at once. You're manipulating fictional characters' lives. Do you have any idea what you're doing here?"

Owen's eyes widened as he read the lines, while at his side, Spike began to growl, low and menacing. Owen hadn't just written those words . . . had he?

And then more text appeared on the screen, without Owen even moving his hands.

"Do not write again," Nobody said. "I don't want to have to tell you this twice." And with that, he disappeared.

A chill went through Owen, and he quickly reread the last few lines. What had just happened? Was that *really* Nobody? And if so, was Owen actually messing with real fictional people's lives? Had he just created another fictional Owen?

He quickly highlighted the entire story, ready to hit the delete button, then froze. What if he *had* created new people, and was now going to delete them? Would that take them out of existence somehow? His finger hovered over the button as he looked to Spike for an answer. But now that Nobody was gone, the cat seemed to have returned to his nap, not paying any attention.

Should he delete the story, or was that worse? If only there was someone he could ask—

"OWEN!" shouted someone from mere inches away.

Owen screamed and tumbled out of his chair, while Spike tore away across the room, hiding under the bed. His heart racing, Owen turned to find Bethany's head sticking out of a piece of paper on his desk, and he gave her the dirtiest look he could.

"Don't *do* that! You scared me half to death!" She'd given him a page from a book she kept hidden under her bed. In case of emergencies (fictional characters escaping their books, libraries burning down, that kind of thing) she could jump in one page, move to the next part of the story, then pop out of his. But it was *not* meant for terrifying him!

"Good, you should be scared!" she said, breathing heavily. "Because that guy is back on the street again, the one who keeps watching my house!"

Owen groaned loudly. "Seriously? This again?"

"Oh, is my being stalked by a crazy person boring to you?" Bethany asked, giving him a sarcastic look. "Get over here and help me spy on him!" She moved her head to the side, and one hand popped out of the page.

Owen shook his head. "No way. Remember what happened last time I came over to check on this guy?"

Bethany rolled her eyes. "He wasn't there, but only because he must have seen us coming!"

"And the time before that?"

"That one, I got the car wrong."

"And we terrified that poor old lady!"

"Then she shouldn't be acting so suspiciously!" Bethany yelled, her hand flying around wildly. "Who sits in their car for ten minutes at eleven at night?"

"She couldn't get it started!"

"That's what she wanted us to think," Bethany said, glancing around suspiciously. "Hurry up, or he might leave again!"

"Which would mean he's not actually spying on you," Owen said, sighing. "Bethany, it's been a while since we jumped into a book—"

"Two months, three weeks, and four days, actually. Now come *on*—"

"And I know it's been hard on you. But you're kind of acting . . . different now."

Bethany's face froze, and she pulled her hand back into the page. "What? What are you talking about? Don't you get it? This could be Doyle, or Fowen again. Maybe Fowen got out of the book where I left him and is back for revenge. Or maybe Doyle remembered everything that happened and wants to figure out how I jump into books. If Kiel were here instead of running off to find out who he is without magic, he could just cast a spell or something to find out who this guy is. But without him, we're going to need a good plan."

Owen groaned again. "No more mysteries. Please? Fowen and Doyle are both still in the fictional world where we left them. And whoever's parked outside your house is probably one of your neighbors, which would explain why he's on your street."

"You think I'm making this up, don't you?" Bethany said, looking suspicious.

"Not . . . entirely. I just think you used to jump into books every night, and now, well, your imagination doesn't have as much to play with, so it's messing with you."

She gave him an evil look and started to say something,

then stopped, shaking her head. "Maybe you're right. I might have a little bit of cabin fever or something. I'll just go to bed and forget all this. See you tomorrow?"

"Yeah, of course," Owen said, breathing a sigh of relief. He'd been worried about saying something for weeks now, but she'd been getting more and more frantic to find something exciting in their fairly boring lives, and it was out of control. "And Bethany? Only use that page for *emergencies*. I might not have clothes on or something!"

Bethany rolled her eyes, then waved good-bye and disappeared.

Owen slowly got back into his chair, and Spike came trotting out from under the bed, then jumped into his lap. He petted his cat for a moment, then sighed.

"Bethany's going after the guy in the car, isn't she."

Spike just purred in response.

"Fine," Owen said, and set Spike on his bed. "I'll go, but this guy better be a murderer or something, or I'm going to be really annoyed!"

CHAPTER 2

Outside in the bushes Bethany put on the infrared goggles she'd pulled out of a military catalog and slowly raised her head.

There in the car was a bright-orange blob, vaguely human-shaped, but evil for sure. Almost every night for the last two months, she'd seen the same car parked across the street from her house, and the same creepy man waiting in it. Could have been even longer than that too. After all, she'd been in books basically every night since she was six until she'd decided to give up . . . to *stop* looking for her father, after everything that had gone down with Fowen.

Unfortunately, being back in the real world didn't mean things felt normal. She couldn't remember the last time she'd fallen asleep on time. Most nights she just tossed and turned, her mind racing with all the places she could be instead of in her bedroom. So many books, so many *worlds*, and she had promised to stay put in this one? She must be insane.

One of her sleepless nights had led her to staring out the window, and that's when she'd first spotted the guy. She noticed a car on the street she'd never seen during the day, and could tell that someone was in it. She only saw him get out once, wearing a hat and long coat, so she couldn't make out his face, but she knew he had to be spying on her. Did he know her secret? Was he planning on waiting for her to jump into a book, then stealing it to trap her? The person who visited her in Fowen's water trap had told her there were people looking for her, and she suspected they'd finally found her.

Owen hadn't believed her, of course. She shook her head at the idea. Why would she make up something like this? Just because she was bored out of her mind and desperately wanted to be jumping into a story didn't mean that she was just going to make up her own plot, right?

Well, when she put it *that* way, it did almost sound like Owen had a point. But clearly this guy was a spy or a murderer and needed to be investigated. And just because Owen hated mysteries didn't mean he should have let her do this alone.

"Is that him?" whispered a voice to her right, and after

almost shouting in surprise, she couldn't help but grin widely at the sight of Owen. He'd even worn dark clothes to better hide in the bushes.

Emotions flooded through her, but this wasn't the time for all of that. "That's him," she said, pulling the goggles off of her eyes. "Now we just need to put this tracker on his car, so we can follow him wherever he goes."

Owen looked like he'd swallowed something rotten. "You're going to bug his car? Do you know how illegal that is?"

"Nope," Bethany said, still smiling at him.

"Okay, I don't either, but it's probably *very* illegal."

Bethany shrugged. "Sometimes you need to take some risks, Owen. Be more fictional, like Kiel used to say."

"That was in a book," Owen hissed. "We're in the real world. Here you should be more *nonfictional* so we don't both get thrown in jail."

Bethany shushed him as the car's engine turned on. The red lights on the back of the car lit up their bush, and immediately they both dropped to the ground. "There's no time to argue," Bethany told him. "I need to get this tracker on the car before he leaves. You need to go distract him!"

Owen's eyes widened. "ME?!"

"He's spying on me, so I can't do it. Hurry up, he's about to leave!"

Owen gritted his teeth like he was trying not to yell at her, but slowly stood up anyway. He started to say something, so Bethany just shoved him out from behind the bushes.

"Go!" she hissed.

He gave her the dirtiest look she'd ever seen, but slowly walked toward the car in front of them just as it began to pull away. "Excuse me?" he shouted, waving his hands, and the car immediately stopped, the driver's window rolling down.

From the bushes Bethany couldn't hear the driver's voice, but Owen must have, as he responded to a question. "Yeah, I'm fine. I just, um, wondered if you lived around here, because I'm a little lost."

Huh, not bad! She silently gave Owen credit for his interrogating methods, then crawled out from behind the bushes. Be more fictional, eh, Kiel? She'd show him. She'd be the most fictional half-fictional person *ever*.

"The library," Owen was saying. "I know it's closed, but I have some books to return."

Bethany shook her head as she crawled forward on her hands and knees. He didn't have any books, or even a backpack. Why hadn't he come up with something more believable?

She reached the back of the car just as the driver seemed to be making the same point to him. Owen looked down at his hands, then shrugged. "Oh wow, I guess I forgot my books! Thanks for pointing that out. I should really go back home now!" With that, he waved wildly, then started walking quickly away from the car.

Bethany powered the tracker on, then slammed her hand up underneath the back bumper just as the car pulled away. She flattened herself on the road as it left, hoping the man didn't look back . . . but Owen came through again, waving over and over at the car as he abruptly changed direction and ran to the other side of the street.

Bethany rolled her way to the relative safety of the other parked cars, then grinned. That had gone even better than she'd hoped. Not only had they gotten the tracker on the car, but Owen had found out information vital to the cause!

"I got *nothing*," he told her a moment later, up in her bedroom. They'd snuck in but hadn't needed to, as Bethany's mom seemed to be talking to someone on the phone in her bedroom. Probably her aunt in California, which explained why she'd be talking so late.

Bethany frowned. "But you asked if he was from around here. What'd he say?"

"He asked me what I was doing out so late!" Owen said, his voice getting dangerously loud. Her mom would hear if he started yelling. "And then I blanked on what to say, so I told him I was looking for the library. The library! It's almost midnight!"

She nodded. "It wasn't great, but we can work on that for next time."

"*Next time?*" Owen's eyes widened. "There's not going to be a next time. I only came over to keep you from getting in huge trouble. Mission accomplished, so let's just count ourselves lucky and forget any of this ever happened."

"Sure," Bethany said, nodding. "As soon as we track him down and see who he is, we'll let it all go."

Owen made a painful sobbing noise, falling backward onto her bed. He put his hands over his face and didn't speak for a minute. "Just promise me you have a normal, nonfictional way of finding him?" he said finally.

"Of course," Bethany said indignantly. "I've got just the thing." And with that, she held up a book and showed it to him.

He peeked out from behind his hands, then groaned loudly. *"My Best Friend, the Assassin?!"*

"Do you have a *better* option than a dog who can track down anything *and* has assassin training?" Bethany grinned. "Exactly. That's what I thought."

CHAPTER 3

"Have I mentioned how much I hate mysteries?" Owen said as he walked next to Bethany and their fluffy, apparently deadly, fictional tracking dog, Kelly, who trotted along with her tongue hanging out, happily wagging her tail. They'd followed Kelly through several neighborhoods already and were heading down Ditko Drive now.

"This isn't a mystery," Bethany said, her eyes on the dog. "Good *girl*, Kelly. Find the bad man's house." Kelly continued trotting along, her long tail blowing in the breeze.

"This is pretty much *exactly* a mystery, and it shouldn't be," Owen pointed out as they passed by house after house. "It should be you admitting that you miss Kiel, and you miss jumping into books, so you're looking for a way to make things right again."

Bethany stopped abruptly, accidentally yanking Kelly to a

halt too. After a quizzical look, the dog started sniffing around in the nearest grass.

"Can Kelly really *kill* someone?" Owen asked, staring at the dog cautiously.

"A person, a charging rhinoceros, and in the series, even a T. rex at one point," Bethany said. "And this *isn't* about Kiel or not jumping into books, okay? This is about a bad guy knowing who I am, and coming after me and my mom. And I'm not going to let that happen. C'mon." Before Kelly could do whatever business she had to do, Bethany clicked her tongue at her and they continued their walk.

"I'm just saying, we could have called the police, maybe. Using a genetically engineered killer dog to track him down isn't exactly the most logical approach."

"Kelly's not *just* an assassin, Owen," Bethany told him, her eyes back on the dog. "She's too sweet to enjoy the killing, anyway. What she likes doing is tracking, and more importantly, she's so advanced, she can pick up radio signals. Signals like the ones from the tracking bug I put on his car." She sighed. "I'm being *subtle*, okay?"

"Oh *yeah*, tracking bugs on cars are totally subtle."

Bethany turned to say something, but stopped as she felt

the leash go taut. Kelly was pulling hard toward the house at the end of the street, a tall, thin house squished between two normal-sized buildings.

Parked right in front of the tall, thin house was the man's car.

"Get down!" Bethany hissed, and yanked Owen to the ground behind some bushes hard enough to almost knock the wind out of him.

"Oh yeah," Owen wheezed. "No one's gonna notice us here."

"I only care if *he* saw us," Bethany said, slowly pulling Kelly behind the bushes with them. The killer dog gave her a happy look, settled into her lap, sighed dreamily, and drifted off to sleep.

"That was quick," Owen said.

"She's trained to go right to sleep whenever she has the chance," Bethany said, her eyes on the house through the bushes. "Conserves her energy for when she needs to fight dinosaurs and such."

Owen absently reached out to pet Kelly's fur while glancing at the car. "So what now? We wait until he comes out and then see what this guy looks like?"

Bethany ignored him, her eyes on the house.

"That's all we're going to do, right, Bethany?" Owen said. *"Right?"*

"Quit joking, Owen," she said. "That would accomplish nothing."

Owen sat back, his head falling into his hands. "We're going to break into his house, aren't we?"

"Of course. It's really our only option here."

"*Our only option—*"

But Bethany shushed him by slamming a finger against his mouth. "Quiet! He's coming out."

Owen pushed her finger away and leaned forward, parting the bush's branches for a better look. He could just make out a normal-looking man in a brown hat and overcoat getting into his car.

"Oh yeah," he whispered sarcastically. "I'm totally getting a serial killer vibe."

"You're going to feel terrible when that turns out to be true," Bethany said, glaring at him. "Get ready."

"You know, I've been arrested before," Owen told her. "In the fictional world. It's not even remotely fun. Do you know how much less fun it'd be here, where we have to *live*? We'd be thrown in jail. Worse, they'd call our *moms*."

"You were fine," Bethany said, her eyes locked on the car. "It's not like you were arrested for that long."

"That's because Moira, a supergenius criminal, broke us out."

"We don't need her," Bethany said, waving a hand. Owen heard the car start and slowly pull away. "Besides, she's got a new series now. Her father sent her to Doyle's boarding school."

Owen's eyes widened. "Wait, *what*?"

"He's coming this way!" she hissed. "Be ready to move!"

Bethany grabbed Owen's shirt and dragged him around the bush, keeping the plant between them and the car as it passed them on the street. Bethany kept peeking through the branches, but whispered something inappropriate under her breath. "Couldn't see his face. Who wears a hat anymore? So suspicious."

"Yeah, unlike tracking some stranger to his house and then breaking in. The *hat's* suspicious."

Bethany responded by picking Kelly up and pushing her back into a page from a book. "C'mon, and don't make a noise."

"Bye, Kelly," Owen said, waving at the book page as he quickly followed Bethany, though at least he didn't crouch along suspiciously like his clearly insane friend.

The mystery man's house looked like it'd been built on a much-too-small piece of land, given how narrow it was. If there hadn't been a house in the spot, Owen wouldn't have thought you could fit one. The three houses were so close that you couldn't even see between them, which meant that getting around to sneak in the back was probably out.

In fact, other than the front door and maybe the lowest window, there didn't seem to be another way in.

"Oh yeah, perfect," Owen said as Bethany glanced around. "We're definitely not going to get caught."

"Shh," Bethany shushed, and strode confidently toward the front door. She held something up to the doorknob, and the lock clicked. "I thought ahead," she said, showing him some sort of metal lock-picking gadget in her hand. With that, she turned the knob, pushed the door open, and went inside.

Great. So not only had she broken her rule about going into books by borrowing a dog assassin, but she'd also grabbed a lock-picking device. *Ugh.* Why had things felt safer when Bethany was still looking for her father? Then, she'd had all kinds of rules to follow. But now, even without Kiel, she was getting completely reckless. He shook his head, then quickly hurried in after her.

Just inside, Owen slammed to a halt to avoid running into Bethany. She had frozen in place not more than a few feet inside the door. Owen started to say something, then noticed what she was looking at.

On the wall in front of them was a photo of two men and a woman, all three adults smiling at the camera as they stood behind a group of kids surrounding a birthday cake.

And behind them all, a banner read HAPPY FOURTH BIRTHDAY, BETHANY!

CHAPTER 4

"Those are my parents," Bethany said quietly, staring at the picture. "I've never seen this photo before, but that's . . . that's them." She pointed at two of the adults.

"But how did this guy get the picture?" Owen asked. "Unless . . . is that him, there in the picture too?" He pointed at the second man in the photo. "That *could* be the guy we saw, right?"

Bethany took a step closer, raising her hand to gently touch her father's face in the picture. "This was when it happened," she said, more to herself than Owen. "This was the night I lost my dad."

There was silence for a moment, and when Owen spoke, he startled Bethany, like she'd almost forgotten he was there. "Okay, well, I officially have to say I was wrong about this guy," Owen told her, pulling her away. "He's *definitely* been watching your house. But it looks like he's a friend of your mom's, so he probably has a good reason. We should just go and ask her. We can lock the door behind us, and no one will ever know—"

"Are you *joking*?" Bethany said, giving him a shocked look. "We're not going anywhere. Not until we find out who this guy is." She yanked her arm out of Owen's hand, and turned to face the rest of the room, while Owen sighed, then quietly closed the front door behind them.

The narrow living room was cramped but cozy, with a large pillow-covered sofa taking up much of the space. Art covered the walls, most of it framed pencil-and-ink drawings, some of the drawings in little squares, while others took up the entire frame.

"Are those comic book pages?" Owen asked, walking over to the nearest one. "Looks like the covers, too." He pointed at a pencil drawing of the cover to something called *Doc Twilight* #1. Doc Twilight seemed to be a superhero in a red-and-purple costume with a cape that wrapped around him, and a mask that covered his entire face. On his chest was a yellow moon and three stars, which was supposed to represent twilight, apparently. "I've never heard of this. It looks pretty ancient, like from before we were born."

Bethany walked over to stand next to him and read from the

cover. "'Doc Twilight. He's giving crime its proper medicine.'" She made a face. "Wow."

Next to the first issue cover were black-and-white drawings of a second, third, and fourth cover, where Doc Twilight went on to fight the Clown, a Joker-looking rip-off, and a few other villains. As they moved, Bethany pointed at the signature on the bottom of the nearest covers: Murray Chase. "That's the artist, I guess," she said. "Maybe that's the guy's name who lives here?"

"Either that, or he's a massive Doc Twilight fan," Owen said. "Who else would own all of this art of a superhero no one's heard of anymore?" He anxiously looked around, jumping at every little creak of the house. "Bethany, we should really get out of here. If he does draw comics, he's by definition awesome. Let's just go ask your mom."

Bethany shook her head and pushed past him. "He knew my father. I'm not done."

Owen sighed. "Of course not."

Bethany continued through the living room to a staircase leading both up and down, with Owen right behind her. Up seemed to lead to a kitchen, from what she could see. But down led to a closed door, and that seemed the more likely place to find . . . what? What was she looking for now? If this Murray Chase person, if that was even his name, had known her father, then was that why he was watching the house? Her mother must have seen him out there, so had to know. But why? And why had her mother not said anything to Bethany?

Whatever the answers were, Bethany wasn't leaving until she found out. And since basements seemed like a better spot for hiding secrets than kitchens, down she went. Owen mumbled something, but she could hear by his footsteps that he was following behind her.

The door to the basement was locked, but Bethany quickly hit it with her lock-picking device, while Owen made pained noises behind her. She opened the door, cringing at its creaking, and found herself in front of a pitch-dark room.

"You ever read those Five Kingdoms books?" Owen whispered. "Those kids went into a basement on Halloween, then got kidnapped and taken to another world. That's, like, *best* case scenario here, Bethany."

"You want to wait outside?" she asked, turning back to look at him as she felt around the wall for a light switch.

"Don't turn your back on a dark room!" he hissed, twisting her around. "You're just *asking* to be killed!"

She rolled her eyes, finally locating the switch, and flipped it. Spotlights clicked on around the room, and behind her, Owen gasped loudly. "You've *got* to be joking me," he said.

Five glass cases, each five or six feet tall, stood around what looked like a manhole cover. Most of the glass cases held super-hero costumes of such high quality that they looked like they'd been made by a movie studio.

"That's Doc Twilight," Owen said, pointing past her at the first glass case, which held a costume that looked exactly like the comic cover upstairs. "Look at that thing! It's even got little setting-sun throwing stars, like those bat-shaped ones that Batman uses!"

Next to Doc Twilight's costume were two smaller cases with mannequins, both wearing costumes. The first had a label: KID TWILIGHT, and the outfit looked like Doc's, just smaller. The outfit in the second case was similar, but instead of a body suit, it was more of a dress. Both mannequins wore masks.

"Who fights in a dress?" Bethany said, looking at the girl's costume with disgust. "That makes no sense."

"All kinds of people," Owen said. "Supergirl, and, um . . ."

"Exactly," Bethany said.

"Looks like it's a theme," Owen said, pointing at the next

case, which held another adult costume. This one had a skirt as well, and was also colored in bright blue and white. The label said NIGHT STAR.

The last case was set off a bit from the others, and just looking at it made her shiver. The label read THE CLOWN, and the case held what looked like an elaborate clown costume, complete with joy buzzer, water gun, and a sword made out of long, thin balloons.

"This guy's *really* into this comic," Owen said, stepping past her to get a closer look. He pointed down at the manhole in the middle of the room. "What do you think he's got in there? The *real* Clown, like in that Stephen King book?"

Bethany turned to look at the manhole cover, and realized that thin chains of silver interlocked over it, locking the manhole down like some kind of prison. The chains all came together in one corner under a number pad. Would her lock picking trick work on that? She kneeled down next to it and brought it close to try—

"What are you doing?" Owen hissed, grabbing her hand and yanking it away. "You're going to let it out?"

"We *have* to open it," Bethany said, her heart racing. Whoever this man was, this was what he was hiding. And there was no way she was leaving without knowing.

"That's it, Bethany," Owen told her, shaking his head. "You're going too far. This guy's got some creepy secrets, yes, but how do you *not know* to never open a locked manhole in a basement? Especially the basement of someone who owns a clown costume like that? This is like Horror Book 101!" He crossed his arms. "I'm sorry, but if you do this, I'm *leaving*."

"I'm doing it," Bethany said, pulling her hand out of his grasp and bending back down to the manhole.

Owen blinked, then shook his head. "Fine! I'm leaving!" He began backing away.

"Go then," she said, running the lock pick over the number pad. The pad began to cycle through numbers too fast for her to see, and then the first number popped up, a one.

"I'm gone!" Owen said from the basement door, not moving. "I'm not kidding!"

"I know you're not."

The second number appeared, a nine.

"Bethany—" Owen started to say, then stopped as they both heard a lock click, this time not from the manhole.

The front door opened, and they could hear footsteps on the floor above them.

Owen quickly slid back inside the basement door and quietly

closed it, turning the lock. "This is what happens when you break and enter!" he hissed quietly to her. "The person *always* comes home. It's like a cliché, it happens so often!"

A three, and then a nine, and the lock clicked open.

Bethany glanced up at Owen with a wide smile, then tore the chains away. "I know where we can hide," she whispered.

CHAPTER 5

Footsteps thumped on the stairs from above, then stopped at the door. The lock turned, and the basement door slowly opened.

A man wearing a long coat stepped into the basement, moving toward the glass cases, only to stop right over the manhole cover.

"No," he whispered. "It can't be."

He abruptly opened the glass case containing the Doc Twilight costume, then took the costume off the mannequin, gathering all the extra weapons and supplies. Finally, he turned around and ran back upstairs.

A minute passed before Owen let himself breathe again from his hiding spot behind the Kid Twilight costume case. "I can't believe he didn't see us!" he whispered to Bethany, who was hiding behind the Night Star case.

"I can't believe we didn't just jump into the manhole," she hissed back at Owen. "He almost caught you!"

"He never would have seen me," Owen told her.

"Your hair is peeking out over the mannequin's head," Bethany said, pointing at the glass case Owen was hiding behind. "At least you didn't hide behind the Doc Twilight costume. He definitely would have caught you then."

Owen blinked, not wanting to think about that. "Still. Thank you for not being completely insane and jumping in there."

Bethany sighed. "You weren't entirely altogether one hundred percent completely wrong, Owen. I know I'm getting a little . . . stir-crazy, not visiting books for the last few months. And the last thing I want to do is just leap without looking. But that doesn't mean we're safe now. We still have to get out without him seeing us."

"He probably just wanted the costume, and now he'll leave," Owen told her, nodding at the door.

The footsteps thumped down the basement stairs again.

"*Why* did you have to say that?" Bethany asked him.

"*I don't know,*" Owen whispered, frantically jumping behind the same glass case again. He pushed his hair down as much as he could, but it refused to hide. "I will shave all of you off if you don't stay down!" he told his hair, but that didn't seem to help.

Bethany glared at him from behind the Night Star costume case. "See?" she hissed. "We should have gone down the stupid manhole. We probably could have hidden somewhere in there, then come out when he's gone."

Owen looked down and realized they hadn't reset the chains. Oh *great*. A second chance to fix their mistake, and instead, they'd spent the time arguing. But still, why would he come right back down now?

The door opened again, and this time Doc Twilight strode confidently into the room in full costume, his cape waving just above the floor as he walked. Owen would have laughed, if the situation hadn't been so terrifying. He was really wearing the costume? The man dressed as a superhero strode to the middle of the room, then stopped, kneeling down, which took him out of Owen's sight.

Please don't notice the chains. Please don't notice the chains. Please don't notice the chains.

The chains rattled as the man picked them up. Metal grated on metal, and then a loud bang made Owen almost jump out of his skin, which probably would have been noticeable. A dank smelling air filled the room as the man grunted, sounding lower this time, then metal scraped again as the manhole closed back up.

Owen closed his eyes and just breathed for a moment, glad that he didn't have to find out what people who dressed up as superheroes did when they found intruders in their houses.

And then someone grabbed his arm, and Owen screamed, "Don't murder me, this was all *her* fault!"

"Hey!" Bethany shouted at him, slapping his arm. "Don't *do* that! And thanks a lot!"

"I thought you were the Doc Twilight guy!" Owen shouted back. "Don't just grab someone like that!"

"Why did you have your eyes closed?"

"Because creepy things were happening!" Owen peeked out from behind the case and saw that the manhole cover was back in place.

Bethany stepped over to it. "He went down there. Let's follow him."

"What?!" Owen shouted, pulling her away from the manhole. "Are you kidding? He's dressing as a superhero. And not for a comic convention or something normal. He's probably trying to fight crime for real, which means he's insane. We're *not* going down there, no way. Down there leads to horrible things, and the last thing we need is a nonfictional adventure. People get killed for *real* in those things, you know, and there's no jumping out of a book to save us."

Bethany stared at him like she was about to say something, then paused, looking down at the ground. "You're right."

"I'm . . . what?" Owen paused, a bit flustered. He hadn't expected that.

"Don't push it," Bethany told him, walking back to the basement door. "I . . . might not have thought this whole thing through. I just feel like I'm about to burst, Owen. I have so much energy, and all I want to do is something . . . *risky*."

"You sound like Kiel," he told her, forcing a smile.

She looked up at him, then sighed. "Probably. But it doesn't matter. The best thing to do is just confront my mother and ask her what's going on."

"Like I suggested upstairs," Owen pointed out quietly.

"What'd I say about not pushing it?" she told him, glaring over her shoulder as she started up the basement stairs.

An oversized overcoat and hat now covered the couch in the living room. Next to the outer garments was what looked like a large envelope that the man must have brought in with him.

Bethany picked it up, glancing at Owen as if waiting for him to say something, but he figured she'd earned this much. He nodded. "Go for it."

She grinned just a bit, then opened the top of the envelope, pulling out some pages that looked a lot like the art hanging on the walls.

"What is it?" Owen said, but Bethany didn't answer, her eyes on the pages as she scanned them.

Then her eyes widened, and she dropped the pages and envelope to the floor, staring at Owen in shock. Without another word, she turned and sprinted back down the basement stairs.

"What is it?!" Owen repeated, grabbing for the pages and scanning them quickly.

It was Doc Twilight, the comic book version, in what must have been his Twilight Cave or whatever. He was alone and talking to himself in a mirror. "The world must never find out my secret identity," Doc Twilight said as he pulled off his mask. "For what would they think if they knew that Christian Sanderson, astronomer of Jupiter City, was actually Doc Twilight?"

Owen glanced at the face, thinking it seemed familiar. Where had he . . . and then his eyes rose to the photo of Bethany's fourth birthday party.

Doc Twilight had the same face as one of the men in the photo. And it wasn't Murray.

From the basement Owen heard the unmistakable sound of Bethany pulling the manhole cover up and dragging it slowly to the side. And for once, Owen couldn't blame her.

Doc Twilight . . . was her father?

CHAPTER 6

Bethany stared down into the manhole, ready to jump in the moment Owen tried to stop her. It didn't matter what he said, not now. This was her dad. Her *dad*. She'd been within a few feet of him without even knowing! He'd been watching over her, keeping her safe for months now, maybe even longer, and she'd never known!

"Don't even say it, Owen," she said as her friend walked up next to her.

Owen glanced down. "I was just going to point out that you don't usually see manholes covering up blue circles of fire."

Bethany gave him a look, then turned back to the fiery circle right underneath the manhole. "Yeah, okay, fair enough. I can't say I was expecting that either. Figured there'd be a tunnel or a ladder or something."

"So what do you think it is?" he asked, peering down into

the darkness through the circle of fire. Whatever was on the other side, it was too dark to make out.

"Doesn't matter. I'm going in. You can come with me or stay here, up to you, but I'm going."

Owen didn't answer at first, and Bethany closed her eyes, hoping he'd just this once be on her side.

"Follow me," he said, moving to the side of the manhole.

Bethany smiled in surprise. "You're going? And you're going *first*?"

"What's there to be afraid of?" he asked, shrugging. "It's just a big blue circle of fire. Doc Twilight knew what it was, and *he* went down there, so what can go wrong?"

"I found him, Owen," Bethany said quietly. "That was *my dad*."

Owen sat down on the floor next to the hole, staring at the blue fire. "All we know for sure is that a guy put on the costume of a guy who looks like your dad. We don't know if that comic superhero is your *real* dad. Or if this guy is him either."

"It *was* him," Bethany said, shaking her head. "It all makes sense now. That's why I couldn't find him, because he wasn't in a book at all!"

Owen's foot reached the blue circle, and he poked it through slowly. "*None* of this makes sense. Don't lie."

"He couldn't come back to us because he had some important mission, obviously," Bethany said. "Look at him, he's a real live superhero! He probably had to save the world, and couldn't put us in danger or something. Villains are always finding out about people's secret identities, aren't they? But he couldn't just leave us alone, so he's been watching over us from a distance this whole time."

"Well, my foot isn't bursting into flames or anything," Owen said, pushing the rest of his leg in. "I'm not feeling anything on the other side to stand on, though. I'm going to try to poke my head through, okay?"

Bethany nodded, not hearing a word he said. "I still have a lot of questions, but at least he must have had a good reason. And my mom must know! They both must have been protecting me. This changes *everything*, Owen."

Owen didn't respond, so Bethany looked over at him. "Owen?"

There was nobody there. He must have already jumped through while she was talking. Bethany dropped to the floor, then slid into the blue circle of fire, ready for anything.

Instead, everything went dizzy, and she crashed against something, landing hard on her stomach. Shaking off the jolt, she looked around into a room lit only by a larger version of the blue-fire ring that had been covered by the manhole, except this one was standing straight up and down, instead of in a hole in the floor. And it was surrounded by metal equipment on all sides.

In fact, there wasn't much of anything in the room that *wasn't* covered in machines.

"I've got a bad feeling about all of this," Owen said from behind her. She pushed to her feet and found him standing over a dimly lit control panel.

"Is someone here?" she asked, then louder, "Da . . . Doc Twilight?"

"I don't see him," Owen said. "But I think this machine is what's making the fire portal thing we just came through. It's all hooked up to it. Where *are* we? You think this is, like, some kind of government thing under the city?"

"Does the government use blue-fire portals?" Bethany asked, looking around.

Owen shrugged. "Probably." He walked around, running his hand over various machines before stopping in front of something large covered in blankets. "What do you think this thing is? It looks almost like a person."

Bethany walked over next to him, moving slowly in the dimly lit room. Whatever he'd found *did* sort of look person-ish. "Maybe it's, like, a robotic suit for someone to wear?"

Owen poked it with his finger. "What, like Iron Man?"

Something began to whir underneath the blankets, and the suit abruptly doubled in height. The blankets fell off, and Bethany gasped as a ten-foot-tall robot with missiles on its shoulder and buzz saws for hands turned on in front of her. It had a giant remote control with a big red button taped to its chest, which must have turned it on when Owen touched it.

"FOOLS!" the robot yelled, holding its buzz-saw hands up in triumph. "You have awakened Dr. Apathy, and now face your deaths!"

CHAPTER 7

Owen gasped, jumped forward, and hit the button on the robot. The robot instantly powered down, its arms and torso hanging limply as the buzz-saw hands slowly spun to a halt.

"What . . . was that?" Bethany said, her eyes wide.

Owen seemed to be trying to catch his breath. "I *don't* think this is a government facility."

She just stared at him. "How is this happening? Where *are* we exactly?"

Owen shook his head, then turned to look at the blue-fire portal. "I don't think we're below that house anymore, Bethany. Wherever that thing brought us . . . it's not good."

Bethany nodded. "Right. Well, we need answers, so . . ." She pushed the robot's button, and it began to power up.

"FOOLS!" it shouted, then powered down as Owen quickly hit the button again.

"What are you doing?" he shouted at her.

"I'm going to ask it where we are," she told him. "Do *you* have a better idea for finding out?"

Owen just stared at her, his mouth hanging open. "It's a death robot!" he said finally. "Named Dr. Apathy!"

"'Apathy' means 'indifference,'" Bethany told him. "So the robot probably won't care enough to kill us." She hit the robot's button, and it powered back up.

"FOOLS!" the robot shouted, its buzz-saw hands spinning up again.

"Stop that!" Owen shouted at her, punching the button. "You're doing it again!"

"Doing what?"

"Taking crazy risks! You're asking a ten-foot-tall robot with buzz-saw hands for *directions*. Literally anyone else would be better!"

"Do you see anyone else?" Bethany asked him. "And we can clearly shut it off whenever we want. So why worry about it?"

"It's a *death robot*. Everything you need to know is right there in the name!"

"Then go hide," she told him, her heart racing. "I'm finding out what this thing knows about my dad." And she smacked the robot in the chest again.

The robot powered up. "FOOLS!" it shouted, holding its hands up in triumph. "*Stop* turning me off and on!"

"Who are you, and where are we?" Bethany asked as the buzz-saw hands made horrible grinding noises. In spite of the danger, her heart was beating faster than it had in months, and she couldn't help feeling excited.

"I am Dr. Apathy, wretch! And you shall pay for invading my laboratory. All of Jupiter City shall pay!" The robot paused, then looked around. "Wait, this isn't the real me." He felt around his body with his buzz saws, leaving cuts in the metal. "This is just the copy of my brainwaves that I stuck in my robot. I must still be in jail, which means I need to go break myself out!"

"Where is Doc Twilight?" Bethany said, ready to shut the robot down at a moment's notice.

"*Doc Twilight?*" the robot roared. "My greatest enemy? Where is he!" The robot stepped out into the lab, a beam of red light searching all around. It passed over Owen, who shouted in terror and dropped to the floor, then continued. "He's not here. What trickery is this?"

"He passed through here," Bethany told the robot. "Where is this place? Where is Jupiter City?"

"I care not for your questions," the robot told her. "Silence them, or you shall meet your *doom*."

"Oh, stop it," Bethany said, and hit the button.

"Don't *do* thaaaaa—" the robot said, trailing off as it lost power again. Bethany ignored it and ran over to Owen, then helped him stand up.

"I thought that was a laser beam or something," he told her.

"I know," she said. "Doesn't matter. Jupiter City was the name of the place Doc Twilight's from, right?"

"Yeah, that's what the comic said." Owen gave her a strange look. "Don't even start with that. We're not actually *in* Jupiter City. We didn't jump into anything."

Bethany pointed at the portal. "We did come through that, though. Think about it. How did my father get into the real world to begin with, before I was born? He never had the power to travel between the worlds like I do. So what if this thing's a portal?"

Owen's eyes widened. "Supervillains *are* always making crazy portals to other dimensions. And this Dr. Apathy guy seems to be pretty good with the fake comic-booky science stuff."

"What do you mean, fake?"

Owen snorted. "Did you hear the robot? It said Dr. Apathy put his brainwaves into it. That's not exactly realistic science. It's a lot more like the science that comic books use that sounds cool, but would never happen." He shrugged. "Think about it. It's like Peter Parker getting bitten by a radioactive spider. That would probably give him radiation poisoning or something in real life, but instead, he becomes Spider-Man. The Hulk gets hit by a gamma bomb, which isn't a real thing anyway, and doesn't die. Comic book science just needs to sound good, it doesn't need to actually be real."

"But if it's real enough in that world," Bethany said, stepping closer to the portal, "does that mean it could actually work? A doorway to the nonfictional world? That could be how Dad got out!"

Owen sighed. "I can't believe I'm saying this, but we could always ask the robot."

Bethany grinned. "You're a brave man, Owen Connors. Just stand back."

Owen shook his head, stepping closer to her. "If this really is a superhero world, I'm probably safer being brave. If you try to run, the villain always gets you. It's always better in comics to stand and fight against bullies and bad guys."

She gave him an odd look, but he just slapped the robot in the button, and it immediately woke up.

"FOOLS!" the robot shouted, raising its hands in triumph. "I'm really beginning to tire of—"

"Where does that portal go?" Owen shouted, pointing at the blue ring of fire.

"Children do not *interrupt* Dr. Apathy when he is pontificating, wretch!" the robot shouted, bringing his buzz-saw hands down close to Owen. "And the Apathy Circle burns a hole between dimensions to a world where there *are* no superpowered meddlers to thwart—"

Bethany pushed the robot's button, shutting him down again. "You were right, we're in the fictional world, then!"

"Only, we didn't jump in," Owen said quietly, his eyes on the robot still.

"So? That doesn't matter. Forget our promise, this is about my *dad*!"

"No, I mean, we didn't get here by jumping into a comic book. Does that mean we can't jump *out*, either?"

Bethany paused, then rolled her eyes. "Of course I can jump us out. It's the fictional world. That's what I do."

Owen gave her a look, then waved her on.

"Fine," she said. "But only to show you how wrong you are." She closed her eyes, took a deep breath, then jumped out of the story.

Except instead of the nonfictional world, she landed right in the same spot.

"Uh-oh," Owen said.

CHAPTER 8

"Okay," Owen said as Bethany jumped into the air over and over, getting more frustrated with every landing. "So we're in a comic book world. How much do you know about that?"

"I read comics," Bethany said between jumps, glaring at him.

"Like what?"

She finally stopped, breathing a bit hard. "*Bone. Tintin. Zita the Spacegirl.*"

Owen nodded. "So no superhero comics then. If we're going to go out there after Doc Twilight, wherever he went, then you need to know how this place works."

Bethany rolled her eyes. "We've wasted a lot of time already. Why don't we just go find my dad before he disappears again?"

Owen pointed at the depowered killer robot. "Because this? This is normal here. In superhero comics, there are alien invasions, entire cities get mind-controlled, and almost everyone has superpowers at one point or another. You really want to just run out into that without knowing what you're doing?"

"*Fine.* Let's just hurry."

"Okay, there are five rules to superhero comics," Owen told her, marking them off on his fingers. "First, like I already mentioned, science works differently here. It's not quite science-fiction, but it's close. Basically, if it would look cool in a fight, it's probably possible here. So don't worry about how someone who can shrink to the size of a bug gets super strong when they're small. They just look cool punching someone out. See what I mean?"

"Nope," Bethany said, shifting her weight back and forth like she couldn't wait to go. "Next?"

Owen sighed. "Second, superpowers come from three different things: You get them just by your genetics, like the X-Men or Superman or someone; you make them yourself, like Iron Man; or you get them by accident, like pretty much everyone else. And the accidents should normally kill you, but here, they don't."

"Accidents are good. Got it."

"Third, everyone has a theme, heroes and villains. A lot

involve animals for whatever reason. Bats and spiders and black widows—"

"Also spiders," Bethany pointed out.

"But whatever the theme, that's usually a clue on how to take them out. If you're fighting Electro, hit him with water. If Hydroman is chasing you, hit him with Electro. See what I mean?"

"Don't you mean Aquaman?"

"Nope. Four, even in superhero comics, there are different kinds. You've got your crime detective stories like Batman, your comedy comics like Squirrel Girl, your—"

"There's not really a Squirrel Girl," Bethany said. "No way."

"Uh, there is, and she's *awesome*," Owen said, giving her an indignant look. "I'm just saying, this Jupiter City place could be futuristic, it could be creepy and crime-ridden, it could be anything. Doc Twilight looked more like Batman or Daredevil than, say, Spider-Man, so we're probably going to be dealing with a *lot* of rooftops and gargoyles and stuff."

"I'll watch out for that. Is that all?"

"You're not taking this seriously, Bethany!" Owen shouted. "And we can't just jump out of here if things go badly. Think about what comic books are like. Huge, all-powerful heroes

54

and villains fighting in the streets. You need to know how to deal with it all."

Bethany looked down. "You're right, I'm sorry. I'm just . . . he's so *close*, Owen. And I'm, like, crawling out of my skin here. I just want to go find him already!"

Owen nodded. "I get it, I do. Last thing to remember: Comics are about heroes. People standing up to bullies and bad guys, helping protect anyone who can't stand up for themselves. So if we *do* run into trouble, there should be someone around to help out."

Bethany's eyebrows shot up. "You're saying to just hope we get rescued?"

"Depending on what's out there, that might be our only hope," he said, taking a deep breath in, then letting it out.

"Okay, Dr. Doom," Bethany said. "But you're not fooling me. You can't wait to get out there either. I know you. You love superheroes."

Owen glared at her, then slowly smiled. *"I'm so excited!"*

She grinned as well, then pushed him toward the laboratory door. "Then lead on, comic book guy. Let's go find my father!"

In spite of all his rules, Owen felt weirdly optimistic as they walked out of Dr. Apathy's lab. This was a comic book world, after all. The place where the good guys always won! And after all this time, Bethany was about to find her father . . . maybe. This might turn out to be a piece of cake, all things considered!

As they left the room, the lights of the blue-fire portal began to flicker, causing the shadows to dance.

Then the shadows pulled away from the portal to follow Bethany and Owen.

CHAPTER 9

They passed through what resembled a round bank-vault door to get out of the lab (it was ajar, so Bethany decided her father had definitely come this way), and emerged to a sight that made them both gasp in surprise.

"We're definitely not in a basement anymore," Owen said, stepping closer to the curved glass windows covering the entire wall in front of them. Apparently Dr. Apathy built his lab at the top of a skyscraper, because beyond the windows an entire city spread out far, far below.

"Jupiter City, the robot called it," Bethany said, leaning forward to put her head on the glass. Owen was a bit more tentative, but got close enough to look as well.

Jupiter City didn't look like any city she'd ever seen before, not in real life or in books. Everything seemed to glow with an eerie red color in the evening hours as the sun went down.

Apartment and office buildings looked a bit like they would in New York or Chicago, but seemed a bit too perfect, like they'd been sketched out with a ruler.

They appeared to be in a downtown area, with a few other skyscrapers around them. One a few blocks away had the words SECOND COUSINS CORPORATION written at the top, with a gigantic "2" next to the words. Another had a giant lightning bolt at the top that blinked, with the words THE DAILY CURRENT.

"That must be a Fantastic Four type team," Owen said, pointing at the first building. "And instead of the *Daily Bugle* or the *Daily Planet*, like in Spider-Man or Superman, it's the *Daily Current*. That lightning bolt is so cool! How many times do you think they've used it to fight off giant monsters?"

Nearby, a giant statue of a man in a duck costume sat on top of some kind of museum, which was strange. Close by that was a domed building with white statues in a courtyard. Not two blocks from there, a mysterious building seemed to appear and disappear as Bethany stared at it.

"None of this seems to really fit together," she said, staring at the disappearing building. "It's like there's no consistency."

"That's because the major landmarks are probably all from

different comic books," Owen said. "Like that crazy invisible house. That's probably a book about a magician or something. And that domed place looks a lot more like a superhero team headquarters, an Avengers or Justice League or something."

"And the duck museum?" Bethany asked, pointing at it.

Owen shrugged. "Got me. Where do you think . . . wait, look!" He pointed down to the right, where the buildings looked a bit more run-down, though still like they'd been built—or drawn—that way. "There's someone on the roofs!"

Bethany covered her eyes against the setting sun's glare and tried to see what he was pointing at. At first, she couldn't make anything out, but then caught a bit of movement on the roof-tops. Someone was moving quickly, watching the streets as they went.

Someone with a cape.

"Dad," Bethany said, banging her hand against the glass. "Come on! We have to catch up to him." She grabbed Owen's hand before he could respond and dragged him toward some elevator doors. She mashed the button over and over until the elevator finally arrived, then pushed Owen inside and jumped in herself, slamming the button for the lobby so hard she almost hurt her thumb.

"Floor three hundred and fifty?" Owen said, pointing at the display above the buttons. "This is going to take forever!"

Bethany opened her mouth to respond, then screamed as the elevator dropped like a rock, the floor numbers flying by faster than she could even see. Owen screamed too, and he grabbed her arm, though Bethany had no idea what good that would do when they hit the ground.

They seemed to pick up speed as they zoomed by floor two hundred, and Bethany found herself grinning in spite of their looming death. They might be about to crash into the floor going a thousand miles an hour, but the fall was still fun!

They passed floor one hundred, and Owen took in a deep breath, then started screaming again, while Bethany began laughing, harder and harder, whether at him or just the sheer excitement of the drop, she wasn't sure.

And then the elevator dinged, and they stopped smoothly. The doors opened, and Owen's scream trailed off into a sort of awkward moan.

"Amazing," Bethany said, her heart almost beating out of her chest. "And it got us down fast! Let's go, Owen. We can still catch him." And she grabbed his hand again, trying to pull him. This time, he seemed to stumble along, letting out

another uncomfortable little high-pitched moan every few feet.

The lobby of Dr. Apathy's building was beautiful, with marble columns and elaborate leather seating. But what it didn't have was any people. Not even a security guard.

"Where is everyone?" Bethany said, turning around as she walked. Behind her, a sign above what looked like a security desk said APATHETIC INDUSTRIES, which must have been Dr. Apathy's company name.

"Some mad scientists in comics hide behind companies," Owen told her, still rattled. "Lex Luthor has LexCorp. The Green Goblin has Oscorp. I guess Dr. Apathy has this."

"That doesn't explain why no one's here," she said, frowning. But there wasn't time to figure that out anyway. Right now she was just thankful she didn't have to explain to security why they were coming out of the building's elevator without ever having come in the front doors.

They pushed through unlocked glass doors to the street outside, and Bethany braced herself for the sounds of a bustling city. Only, other than the hum of some electrical boxes, the city was almost completely silent. No pedestrians walked the sidewalks, and there were no cars driving in the streets. A few were parked on the sides, but they looked like they hadn't been moved for a good long while.

"This doesn't feel right," Owen said. "No city full of super-heroes would ever be quiet. There's always a bank robbery or an invasion by the mole people or something." He gasped. "Unless maybe that's why everyone's hiding at home? Because there *is* an invasion going on?"

"We'll watch out for it," Bethany said, trying to orient her-self on the street to where she'd seen her father. "I think we need to go up this street for a few blocks, then find some way to get to the roofs. Or maybe he'll see us first? He looked like he was searching for something." She set off in that direction, and Owen hurried to catch up.

"He could be on patrol," Owen said, looking all around, like he was a tourist. Which he was, she supposed. "Do you think we'll see any superheroes fly by?"

"I didn't see any upstairs," she said, reaching a street corner and stopping at the red light, then shrugging and crossing any-way. It's not like there were any cars on the streets. Where *was* everyone?

A few empty blocks later they reached the familiar-looking buildings that they'd seen Doc Twilight on from the window.

Well, Bethany hoped they had, at least. Matching rooftops to street-level buildings wasn't the easiest thing in the world. Everything seemed more sinister here, like someone might rob you around any corner.

"This feels right," Owen said, shivering. "Like where a Batman-type superhero would patrol the roofs. Less other-dimensional stuff and more muggings." He looked over his shoulder. "Don't flash any cash or anything."

"I'll keep that in mind if I see anyone," Bethany said. "Or if I had any cash."

"Wait," Owen said, tapping Bethany's arm and pointing. "There's someone!"

Up ahead on the steps of an apartment building, an old woman stood, holding a walker. She seemed to be staring at them, even from a distance.

They walked closer, and Bethany waved. "Hello!" she said. "We were just wondering where everyone was?"

The old woman didn't respond at first, but just stared at them. Bethany frowned, moving closer, but Owen pulled her to a stop. *"Look at her eyes,"* he hissed.

Bethany squinted, then took a step back involuntarily. The woman's eyes were entirely black.

"Is she a zombie?" Owen whispered, breathing faster. "Sometimes there are comic book crossovers, and superheroes meet zombies. It never ends well, trust me."

"We need to get to the roof," Bethany said, backing away from the woman. "Maybe we should—"

"Out after five p.m.?" the woman shouted at them. "You're breaking curfew, so must be little hooligans! You want to take my money, I bet! I'll show you what we do to lawbreakers in Jupiter City!" She picked up her walker and tossed it down the stairs, then slowly began making her way toward them.

"This is . . . odd," Owen said, backing away. "But at least she's not a zombie."

"I'll show you who's a zombie!" the woman shouted as she reached the street. "You'll wish that undead magician uptown had gotten ahold of you when I get through with you, you little criminals!"

"Undead magician?" Owen said, his eyes widening. "That's so cool."

"How about we concentrate on this woman?" Bethany said, pushing Owen backward. The street seemed to darken around them, but not from the sun going down.

"Uh, Bethany?" Owen said, stopping short behind her. "We have a bigger problem."

Bethany turned, and watched as a shadow rose up off the street, wrapped itself around a street lamp, and silently extinguished the light.

Shadows began moving all around them, pulling up off the ground like they were made of paper, but standing upright.

"This is what you deserve!" the old woman shouted behind them, and Bethany looked back, only to find shadows on either side of the woman as well. "The Dark has you now, you little crooks. And he'll teach you what happens to people who break the law in Jupiter City!"

CHAPTER 10

The two-dimensional shadows began to glide toward them, some looking vaguely human, others like something out of a nightmare. All had long shadow tendrils that connected them back to the mass of darkness that loomed like fog rising over the entire city.

"They're all around us," Owen whispered.

"We're not criminals!" Bethany shouted at the shadows, but they didn't respond. Either they chose to remain silent, or they couldn't speak. The closest ones began to reach out with long black fingers.

"Lies!" the old woman shouted. "You're rotten little kids, and you need someone to teach you a lesson. I'd hate to be in your shoes now!" She grinned evilly at them.

Bethany turned to Owen, her body going cold with fear, but before she could say anything, he grabbed her hand and yanked her straight at the old woman, the one place where there weren't any shadows.

"Get away from me!" the woman shouted, her black eyes filled with rage and terror as Owen pushed her aside, then sprinted toward the building stairs she'd been standing on earlier.

They banged into the front door hard enough to send a shock through Bethany's bones. While Owen frantically struggled against the locked handle, Bethany looked up to find shadows slipping down the building's walls toward them, while the ones on the street grew closer and closer. "Here!" she shouted, shoving the lock-picking device at Owen. She heard a click, then almost fell inside as the door opened.

"There's no escape!" the old woman yelled. "You'll get what's coming to—"

Bethany kicked the door closed behind her, cutting the angry old woman off, then ran behind Owen toward the closest stairway. "Get up to the roof!" she said. "We have to get above them. They're everywhere down here!"

Owen took off up the stairs as Bethany threw a quick look over her shoulder, then gasped.

The door hadn't even slowed the shadows down. Instead, they'd slipped right beneath it, while the shadows on the walls from ceiling lamps began to move after them as well.

"How can shadows move?" she shouted at Owen, who didn't stop running as he reached the next floor.

"I don't know, but I hope Doc Twilight knows how to fight them!" Owen said, leaping over a shadow on the ground that reached for him with a two-dimensional hand.

As soon as Owen passed, the hand turned to grab for Bethany, and instead of jumping it, she launched a hard kick right at the palm. Her foot passed through the shadow like it was nothing, and she lost her balance, skidding forward, one hand falling to the floor to hold herself up.

The shadow grabbed for her hand, and this time it was as solid as she was, only its grip was ice cold.

"Let go!" she shouted, trying to pull her hand away, but the shadow held her fast. She punched at the hand, but the shadow split in two around her fist, and now the second shadow reached out and grabbed her other wrist, holding it firmly in place. "Owen!"

But there were so many shadows around her now that she couldn't even see her friend. They rose up from all sides on the floor and walls, surrounding her, reaching for her. She could feel a strange sort of anger and hatred radiating off of them before they even touched her. *"No,"* she whispered, flinching away from their touch.

And then a bright light blazed through the shadows, and Owen grabbed her hand, yanking her through the chilly darkness and out the other side. "Come on!" he shouted, and pulled her toward the stairs.

"How . . . how did . . . ," she tried to say, but couldn't get the words out. The rage she felt from the shadows seemed to almost burn her, even now.

He held up the flashlight on his phone. "Shadows don't much like light, do they?"

She smiled as she forced her feet to move up the stairs, struggling to shake off the shadows' aura. "Thanks," she managed to say.

He looked back at her, still running up the stairs, and almost laughed. "Whenever I've dreamed about having superpowers, they never included using a cell phone flashlight." Not watching where he was going, he immediately tripped, faceplanting right at the top of the stairs.

Bethany barely slowed down as she passed over him, pulling him up by his underarms as she went. "No stopping, Captain Flashlight," she said, and led him up the last flight of stairs, the shadows just a few steps behind.

The door to the roof was locked as well, but Owen used the lock pick, and they burst out into the night air right before the darkness poured out of the door like a flood. "There!" Bethany shouted, and pointed across the roof.

One lone light hung over the roof on a strand, the others having all burned out. This one gave off just enough of a glow to illuminate a small circle below it, which Bethany made for, Owen right behind her.

As soon as they entered the circle, she whirled around, waiting to see if the shadows would attempt to follow, but they didn't. Instead, they pooled around the circle of light, rising into the air like some kind of horrible slime monster, enclosing them from all sides.

Within seconds, they couldn't even see the roof door anymore. Nothing existed past the edge of the circle but shadow and darkness.

"I don't think my flashlight is going to help us here," Owen told her, his hands shaking.

Bethany just stared at him. What could she say? That this was all her fault? That she should have listened to him from the beginning? That clearly this was a horrible idea, but that she just couldn't, she *couldn't* let her father get away again, not after all this time?

But where would that get them? Trapped on a roof by some kind of demon shadows, waiting to infect them with hatred and rage, probably like they had the woman on the street, if her insane anger and black eyes were any indication. But why? What did they want? Why were they here?

"Just let us GO!" Bethany shouted, putting all of her frustration and fear into her scream. "This isn't right! We didn't *do* anything!"

One of the shadows seemed to separate from the rest, even darker than the others, which shouldn't be possible. The new shadow stepped forward into the circle of light, but somehow didn't disappear.

And this shadow had red, glowing eyes.

"Children aren't allowed out after dark in Jupiter City," said a grating, awful voice from somewhere within the darker shadow. "It's not safe. Which means you're breaking the laws, and so you must pay. That means you're now *mine.*"

The darker shadow reached out a hand toward Bethany, and just like that, everything disappeared into a light bright as the sun.

CHAPTER 11

It was like a star fell from the sky and exploded in front of their eyes. Owen shouted in shock and pain, as the light was so bright he could see it through his closed eyelids.

A hand grabbed him from behind, clicked something on the waist of his pants, and shoved. *Hard.*

He stumbled forward a few feet, right into the spot where the shadows *had* been, and then suddenly there was nothing beneath his feet except empty air. He shouted again, this time in terror as he fell into nothingness, completely blind.

Wind whipped by his face as he frantically waved his arms, not even having the time to realize how stupid that was. But whatever it was on the waist of his pants yanked hard, and he slammed to a stop.

Unfortunately, he wasn't touching the ground yet. Instead, he seemed to be hanging by his pants, slowly turning in a circle.

"Um," Owen said. "What just happened?"

Above him, he heard Bethany scream as she fell just to the left of him, then groan as she jerked to a stop too. This was followed by what sounded like a quick gust of wind, and Owen heard something land lightly on the ground nearby.

"I'm releasing you both," said a deep male voice. "When I do, you need to *run*."

"We're blind," Owen pointed out, moving his hands in front of his face. Or at least he thought he was. "How are we supposed to run?"

"*Fast,*" said the voice, and the thing on Owen's waist clicked. Before Owen could even shout, he hit the ground, landing hard on his hands and feet. In spite of the sting, he still was shocked. The ground had only been a few feet below him? He'd come that close to hitting the street?

He heard Bethany touch down, and then someone lifted him to his feet. "GO!" the man shouted, and pushed Owen forward.

"But—" Bethany said, then went quiet as she got pushed too.

"*Now!*" the man shouted. "There's no time, they're already regrouping!"

Owen reached back to where he'd heard Bethany's voice,

grabbed out, and caught her arm. "Talk to him later," he whispered. "We have to go."

She didn't respond, but pushed her hand into his, and together they set out jogging as quickly as they dared, not able to see the ground in front of them.

Somehow, miraculously, Owen made it a good thirty seconds before tripping and landing on his face. He unfortunately yanked Bethany down with him, and it took both of them a few seconds to regain their feet. By that point, Owen had no idea which way they were supposed to be running.

"Can you see yet?" he asked her.

"Does a big yellow circle count?" she said, sounding like she was facing a different direction.

Owen blinked a few times, rubbing his eyes, but it didn't help. Everything was completely dark except a yellow blotch in the middle of his vision. Hopefully that was from the blindness, and not because there were shadow monsters everywhere.

Behind them they heard a small bang, and a moment later someone grabbed both of them around their torsos and picked them up. "*Whoa*," the voice said, grunting from their weights. A few steps later they stopped, and the man dropped them both to the ground. "Okay, you're too heavy.

Plan B, then. Do what I say, and go where I lead you."

"Wait. Plan A was just *carrying* us?" Owen said, then yelped as the man jerked his hand forward, almost yanking him off his feet.

"Up!" the man shouted. "Curb!" Owen jumped to make the curb and still almost knocked himself off balance, but managed to make it up onto the sidewalk. Then they were off again, running much faster than when it'd just been him and Bethany.

"Left!" the man yelled, then, "Right!" At each turn, Owen barely kept his feet, but when he did stumble, the man's grip kept him from hitting the ground.

Were the shadows chasing them? Or worse, the darker shadow with red eyes? Why couldn't shadows make more noise so Owen could know for sure? For all he knew, they were two steps behind and reaching out. The thought made Owen move faster, which meant another stumble as his calf scraped against what felt like a fire hydrant.

"Where are we going?" Bethany asked, sounding strangely calm given what was happening.

"Back where you two belong," the man said. "First to Dr. Apathy's Lab, then through the portal. After that, we're closing it down for good. I told your mother you'd end up here someday. I'm just sorry you picked the absolute worst time to visit."

Bethany tried to say something, but the man interrupted her. "There's no time for questions. Wait until we're safe. He's coming."

"Who is?" Owen asked, struggling to keep up with the running while talking. "Red Eyes?"

The man paused. "The Dark," he said finally, jerking them down yet another street. "He holds power over the shadow creatures. Don't let them touch you, they'll take over your mind and fill you with hate, just like him. It's all Mason Black's fault, he rewrote all of this to be more edgy. I'm going to throw him in here himself, see how he likes it."

"Mason Black?" Owen asked. "Who's that?"

"Are you . . . Doc Twilight?" Bethany said quietly.

The man went silent, and they all slowed to a stop. "We're here," the voice said. "Apathetic Industries." Owen heard the man step forward and a door open. "Go in. I have to lock it down."

Owen stepped forward with his arms out, feeling for a wall. His hands smacked into something that felt like glass, and he maneuvered along it until he found a doorway, then stepped inside. The building's lobby actually looked a bit lighter, which hopefully meant his eyesight was starting to return.

"I think I can almost see now," Bethany said, making Owen jump in surprise, since he hadn't realized she'd beaten him in.

And then they heard a new voice outside, this one low and grating and familiar. The voice of the red-eyed shadow from back on the roof. "You *dare* mock me with that costume?"

"Get back!" the man who rescued them shouted. There was a loud bang from just inches in front of them, and suddenly everything was muffled. "Run, kids!" they heard from the other side of the glass door.

"You will *suffer* for this," shouted the other voice, and their rescuer began to shout in agony. The glass in front of them creaked like it was going to shatter. "You and anyone else who refuses to follow my laws!"

"*Run*, Bethany!" their rescuer shouted again, and then everything went silent outside.

Owen just stared blindly ahead, not sure what to do or say. And then, just like Doc Twilight had warned, Owen felt a kind of radiating fury from all around them. Even just being close to it, he felt himself growing angry.

"The shadows," he whispered. "They're coming inside."

CHAPTER 12

Bethany shivered to her very core in fear, but her eyesight was returning just enough to see which direction the glass doors were. She ran back to them and pushed on them hard, but the doors stayed locked. Doc Twilight must have done that when they arrived. "Owen, help me!" she shouted. "We can't leave him out there!"

"He saved us so we could get *away*, Bethany!" Owen said to her, his hands awkwardly grabbing for her arms but hitting her shoulders instead. Apparently he couldn't see as well as she could yet. "We need to reach the portal before these shadows get us. Or worse, before they make their way into *our* world!"

Bethany shook her head, not even caring that he couldn't see it. "I'm *not* leaving him. Not again!"

"We'll come back, I promise!" Owen told her. "But we can't

do anything for him now. We need to get help. I swear we won't leave him here. But if we get captured, then we're not going to be rescuing anyone!"

Bethany thrashed her way out of his grasp, then stopped, feeling the shadows' anger as they slid beneath the door. No! She couldn't just leave her father here, not after she'd been so close, right next to him. She hadn't even said anything she'd meant to say when she finally found him. None of it!

"We'll come back," Owen repeated, sounding a little irritated. "We *will*. No matter what."

Bethany rubbed her hand against her cheek, surprised to find it wet. "Yes, we will," she said, shaking her head, then sighing. "Let's go." And with that, she took off toward the back wall, where the elevators were.

She hit the button as soon as she arrived, and the doors opened with a ding. She threw Owen inside, as he was still facing the wrong direction, then jumped in herself, hitting the button for the top floor. Her vision seemed to be returning enough to make out the buttons, but outside the elevator everything was still dark. . . .

Except it wasn't. It was a wave of shadows, crashing toward them.

"Close-close-close-close-close," Bethany repeated, banging on the close-door button.

"That thing never works," Owen said, facing the back of the elevator.

"It better!" Bethany shouted as the shadows grew closer. The wave of monsters crashed down at them as the elevator doors closed, just in time to keep the creatures at bay.

The elevator started rising just as quickly as it'd fallen before, and for a moment Bethany thought they might be safe. After all, there was no way the shadows could move so quickly.

"Did you feel it?" she asked Owen quietly. "What *are* those things?"

"I don't know, but they're definitely cranky," Owen said, waving his hand in front of his face. "Hey, I can kind of see!"

"Good," Bethany said as she watched the floors climb higher. "'Cause we're just about there. At least we left those things behind." But right when the doors opened at the top, shadow tendrils began to seep in from the floor.

"Time to go!" she shouted, pulling Owen out the door as the floor of the elevator broke apart, revealing shadows covering the cables and elevator shaft.

They ran back through the laboratory vault door, while the

shadows climbed onto the floor and began gliding after them. Bethany shoved the lab door closed, then locked it, but that wouldn't hold them for long.

"How do we keep them on this side of the portal?" Owen shouted.

"We can't turn off the machine," Bethany said. "If we do, we won't be getting out either."

"The chains!" he yelled as the shadows began to seep under and around the door on all sides. "In the basement, the ones that covered the manhole. Maybe the chains can keep anything from coming through?"

"Shadows, or my dad," Bethany said, shaking her head. Owen started to say something, but she stopped him. "We'll figure it out. Let's just get through this."

The door went flying off its hinges as a wave of shadows crashed in. Bethany turned and sprinted toward the portal, Owen right behind her, but she stopped just before it, jumped to the side, and slapped the button on Dr. Apathy's death robot.

"FOOLS!" the robot said, powering up as Bethany shoved Owen through the portal. "What madness is this? Creatures formed of hatred, invading my laboratory?! You will pay!"

The robot strode out into the lab, and Bethany watched

for just a moment as the shadows turned to address this new threat. The robot's buzz-saw hands sliced down into the creatures, but just as had happened back in the apartment building, the shadows split apart around the buzz saws, then reformed right after.

"Stay solid, you fools!" the robot shouted. "Dr. Apathy would crush you like the wretches you are!"

The shadows began to form up around the robot, and Bethany swallowed hard. They'd have the death machine down in moments, and she had to go.

She ran to the portal, then dove through it, flying up out of the manhole . . . only to stop in midair. Her flailing hands caught the edge of the manhole on the nonfictional side as something dragged her back down, and she held on as tightly as she could. "Help!" she shouted at Owen, who was gathering the chains. "They're pulling me back!"

Owen looked down at her in shock, even as the shadows reached up through the portal, latching on to Bethany's fingers. "I'll be right back!" he said, then disappeared out of her sight.

"What?" she shouted, feeling the rage of the shadow creatures fill her mind. "Where are you going?!"

One by one, the shadows slowly pulled at her fingers, and all

she wanted to do was attack them, fight them, *pull them apart.*
She felt her vision begin to turn black, but she didn't care. She
wanted *revenge* on these things, to show them that she wasn't
afraid of them, that she wasn't afraid of the Dark, and *she'd tear
them to pieces—*

"Duck!" Owen shouted, and Bethany begrudgingly shoved
herself as far against the floor of the lab as she could. She felt
something fall past her head, and then . . . nothing happened.

"What—" she started to yell, only to have the shadows all
around her abruptly disappear and her rage faded away. The
shadows pulling on her bottom half also vanished, and she
quickly dragged herself up through the manhole. "What did
you do?"

Owen grabbed her arms, helping to pull her up. "I have no
idea! I just grabbed the utility belt from the woman's costume
up here, banged it on the ground a few times, then threw it
down the hole."

Bethany almost choked. "What if there'd been explosives
in it?"

Owen grunted as her feet passed through the manhole, then
dropped her on the floor so he could push the manhole cover
closed once more. "No one would keep real bombs in a utility

belt. That's too dangerous. I just figured it was smoke grenades and hopefully some flash-bangs, like Doc Twilight used on the roof. Looks like I was right!"

Bethany dropped on top of the now-closed manhole cover, breathing hard as her heart beat way too fast. She'd been so angry! "I guess so," she said, "but now we don't have those to use when we go back."

Owen shrugged. "It won't matter. I've got some ideas that should help us. But can you roll out of the way or something? I want to get these chains back on before anything comes through."

Her eyes widened. "Whoops!" She quickly moved away as Owen went to work tying the chains back onto the manhole cover. "There," Owen said, clicking the chains back into the lock. "We should be okay now."

He stood up, admiring his work, then leaped back in surprise as the manhole cover jumped a half-inch in the air like it'd been hit by a bulldozer.

The chains held, though, and the manhole cover didn't come loose enough for anything to get through. Bethany crept forward to investigate, just to make sure, then jumped a bit too when the manhole cover rose again with an enormous bang, followed by a series of hits, over and over.

"They don't seem happy," Owen said. "Maybe next time we go in, we think things through first?"

"Fine," she said, not having the energy to argue. "What do we do? How do we defeat these things?"

"We don't go back alone, first of all," Owen told her. "We're going to need help. Maybe recruit a few friends. That's what superheroes do best after all . . . they team up. And if we're going to beat this Dark guy and rescue, um, Doc Twilight, then we're going to need all the friends we can get."

"Who, the Avengers?" Bethany said.

"Oh no," Owen told her. "I was thinking someone with a bit more *magic.*"

And despite the situation, despite everything, Bethany couldn't help smiling.

CHAPTER 13

The library felt lonelier than it used to. Bethany ran her hands along the books, just to say hello to old friends. At the time, giving up on finding her father seemed like the best thing to do for everyone, but she just felt so . . . *lost* without books.

Still, if she hadn't stopped, she'd never have noticed the man parked outside her home every night and so wouldn't have actually found her father. Which brought up a lot more questions, granted. Her mother must have known, but for how long? And why not tell Bethany, even if her dad couldn't contact her for fear of putting her in danger somehow?

"I'll get the lights," Owen said, interrupting her thoughts as he moved behind the counter.

"Call your mom," Bethany told him, picking up her phone.

Owen paused. "I don't think she can get the lights from

there? And then she'd know we were here, and—"

Bethany rolled her eyes. "Tell her you're staying at my house tonight. I'll tell my mom I'm staying at yours. That way we won't be missed if we don't come back—"

Owen swallowed hard. "Ever?"

"In a few hours," Bethany said, glaring at him.

Owen nodded and went into his mom's office, the lights clicking on a moment later. Bethany waited to make sure he wasn't coming right back, then dialed her mom.

"Hey, Beth," her mother said when she picked up. "How are things at Owen's?"

Bethany tried to speak, but for a moment nothing came out. *Just tell her everything. She already has to know that Dad is alive and well, and watching over us. Find out the truth from her!*

But if she did say all of that, there was no way her mother would let her go back to Jupiter City to rescue her father. More likely, her mom would lock her in her room without even a school book to jump into for the next ten years.

"Things are good," Bethany said finally. "I'm going to spend the night here at Owen's, if that's okay. His mom already said yes."

"Oh, sure," her mom told her. "I'm in the middle of a few things anyway."

"Okay, then," Bethany said after a pause. "I'll see you tomorrow."

"Okay, love you!"

". . . Love you too."

She pushed to end the call, then just stared at the phone for a moment, only to almost jump out of her skin as Owen clapped a hand on her shoulder. "Ready?"

"Don't *do* that," Bethany shouted, whirling around.

Owen's eyes widened in surprise, and he put up his hands in surrender. "Sorry, really. I know you're on edge with all of this. But it'll help if we come up with a plan to rescue Doc Twilight. That way—"

"We don't have time," Bethany said, moving off into the stacks.

"We need a plan, Bethany," Owen said, following behind her. "We can't just jump back in with no idea what we're doing. That's what almost got us captured!"

Bethany shook her head, heading straight for the children's section. "The longer we wait, the more chance my father ends up like that old woman. No, we get some help, then jump back in and hit the Dark hard."

"We don't even know who the Dark is," Owen said as

Bethany grabbed a copy of *Kiel Gnomenfoot and the Source of Magic*, the final volume in the Kiel Gnomenfoot series, then put it down on a nearby table and started flipping to the end.

"He's a supervillain, who cares," Bethany said. "Kiel's magic will take care of it."

Owen put his hand on the pages, and she looked up at him in annoyance. "You said you agreed that we needed to think things through."

"And we did. We thought that we needed help, now we're getting it. It's a comic book world, Owen. They're not exactly hard to figure out, right? Good versus evil, with people wearing their underpants on the outside. I get it. Now let's go find Kiel."

Owen sighed. "I looked up Doc Twilight comics while I was on the phone with my mom. They're apparently so rare that the Internet didn't even have pictures. But I did see that a new series by the same writer is coming out in a month. Remember how Doc Twilight mentioned a guy named Mason Black?"

Bethany scrunched her eyes closed. "So?"

"He's the writer," Owen told her. "And guess what the comic is called."

"I'm not going to guess."

"*The Dark*," Owen told her. "He's the hero. Or the main character, or whatever. I have no idea if he's supposed to be the *good* guy—"

Bethany slammed her hand down. "He took my *father*. You think he's a *good* guy?"

"Who knows, in the comic story," Owen said. "There are plenty of bad guys who get their own comic books. The Joker even had his own title for a while. So we have to be careful—"

"No," Bethany told him. "We don't. I don't care who sees us. I don't care if the entire world knows what I can do. We're going in, getting my dad back, and getting out. Hopefully without being seen, but if we are, then so be it. I don't care anymore, Owen. This is *too important*."

Owen paused, then pointed at the Kiel Gnomenfoot book. "Do you know how we find Kiel?" he asked. "Didn't he say he'd get back in touch with us when he was done finding out who he was without magic?"

Bethany nodded. "He told me to give him a year, in the book time, and to meet him there afterward if I needed help, or just to say . . ." She trailed off, then shook her head. "And we do need help."

"Help, and his magic," Owen said, staring off into space. "I just hope he's got spells that'll give us . . ." Then he trailed off as if realizing just now he'd been talking out loud, and coughed to cover it.

She looked up at him suspiciously. "You're planning something, aren't you? *This* is what messes things up, Owen, every time. We need to just do something, and not come up with clever twists for everything."

He threw his hands up. "It's nothing crazy! Just . . . let's wait and see if it's possible, first. If the magic won't work, there's no reason to freak out."

Great. That sounded *exactly* like a reason to freak out. But now wasn't the time. She held out her hand to him, her other hand holding the book open. "Ready?"

"Not really," he said, but she grabbed his hand anyway and pulled them both straight into the book.

Quanterium looked different from the first time Owen had seen it (the only other visit being Five-Years-Later Charm's presidential speech). Then, he'd been disguised as Kiel Gnomenfoot, who was in turn disguised as a Science Soldier robot, trying to find the Source of Magic to use against Dr. Verity. Charm's ship had just crashed, and Charm herself had almost died. Science Soldiers were everywhere, and the entire world had been gearing for war.

All in all, it wasn't the greatest trip.

Now, though, what was apparently a year later, things seemed to be a lot more peaceful.

Instead of robotic killing machines, real live actual people strolled around on the bright-blue electricity-filled streets. Most were dressed like Quanterians, wearing futuristic-looking clothes with sharp angles and silver sheens, but here and there Owen saw people wearing robes followed around by hovering spell books.

"Magisterians here?" he said, pointing. "Things really *have* changed. Back during the series, they were at war with the Quanterians."

"Charm's going to be elected president in a few years," Bethany said, glancing around. "Things aren't perfect yet, but they're headed there. Kiel and I talked about it a few times when we came in."

"Wait . . . you jumped into Kiel's series *without* me?"

Bethany froze, then cringed. "Sorry," she said. "I wasn't supposed to mention that. We knew who you'd want to see, and I thought we'd caused enough damage to the books already."

Owen just stared at her. *Bethany* was the one who hired a

fictional detective, looking for her father. *She* was the one who'd just gotten her maybe-father kidnapped by a crazy supervillain because they'd broken into his maybe-house. And she thought *Owen* had caused too much trouble?

Whatever. Now wasn't the time, surrounded on all sides by fictional people. "*Fine.* So where's Kiel, then?" he said, realizing his voice sounded a bit pouty, but not caring.

"He said he'd meet me on the spot where he surrendered to the Science Police," she said, and led the way through the crowds as if she'd been here a hundred times.

Owen followed along, glaring at the back of her head. How often had Kiel and Bethany jumped into books without him? Was it just the Kiel Gnomenfoot series, or were there others? And what did that even mean? That they wanted to spend time alone, without him?

The city grew more and more elaborate as they approached the Presidential Palace, where Owen had been captured by Dr. Verity, and then Kiel had jumped in and switched places with him. As memories flooded back, Owen put a hand over his heart, just to feel it beating. It seemed so normal that he often forgot that he had a fictional robotic heart, thanks to Charm.

When Owen had last seen the palace, it'd been surrounded by Science Soldier armies from an infinite amount of dimensions, so he hadn't quite noticed how beautiful it was. Now, with Quanterians both real and holographic walking its steps, he could appreciate the enormousness of the building and how stunning the transparent walls were, filled with crackling electricity.

All in all, it reminded him of how much he missed Charm, and his robotic heart ached.

They quickly climbed the steps and stopped at the palace's entrance, the spot where a year earlier Kiel Gnomenfoot had surrendered Charm's unconscious body to the Science Police, turning himself in to save her life. Escaping hadn't been too hard, of course. Not when your half-fictional friend could pull you out of a Science Police jail cell and into the real world, but still, it'd been a heroic thing for Kiel to have done.

"Where *is* he?" Bethany whispered, turning around in a circle. "He promised he'd be here!"

"You sure you got the right place?" Owen asked, bitterness creeping back into his voice. "I mean, the right page?"

"Of course," she snapped, and Owen realized she wasn't just concerned about her father anymore. "He wanted to meet here because they're going to be putting up a statue of him in a year or two, so he loves sitting here and imagining what it'll look like."

Owen nodded. *That* sounded like Kiel. "Maybe he's just late. Should we jump out and try again at a different time or something?"

"He wouldn't be late, he promised," Bethany said, still searching the crowd. "Something must have happened to him. Something's wrong."

"We don't know that for sure. He didn't have his magic when he left, so maybe he still doesn't. It could just take him a while to get places."

Bethany started to reply, then yanked Owen behind a column, her eyes wide.

"What?" Owen said, but she covered his mouth with her hand. He tried to push past her to look, but she slammed her arm into him.

Two Science Police robots walked past the column, not seeing them. The sight of their robotic walk and laser weapons filled Owen with a kind of dread, but he reminded himself that they weren't trying to kill him anymore. "They're the good guys now, aren't they?" he whispered to Bethany.

"They have my picture on file," she whispered back. "Kiel and I *may* have gotten into some trouble once."

"*How many times* did you come here?" he shouted.

Bethany glanced fearfully at the robots, who stopped at the shout. She quickly pulled Owen around to the other side of the column. Unfortunately, she wasn't looking where she was going and succeeded in shoving Owen directly into a Quanterian. They both crashed to the ground, and Owen sheepishly looked up to apologize, but all the thoughts in his head immediately leaked out his brain.

A fully human-looking Charm Quantum stared up at him from the ground with an annoyed expression. "Nice going," she said. "Walk much?"

CHAPTER 14

Owen froze, still right on top of Charm, so Bethany reached down and helped pull him up. "Sorry about my friend," she told the future president of Quanterium. "It's been a while since we've visited, so he was looking at the buildings, not where he was going."

Charm pushed to her feet, staring at Owen's face. "You look familiar, somehow," she said, a red grid passing over her eyes briefly. "But I've got no memory of you. Neither does the Nalwork."

"Owen!" Owen shouted too loudly. "I'm him! That's me, I mean! My name's Owen."

Bethany and Charm both stared at him as his face began to glow bright red, and he finally turned to Bethany with a pleading look. Clearly he was having some trouble. "We're friends of Kiel Gnomenfoot," Bethany explained.

Charm looked even more irritated at the name. "Where *is* he? I just got alerted that the robotic heart I gave him finally showed up on Quanterium right around here, but I can't pin it down. I haven't seen him for a year now, and I have a *lot* of things I want to say to him."

Bethany exchanged horrified glances with Owen, who clapped his hands over his own heart before turning to Charm. "You could . . . tell those things to me, maybe," he said quietly, and Bethany rolled her eyes.

"Sorry," Charm said, the grid falling back over her eyes as she glanced around. "They're a bit impolite, and very specifically for Kiel."

"Wait. You're *angry* with him?" Owen asked.

"He left me in a hospital without even a *note*," Charm said. "And now I hear all these stories about him off in strange places, specifically not in *jail*, by the way, where he's supposed to be. He's got thirteen thousand and five spells in his spell book, and he can't send me one magical message, one telepathic note to say he's okay and he'll stop by when he's done wasting time?"

"He gave us a message for you!" Owen said quickly. "That's why we're here. To find you."

"No, it's not," Bethany hissed in his ear.

"This better be good," Charm said, narrowing her eyes.

"First, he wanted to say how much he . . . he misses you," Owen said, blushing again. "It's been so long since he's seen you, and he thinks about you. A lot. A *lot* a lot."

For a moment Bethany could have sworn she saw Charm's look soften just a bit, but in a blink it was gone. "So why isn't he here to tell me in person?"

"*Great* question," Bethany said, glancing around again. "Don't you have another, non-heart-related way of tracking him down? Like what if he magicked his heart back to normal? Isn't there some kind of science radar or something that can find him?"

Charm gave her an annoyed look. "If I had a better way of locating him, do you think I'd be sharing my innermost annoyances with you right now? I'd have sent hordes of Science Police out after him, then thrown him in jail for a few more years, just so he'd learn his lesson about skipping out on friends. And anyway, his heart is still beating, and hasn't ever been removed. It's sending out a clear signal, so he's got to be here *somewhere*."

"Maybe he is," Owen said to her nervously. "Maybe he's closer than you think."

"Who are you again?" Charm asked, and Bethany pushed Owen out of the way.

"*He* doesn't matter right now," she said. "If you can't help us find Kiel, then we need to be on our way. Kiel might be in danger. He promised he'd meet us here, and since I don't see him anywhere—"

"Kiel Gnomenfoot makes a lot of promises," Charm said, shaking her head. "A few he might even bother keeping, *if* he remembers them. I thought he'd changed a bit, there at the end, but no. Same old Kiel, same old disappearing act. Just like a Magisterian to turn invisible."

"No, but he *told* me he'd be here," Bethany said, getting annoyed with the formerly half-robotic girl. "If he said he would, he'll *be* here. We're really close."

"I saved two entire *worlds* with him," Charm said, her voice rising. "And trust me, he's lied more to me than to *anyone*."

"Not *all* the time," Owen said, and Charm glanced in his direction.

"Okay, I definitely know you from somewhere," she said.

"*Kiel didn't lie,*" Bethany said, her voice rising too. "If he's not here, that means something's keeping him away."

"Oh really?" Charm turned back to her. "Dr. Verity couldn't

beat Kiel. Neither could a bomb that was going to destroy his entire world, as well as anyone who'd ever used magic. So what, you think he tripped and twisted his ankle? Grow up, kid."

"Kid?" Bethany said, her eyebrows rising.

"Maybe *you* can help us," Owen said, stepping between them.

"I don't *know* you," Charm told him. "So why would I help you again?"

"I'm Owen, like I said," Owen told her. "This is Bethany—"

Bethany slapped her forehead with her palm.

"And we're looking for Kiel because we need his help," Owen finished. "He's helped us in the past, and we're in some bad trouble now."

"Knowing Kiel, he probably caused it," Charm said.

"No, actually," Bethany said, glaring at Owen. "My father's been captured by a . . . powerful magician, who can manipulate darkness. He's taken over an entire city, and we need Kiel's help to fight him."

Charm paused. "Magic, huh? I guess I see why you'd go to Kiel. Did you try the Magister?"

Bethany looked at Owen with wide eyes. Owen just coughed, hiding his blush. "Um, we did, yes," Bethany told her. "He . . . wasn't a big help."

Charm shrugged. "Not surprising. I never liked him much. Everything was always so mystical and obnoxious. Half the time I thought he was hiding something."

Owen coughed again, harder this time, and Bethany shrugged. "You might be right."

"Nothing new about that," Charm said matter-of-factly. She turned and gave Owen a careful look, her eye grid blinking. "So . . . listen. It sounds like you've been left in the lurch by Kiel. I have too. Since he disappeared, now everyone's looking to *me* to unite these two stupid worlds, and right now, all I want to do is some nice, quiet ray-gunning of robots or something." She stepped closer to Owen, staring even more intently at him. "You know, maybe I *will* come along with you two for a bit and take care of your problem. It'll be fun to take down some magic-users. Been a while."

"YES!" Owen said, so loudly that both Bethany and Charm turned to stare. "I mean, that'd be really sweet of you," he finished.

"Sorry, we can't accept your help," Bethany said. "Kiel's the only one who knows what's happening here."

"You know why he's hiding, don't you," Charm said quietly.

"I didn't say that."

"You *do* know. Fine. I'm definitely coming with you now.

And you're going to take me to *Kiel*," she gave Owen a long look, "when we're done."

"If I knew where Kiel was, don't you think I'd go get him right now?"

"C'mon, let's go, then," Charm said, grabbing Owen's hand and trudging off a few feet before stopping and pulling him back to Bethany. "Okay, I don't actually know where your ship is. But I'm coming with you, and we're going to take care of this magician, and then we're going to have a long talk about where *Kiel Gnomenfoot* actually is." She gave Owen a long, suspicious look.

"I'd like that," Owen said quietly.

Charm sighed, deeply annoyed.

"You want to come?" Bethany shouted in frustration, then grabbed both their hands. "I'm tired of arguing. If you're coming, then you're coming! And you can just deal with *this*!" And then she jumped all three of them out of the book and back into the library. "There you go. *Happy now?!*"

"More than I can even say," Owen said.

CHAPTER 15

Charm pushed Bethany away and opened up her completely human-looking arm, revealing circuitry beneath it. A small radar dish pushed up out of Charm's forearm, and she glanced up in confusion as it twisted around. "Where *is* this place?" she said. "We're nowhere in the known universe. Is this another dimension?"

"*Yes,*" Owen said quickly. "It's just like in *Kiel Gno* . . . like when you and Kiel found the infinite dimensions that Dr. Verity gathered all of his Science Soldiers from. This is another dimension, only in this one, there's no magic, and science is a lot less cool."

"I'm not even picking up warp signatures," Charm said, a disgusted look on her face. "No magic *and* no science?"

"There's plenty of science," Bethany said, taking out her cell phone to show to Charm. After her outburst, she seemed a little embarrassed, but it wasn't like Owen was going to get on her case about it. She'd brought Charm into the real world, after all!

Charm looked at the cell phone, then at Bethany, then back at the cell phone. "No magic *and* no science beyond toys for infants? Where exactly have you brought me?"

Owen stepped in front of Bethany, who went from embarrassed to violently angry far faster than Owen could believe. "This is a sort of nexus between worlds," he said, gesturing around at the books. "All of these books lead to other dimensions, and Bethany's the one who can take us there. That's *her* form of magic."

"It's not magic," Bethany said.

"It's close enough," Owen said, throwing her an annoyed look. Couldn't she just play along for two seconds?

"So we needed to come to this nexus first, and from here we can teleport to the other world you spoke of," Charm said, nodding in understanding. The radar dish collapsed back into her arm, and the skin restored itself as if nothing had happened. Apparently she'd gotten some upgrades after the war ended. "I see. Well, let's get on with it, then."

"It's not that simple," Bethany said. "You don't know what

we're getting into. That's why I wanted Kiel, because his magic could—"

"Anything Kiel can do, I can do better," Charm said, giving Owen a look that basically dared him to disagree. When he just smiled at her, she sighed. "Besides, I don't *see him here*, so I guess you're stuck with me." She glared at Owen again, and he swallowed hard.

Bethany growled in frustration, dropping her head into her hands. "You don't get it, and it's not your fault, because you shouldn't even be here, but still. The place we're going? It's a whole *city* of people with powers. Like if they each knew one really dangerous magic spell and could cast it as many times as they wanted."

"You know I'm not an infant, right?" Charm said, finally turning away from Owen to glare at Bethany. "I'm aware of what powers mean. The Volka of Magisteria gave themselves the power to speak to animals through magic."

"Exactly!" Owen said. "Just imagine that instead of talking to animals, people in this city will be able to control shadows, or are as strong as Science Soldiers, or can fly."

Charm shrugged. "And?" She clicked her hips and two ray guns popped out. "I can lift half a ton with my robotic arm, and my ray guns will cut through steel. I'm not worried."

"You should be," Bethany said. "*I* am. I can get us there, yes. But other than that, I've got no real powers. And neither does Owen."

"I wouldn't say *no* powers," Owen said quickly. "I've done magic before."

Charm sighed. "Are we really going to keep playing this game?"

Owen turned bright red. "I don't know what you mean?"

"*Fine,*" she said, throwing her hands up in surrender. She grabbed a chair from the nearest table and sat down. "Tell me what you need, and I'll make it for you." She began sketching lines on the table as if she were using a touch screen. Wherever she moved her fingers, electric-blue lines appeared.

Bethany narrowed her eyes. "What are you talking about?"

"You said you wanted powers," Charm said. "I'm going to make them for you." She looked up at Bethany, and the red grid in her eye lit up for a moment. Back on the table a full sketch of Bethany appeared. "That's what science does, you magical hea-thens. Science makes things using logic and electricity. Magic makes things up, science makes things *work*. Now what do you want to do?"

"What powers do we want, you mean?" Owen asked.

Charm just sighed, tapping her foot.

Bethany paused, then looked off toward the book stacks. "Would you be able to give someone the power to fly?"

Charm raised an eyebrow. "Like in a spaceship?"

"No, just by herself?"

"Of course," Charm said with a snort. "You're talking about jet packs. I made those in kindergarten. I'd just need some materials." She tapped the table in a few places, and an elaborate list of items appeared, then came together to form what looked like a jet pack on Bethany's back in the image.

"Be right back," Bethany said, smiling out of nowhere, and disappeared into the bookshelves, leaving Owen and Charm alone.

"And what about you, magic boy?" Charm asked, scanning him in as well. "What power do you want? Since you're apparently *not* using magic. Try to make it at least a bit challenging. I'm getting bored quickly."

Owen felt his entire face burn as he looked at her. She obviously suspected that he was Kiel, if just from his heart. Couldn't he just say who he was? Well, who he'd been pretending to be? *I was Kiel Gnomenfoot, Charm, but not the real one. I was the version that you actually kind of liked, the one who saved you, and you saved right back. I have the robotic heart that you gave me. And I've missed you so much!*

"I'd like to run really fast," he blurted out.

Charm stared at him. "You want to run . . . fast."

His face turned even redder, and he nodded, trying to make it sound good, while inside, he just screamed at how stupid he was being. "You know, *really* fast."

"Not helping," Charm said. "What are we talking, the speed of sound? The speed of light? *Faster?*"

Owen's heart began to race with excitement. "Yes! Is that possible?"

"No," Charm said, giving him a pitying look. "Not unless you want to gradually become so heavy that you suck the whole world into the black hole you create. You'd need warp technology to avoid that, and I don't see us getting an entire warp engine on your back." She paused. "Though *that'd* be fun to try. I wonder if . . ." She tapped the desk a few times, and Owen's image began to spin around as various lights ran up and down him. "Would you be okay if I made you move faster *without* running? It'd be cheating, but it'd get the job done."

"Uh, yeah, that sounds amazing!" She was going to give him speed powers like the Flash? This would be the greatest thing ever! Maybe he could move faster than the speed of dark, not even letting the shadows touch him.

"Give me a second, I just need to think through some variables," Charm said, nodding. She tapped the desk a few more times, her robotic fingers leaving more trails of light.

And then the Owen on the screen burst into flames, began screaming, and collapsed into a pile of ashes.

"Huh," Charm said, erasing the image. "I must have forgotten to carry the one."

Owen's eyes widened and he backed away. Maybe it was time to give Charm some room to plan? He glanced around, suddenly realizing Bethany hadn't come back. Was now really the time to just disappear? What was more important than coming up with their superpowers, anyway?

CHAPTER 16

Bethany floated into the air over Argon VI, a planet whose green sun granted anyone from Earth superpowers. She spun slowly in a circle as she scanned the horizon. At first she couldn't see anyone, but then realized she could use her enhanced zoom vision to get a closer look.

There. Off to the east, a girl in a T-shirt with a symbol of the Earth on it was doing loop-de-loops in the air.

In spite of everything that had happened that day, Bethany grinned and took off so fast she left a sonic boom in her wake. EarthGirl had just enough time to look up and scream in joy before Bethany slammed into her, hugging her close as both girls laughed.

"Bethany!" Gwen shouted, squeezing Bethany hard enough to almost crack her ribs. "I can't believe you're back. I'm so happy to *see* you!"

"I've missed you too," Bethany said, and really meant it. After Kiel not showing up, and being so worried that he was hurt . . . no, that wasn't worth even thinking about. Now it just felt good to see Gwen, who'd been sent to Argon VI as a baby when her Earth had supposedly been destroyed, and here she'd become a superhero.

If Owen wanted superhero help, EarthGirl was perfect . . . at least, once Charm gave her some non-alien-planet-related powers. Gwen herself being awesome was just a huge bonus.

"What brings you to Argon VI?" Gwen asked, raising an eyebrow. Then her face lit up. "*Tell me you're here just to visit. I have so many things to show you!*"

Before Bethany could speak, EarthGirl grabbed her hand and pulled her into flight fast enough to take Bethany's breath away. They sped through cloud banks made of every color not in the rainbow, dove to the very bottom of the sea and saw the great fish queen Poi Poi Gan, then floated above Gwen's home city on Argon VI, just high enough in the clouds for no one on the ground to make out their faces as EarthGirl pointed out the sights, all faster than the speed of sound.

Finally, Gwen led them straight up, up and away, right out

of the atmosphere and into outer space. Bethany immediately held her breath, but Gwen shook her head, smiling. "You don't need to worry!" she said. "Argon's green sunlight actually causes human cells to create oxygen, among other things. Look!" She pointed down at Bethany's arm, and Bethany followed her gaze, using her enhanced vision.

Her eyes widened, and she looked up at Gwen. "They *are* making oxygen," she whispered, staring at her cells. "I can actually see them doing it!"

"C'mon!" Gwen said, then flew off ahead of Bethany, just slow enough for her to keep up. She led Bethany to one of Argon VI's twin moons, then landed down next to what looked an awful lot like a small house made of moon stones with the word WELCOME carved into the dirt at the door.

Bethany just stared at her. "Is this . . . your Fortress of Solitude?"

"Solitude? No, I call it my Friendly House of Welcoming!" Gwen said, gesturing for Bethany to enter.

Bethany quickly floated inside, unable to stop smiling. Everything was just so cozy and wonderful and adorable, from a brick fireplace with some kind of blue flame (how did *that* work without oxygen?) to a twenty-foot-long bathtub to a whole row of hot chocolate makers. "How did you do all of this?"

Gwen shrugged, leaping into what looked like an incredibly comfy beanbag chair. "It doesn't take long when you can move as fast as we can!" She pointed to another beanbag chair. "These are filled with moon rocks that I pulverized, so let me know if it's not comfortable and I'll punch it a few more times."

Okay, none of this was in the books. When had she made it? Bethany settled into the chair, then gasped at how comfortable it was. "This is *amazing*," she said, feeling more relaxed than she had in days. "You should sell these!"

Gwen laughed. "Stop it, it's not that great. I just wanted this to be nice and welcoming, if you ever came back. Like a clubhouse for my friends, you know?"

Bethany froze. "You made this for *me*?"

Gwen blushed. "Well, for both of us, and anyone else you brought along from Earth. I know you were worried about not being seen down on my world, so you don't accidentally break the timelines and all, so I figured this would make things easier on you."

Right. Bethany had told Gwen when they'd first met that she'd come from the future and was searching for her missing father. That was before Bethany had taken Gwen to the non-fictional world, just to give Gwen a glimpse of an Earth she'd never known. Not Bethany's wisest move, but that, at least, was one thing she didn't regret.

Gwen continued the tour. "There's a kitchen back there, and nothing ever goes bad because it's all frozen in the vacuum of space. Just use your heat vision to cook it. I built a plumbing system that should work, but I might need to unfreeze some of the water, just to get it started. I'll go check on that in a second. Can I get you anything?"

"No, I'm fine," Bethany said quickly, holding out a hand to stop Gwen from getting up. Was this really all true? Gwen had done all of this for *her*? "I just . . . I don't know what to say."

"Don't say anything," EarthGirl said. "You did the nicest thing in the world for me, when you brought me to Earth. This is really the *least* I could do. I wish there were more, honestly."

Ugh, seriously? Bethany felt even worse now about asking for a favor. "Speaking of that," she said, sitting forward in her moon rock–bag chair so she didn't have to look Gwen in the eye. "I actually *could* use your help."

"Done," Gwen said, leaning forward too. "Are we heading back to the future? Is this about your father?"

"No. Yes. It's a bit complicated." Bethany gritted her teeth, the day's events all flooding back. "I *did* find my father," (Gwen gasped), "but he's being held captive by someone, and I need help to rescue him."

"That's awful!" Gwen said, looking shocked. "I'm so, so sorry. But don't worry, we're going to rescue him right now!" She leaped up to her feet, and almost flew out of the house before Bethany grabbed her hand to stop her.

"Here's the thing," Bethany said. "This guy who's holding my father . . . he has powers just like yours. The whole city there does. The powers aren't exactly like yours, some are really different, but—"

Gwen gasped. "Are they all Earthers? Is the sun green as well?"

"They *are* from Earth. This city's actually on Earth, sort of—"

"You're taking me back to Earth?!"

"But the sun is yellow," Bethany finished. "So if you *do* help . . ."

"I'll be powerless," Gwen finished, then shrugged. "So when do we leave?"

Huh? How could she be so confident in her decision? "You'd come help me without any powers?"

Gwen looked confused. "Of course. Why wouldn't I?"

"Because it's dangerous, and you'd be . . . well, normal!"

Gwen laughed. "So? I'm not helping you because I'm super strong, Bethany. I'm helping because you need it and you're my friend! So how do we take down this bad guy and rescue your dad?"

"There actually might be a way to keep at least one of your powers," Bethany told her, feeling so thankful she could burst. "But just to warn you, you're going to meet some odd people. One Earther, yes, as well as someone who looks like she's from Earth, but isn't so much, and is also incredibly obnoxious."

"Stop it, you're getting me so excited!" Gwen shouted, jumping to her feet. "I mean, not the part about this bad guy and your dad being held captive, but that's all fine. We're going to stop him and rescue your dad, and maybe spend a little extra time on Earth, just to visit some places!"

Bethany grinned, stood up, and gave Gwen the biggest hug she could.

Gwen hugged her back, then gave her a questioning look. "What was that for? Not that I mind . . . hugs are obviously amazing."

"Don't ever change," Bethany said, then grabbed her hand and jumped them out to the real world.

CHAPTER 17

Got someone else to help!" Bethany shouted from the stacks, and Owen looked up in surprise to find a girl wearing a T-shirt with the Earth on it standing next to Bethany, looking incredibly shocked.

"So many books," said the girl as she ran her hands over the shelves. "I never thought I'd actually see this many! My parents left me a few, but they're all I had. There are more books than just detective novels?"

"A lot more," Bethany told her. "Though see that section over there? Those are all mysteries. Maybe you can borrow some more detective novels if you want!"

"Um, take all you want," Owen said, trying to decide which story he knew her from, and how he felt about Bethany just pulling random characters out to help her. Hadn't that been against *her* rules? "The fewer mystery books we have here, the safer I feel. I'm Owen, by the way."

The girl turned to stare at him with a huge grin. "So you're from *Earth*," she said, sounding amazed. "I am too! I don't live there anymore, though. I'm Gwen! Some people call me—"

"EarthGirl?" Owen's mouth dropped open as he finally made the connection with her T-shirt/costume. Bethany had pulled out *EarthGirl*? Then why exactly couldn't they ask Batman for help?!

Gwen gave Owen a confused look. "You've heard of me?"

"He's from my time," Bethany explained, giving Owen a dirty look. "Everyone in the future knows about EarthGirl. You're famous!"

Gwen began to blush, and Owen flashed Bethany a *whoops* look. Still, he wasn't going to take the blame for anything now that Bethany was pulling fictional people out of books left and right. And another fake story, this time about being from the future? How was he supposed to keep track of all of these?

"What's an Earth?" Charm said, rifling through a book on quantum physics. She shook her head. "This thing's so out of date. No wonder you people need my help."

"So you must be the one *not* from Earth," Gwen said to Charm, sticking out her hand.

"I'm from Quanterium," Charm said without looking up. "It's a different dimension. Don't worry about it. I'm just here to find a friend of mine and yell at him." She looked up and gave Owen another dirty look.

Gwen nodded, then whispered to Bethany, "Is her friend your father?"

Bethany sighed. "Let's all just stop asking questions that no one really should have the answers to, if that's okay. I shouldn't have brought you all together, since—"

"Time travel," Gwen said, nodding again. "We don't want to reveal too much about the future."

Charm's eyes narrowed. "Wait a second. You didn't say *anything* about time travel. And this doesn't look anything like the future Kiel and I visited."

"Different dimensions," Owen told her, thinking quickly. "This is the past of Gwen's dimension, and Bethany's from the future."

Charm stared at him for a moment in silence, then shook her head. "Don't care. It's not relevant. Are we enhancing you two or not?"

"She needs something to help her fly," Bethany said. "And Owen could maybe use some kind of weapon, too."

"We covered what I'm going to get already," Owen said quickly, not looking at Bethany. The last thing he wanted to do was give her the chance to veto his awesome new super-powers. After all, if he *had* to have a robot heart, the least he could do was also have the ability to move faster than light. It was only fair.

Bethany gave him a suspicious look, then sighed. "Fine. Charm, what do you need for—"

"A laboratory," she said, slamming the quantum physics book shut and tossing it over her shoulder. "We can use mine, if you teleport us back to my dimension. I have everything we need there."

"Can I talk to you for a second?" Owen whispered to Bethany as Gwen sat down cross-legged in front of the nearest shelves and began pulling out books one by one. He dragged Bethany aside, just out of Charm's hearing.

"I know what you're doing," Bethany whispered back. "You *can't* have permanent superpowers."

"That's not what this is about," he said, inwardly cursing. "We can't let Charm use her Quanterian science to give us powers. Science in Charm's world *works*, and that's the last thing we want."

Bethany just stared at him for a moment. "Did you go insane since I left?"

"We need comic book science for this," he said. "How do superheroes get their powers? *By accident*, and almost always in a science experiment gone wrong. But it's not normal science, not in a comic book world. If a radioactive spider bit us here, or in Charm's world, it'd just make us sick from radiation. That, or kill us. But in the comic book world, we'd have Spider-Man's powers and be the star of, like, five movies by now."

Bethany gave him an incredulous look. "So let me see if I'm hearing you right. You're suggesting we go back into Dr. Apathy's lab, which is filled with shadow monsters by the way, so Charm can use machines she's never seen before and do crazy things to us which might give us powers if we first cause an *accident*? That's what you're telling me?"

"Pretty much," Owen told her, shrugging. "It's how super-heroes get their powers, and if we want to beat the Dark, we're going to have to play by the same rules he does."

Bethany just shook her head, her mouth hanging open. "This might be your worst idea since you saved the Magister."

Owen nodded. "Probably. But I'm right about this, and you know it."

"I know you're *crazy!*" She sighed. "How are we going to get the shadows out of Dr. Apathy's lab, then?"

"Well, we don't have to play by *all* the rules," Owen said. "Grab some flash-bangs or something from other books. We'll toss a few dozen in there, light bomb the shadows, and walk in with no problem."

"This is a horrible idea," Bethany whispered.

"Yup," Owen said, nodding. "But we're doing it to rescue Doc Twilight and see if he's your father, and I don't know any other way to do that."

"He *is* my father, you saw the comic," Bethany said, then paused. "Captain America didn't get his powers in an accident. He volunteered for them."

"He's the greatest superhero ever," Owen said. "We can't all be that awesome."

"Fine," Bethany said. "But don't blame this on me if you get, like, six arms or turn into a mutant or something."

"Like in *X-Men!*" Owen said, looking off into the distance dreamily. "You know, mutants get their powers around age twelve or thirteen, without having to do anything else. Do you know how many times I tried walking through walls like Kitty Pryde on my last birthday?"

"Based on what's left of your brain, I can guess," she said.

"Hey!" Owen said, but she had already turned back toward the others.

"The whole planet collapsed," Gwen was telling Charm. "The reason's a bit hazy, since my parents didn't have time to record it all in my ship's memory, but something about supervolcanoes?"

"A supervolcano wouldn't collapse a planet," Charm pointed out, sketching plans in midair now. Apparently she didn't even need a desk. "It might kill all life, but the planet would still be there."

"So you think *my* Earth might still be out there?" Gwen said, her eyes widening. "I always had hoped, but—"

"Don't answer her!" Bethany said quickly, trying to keep Gwen from spoiling the rest of her series for herself. As EarthGirl's face fell, Bethany put a hand on her shoulder. "I'm sorry, but it's time travel. You shouldn't find out too much. That includes hearing from people who really don't have any idea what they're talking about."

"Is that right?" Charm said, raising an eyebrow. "Then how about we talk about *you*, mystery girl? Because according to my instruments, you're giving off some strange readings—"

"She *always* gives off the strangest readings," Owen said quickly as he rejoined them. "So we have a different laboratory for you, Charm. It's actually perfect for our needs. Does that work for you?"

"Fine, whatever," Charm said. "Let's just get this over with."

"First, you need to know what we're walking into," Bethany said. "Jupiter City is the home to people with strange and wonderful powers, and not all of them use those powers for good. There's a man—"

"Or monster," Owen supplied.

"Named the Dark that somehow controls shadows," Bethany said, pointing at her own shadow on the wall. "He—"

"So we shoot them," Charm said, pulling a ray gun out and aiming it at Bethany's shadow.

"No!" Bethany yelled, jumping forward and shoving the ray gun down. Charm just glared at her. "Not the shadows here, just in Jupiter City. I'll tell you when to start worrying, okay?"

"Make up your mind," Charm said, pushing her ray gun back into her hip.

"That's so cool!" Gwen whispered to Charm.

"These shadows can take any shape," Bethany continued. "And they seem to have the power to infect your mind. We met a woman who looked like she was controlled by them somehow, and her eyes were covered in blackness."

"It was so creepy," Owen said. "Also, she was *cranky!*"

Bethany nodded. "They got close to me, and I could feel them taking over, making me furious." She paused and unclenched her fists, not even realizing she'd done that. "Doesn't matter. Just stay away from them if you can."

"Or destroy them," Charm said. "We're not here to run, after all. So is that it?"

"The Dark has my father," Bethany said. "That's who we're there for. No matter what, we're bringing him home. Anything other than that doesn't matter."

Owen frowned. "What about Jupiter City? We can't just leave it under the Dark's control."

Bethany shook her head. "My dad is all that matters, Owen. We're not heroes here. This is *only* a rescue mission. So don't do anything crazy and heroic. Get in, grab my father, and get out. Got it?"

Owen looked over at Gwen, who also seemed concerned. Charm, though, just sighed. "I've saved two planets in less time than you've been talking. How about we just get to the raygunning part?"

CHAPTER 18

Owen opened the door to Doc Twilight's house slowly, bracing for a shadow attack, just in case the creatures had found a way up through the manhole cover.

The house *was* dark, but none of the shadows seemed to be moving, so that was good. The Dark must not have been able to get through . . . yet. Whatever those chains were doing, Owen hoped they kept it up. Given how thin they were, maybe they were made of superhero metal or had been magicked or something.

Bethany pushed past him and flipped on the lights to the basement, and Gwen led the way down the stairs, then went completely silent in awe at the costumes. She ran a hand along the glass cases reverently, then turned back to them, her eyes wide. "*These* are the vestments of my people?" she said, pointing at the one labeled Night Star and the costume's flashy cape. "I've been doing it all wrong, haven't I?"

Bethany shook her head. "Trust me, you're doing fine. Ignore these. They're more like a museum piece than anything."

"You're kidding me," Charm asked, pointing at the chains covering the manhole cover. "This is the level of technology you people are reduced to? You're worse than Magisterians. I'd feel pity, if my heart still existed."

Owen laughed loudly at this, and the others all turned to look at him. His face exploded with redness, and he quickly moved over to the smaller costume case with the boy's costume in it and opened it. "Hold on one second."

"What are you *doing*?" Bethany asked him, slamming the case closed again.

"We're going to need costumes for this, Bethany," Owen said, not looking her in the eye, just in case she could see how much he really, *really* wanted to be wearing a real live superhero costume. "We need to follow the rules, remember?" He lowered his voice. "And more importantly, we need to cover our faces, in case people reading this comic might recognize us."

"I told you, I don't care about that. Not anymore. And you're *not* wearing that."

"Don't you trust me?" Owen said as he opened the case and

pulled out a Twilight throwing star, which he immediately dropped on his foot, cutting a small hole in the tip of his shoe. He looked up to find her glaring at him. "Hey, it's not like I hit a toe or something!"

Bethany gritted her teeth, then whirled around as Charm ripped the chains off of the manhole with her crazy robotic strength. "What are *you* doing?!"

"Getting on with things?" Charm said. "I'm sorry, did you want me to hold everything up while you opened your lock from ancient times? I can put them back if you want." She dropped the chains loudly back on the manhole cover, then crossed her arms, waiting.

"We're going to need to lock this again when we come back out!" Bethany shouted. "How are we going to do that if you rip up the chains?"

"I'm sure we can figure something out," Gwen said, stepping between them. "It'll be fine."

"Or I could actually just lock it for real," Charm pointed out. "You know, using actual science instead of a toddler's toy."

"How do I look?" Owen said, and the three turned to stare at Owen, in his normal clothes, but now wearing the boy costume's mask, cape, and utility belt. He whirled around once, making the cape fly out majestically, only it wrapped around his shoulders and he had to fight to get out of it.

"What did I say?" Bethany shouted.

"Okay, I'm going home," Charm said.

"I love it, Owen," Gwen said. "It's maybe the most amazing thing I've seen in my whole life."

"Thank you," Owen said. "Look at all the cool things in this belt!" He opened a pouch and pulled out three pellets. "What do you think these are?"

It took a few minutes for the smoke to dissipate, and when it did, Owen realized his utility belt was gone. "Hey!"

"You're not keeping this," Bethany told him, strapping it on herself. She rummaged through the pouches, making sure there was nothing that was going to explode, then dropped the collection of flash-bangs she'd brought from other books into some pouches. "I hope this is going to be enough. And take those other things off."

"It should be fine," Owen told her as he reluctantly pulled off the cape and mask. "I dropped your mom's belt in before, and that had a lot less than you have now."

Bethany's eyes widened, and she slowly turned to look at the last two glass cases. "My mom's belt?" she said quietly.

Had she not realized that? "I mean, I don't know for sure," Owen said quickly, "but it seems like that would be what it was. I just kind of assumed your mom would go back into your dad's world with him, at least at the beginning, and they'd fight crime together. Who *wouldn't* want to do that?"

Bethany slowly opened the glass case with the woman's costume in it and put her hand on the star symbol. She didn't say anything for so long that Owen started to get nervous. "Are you okay?" he asked her quietly.

Bethany didn't turn around. "Nope."

Uh-oh. Owen looked around for a change of subject, and tapped the one glass case with a mannequin of a younger girl. "Hey. This one looks like it might have been meant for you. How cool is that?"

Bethany turned, and Owen noticed that she had tears in her eyes. She glanced at the mannequin of a girl in the glass case, then wiped her hands over her eyes and shook her head. "Doesn't matter. Let's just get this over with. I don't want to leave my dad with the Dark one more minute."

"Are we finally ready?" Charm said with a heavy sigh, her hand on the manhole. "Or does everyone need to have another moment first?"

Gwen giggled, and Charm smirked. "*These* people, huh?"

"I've literally never been this happy," Gwen said, and Charm groaned.

"Everyone be prepared for what's on the other side," Bethany said, her voice a bit choked up as she stepped over to the manhole next to Charm. "There could be anything, up to and including either the Dark himself, or just a whole host of his shadow creatures. If anything's in there, we throw a bunch of flash-bangs in, close the manhole, then wait for the light to fade. Agreed?"

All three nodded, even if Charm did so in annoyance. "Okay," Bethany said. "Open it up."

Charm ripped the manhole cover up and tossed it aside with a heavy clang, then bent down eagerly to see what awaited.

The hole immediately exploded with darkness, filling the room before any of them could move.

CHAPTER 19

A terrible mixture of fear and rage filled Bethany's mind, and she felt her vision going black again. Rescuing her father, protecting her friends, all of that disappeared in a flood of anger. All she wanted to do was *attack*.

"I'll destroy you all!" she screamed at the shadows, then tossed her flash-bangs to the ground as hard as she could, covering her face with her other arm.

Even through the cover, the bright explosion still almost blinded her. The awful anger and fear instantly faded, though, and she took a deep breath to try to calm herself. She dropped her arm and blinked, at least able to see this time, even if there were some spots of light still imprinted on her eyes. "Is . . . everyone okay?"

"I thought you were exaggerating," Charm said, staring down into the manhole. "This really *is* some magic garbage again, isn't it?" She seemed calm enough, but Bethany noticed her hands were shaking. "Better see if there are more of them," she said, then leaped into the blue flame portal.

"Wait!" Owen shouted, and jumped in right after her.

"What is everyone doing?!" Bethany said, grabbing Gwen before she could follow. "Hold on! We don't know what's in there!"

"Yes we do," Gwen told her, somehow completely unshaken by the shadows' attack. "Our friends, and they need our help. Coming?" She held out a hand, and Bethany took it, shaking her head as they leaped through the hole together.

The two of them shot out of the blue-fire portal just as quickly as they'd fallen, skidding across the floor. Or at least Bethany assumed it was the floor, because she couldn't see anything. Though this time, it wasn't because of the shadows or blindness from flash-bangs.

"What is this?" she started to ask, but ended up coughing too hard to say anything.

"Smoke . . . bomb!" Owen said from somewhere nearby, coughing as well. "I think I . . . landed on your mom's . . . utility belt. A bunch of things went off."

"Interestingly, the shadows aren't approaching," Charm

said. She didn't seem to have any trouble breathing. Being half robot apparently had some advantages. "The smoke must not let them pass through it, I suppose. Hold on." Something metallic clicked, and then Bethany heard an electronic whine. "Now let's see how these things like a little science!"

As the smoke began to dissipate, the angry feelings began to seep in, and Bethany realized Charm had been right: The shadows *had* held back. But now they were on the attack again, and she was out of flash-bangs. Before she could move, though, a bright white light shot through the smoke just inches from her face, and she almost fell over in surprise.

"Ha!" Charm shouted. "You like that, shadow thing?"

"Whoa, it exploded!" Owen said from somewhere over by Charm. "How did you do that?"

"Light can be either a wave or a particle," Charm said, shooting a few more times. "I just modified my ray guns to send out waves that become particles as soon as they hit one of these things. Basically they're light bullets. It's like elementary school stuff."

"How can you see?" Bethany said, struggling not to cough in the smoke.

"Infrared in the eyes," the half-robotic girl said. "Why, do you not have that yet?"

Bethany started to say something but was yanked backward instead, then slammed to the ground by a shadow. As its rage and fear filled her mind again, she tried desperately to get free, but the creature's hand covered her face, and the darkness began to seep into her mouth.

"Bethany?" Gwen said from what sounded like many miles away.

The shadow pulled her away from the others, but Bethany barely noticed as anger and terror began spinning around and around in her brain. She thought she could see the darkness moving as more of the creatures grabbed for her, but then a larger wave of hatred and fear hit her like a punch to the face. She gasped at the intense feelings, then began thrashing around violently. *Who did these creatures think they were, scaring her like this? She'd destroy them, wipe them off the face of the Earth along with anything else that thought it knew better than her, thought it could scare her. She'd make the world safe by burning it to the ground if she had to!*

Someone shouted from very far away, but she couldn't hear, not over the sound of her pounding heart. *Get off of me! Let me go, you can't have me! I'll rip you apart, all of you!*

A bright light exploded just past her head, bringing her back to reality. The shadow over her face disappeared, and she collapsed to the floor, her whole body limp. Though she was still scared, somehow it wasn't so intense, and the hate-filled rage dissipated quickly.

What *were* these shadow things? And more importantly, what would she have done if the thing had completed its takeover of her?

Someone yelled again, closer now, and another light shot past her. Shadowy bits exploded around her, and she tried to move to see who was doing all the rescuing, but couldn't.

Finally, the darkness disappeared, and a bit of energy returned. Bethany managed to lift her head just enough to see Owen and Charm standing over her, Charm aiming her ray gun above Bethany's head.

Someone from Bethany's side gently pushed her head back down. "You had us worried for a minute there," Gwen said, leaning over her with a smile. "You're sure you're feeling all right?"

"No," Bethany said, trying to smile and failing. "Are the shadows all gone?" Almost against her will, she remembered the flood of hatred and fear she'd felt, and shivered.

"I got rid of them, no thanks to the rest of you," Charm

said, finishing up her ray-gunning at Bethany's feet. "You're not wrong. You really *do* need me to give you powers."

"Or just let us borrow your ray guns," Bethany said, trying to forget the emotions the shadow had pushed on her.

"No one touches my little princesses," Charm said, clicking the ray guns off. "But that's all there were, right? No more shadows?"

"The entire city is filled with them," Owen said quietly.

Charm sighed. "I really, *really* do hate magic."

"That's okay," Bethany said, groaning as she stood up. Gwen rushed to help, and Bethany got up to her feet. "I can go grab more flash-bangs. I just have to jump back through the portal real quick and grab some book pages from the library."

"The portal," Owen said. "Um, what happened to it?"

"What's wrong?" Bethany said, turning around to look.

The portal was gone. And with it, any chance of them getting out of Jupiter City.

CHAPTER 20

They all stopped and stared at the spot where the blue circle of fire had been before the shadow attack. Charm opened her arm up and began scanning the room. "The machine powering the trans-dimensional gate is gone," she said, nodding at a now-empty spot near the wall. "The shadows must have taken it when they fled."

"While we were fighting them off Bethany, probably," Owen said quietly. He looked over at her, unsure what to say.

Bethany gritted her teeth, staring at the floor for a moment, then shook her head. "Doesn't matter."

"Doesn't matter?" Owen said quickly. "We might be *stuck* here."

"We're going to rescue my father," she said, glaring at him. "And when we find him, we find the portal machine too. This doesn't change anything."

"Except that now we have no way to escape or get more help," Owen said, spreading his hands. "Shouldn't we maybe think about finding another way home before doing anything else?"

Bethany's eyes narrowed, and she opened her mouth to yell, when Gwen stepped between them with her hands up. "Hey, this is going to be okay," EarthGirl said, looking back and forth between Bethany and Owen. "The last thing we should do is argue amongst ourselves. How about instead we prepare in case the shadows come back?"

Owen paused, then nodded, and Bethany did too. Gwen grinned. "See? We're all on the same side, even when things go wrong. We can do this as a *team*!"

Charm sighed deeply. "If I hear anything else about a team, I'm going to throw up. But she's right. Who wants to be genetically engineered first?" She wandered past the killer robot with Dr. Apathy's brainwaves, giving it a derisive snort, then moved over to the remaining machines, taking inventory of what they had. "Wow, I haven't seen one of *these* since a museum trip to Quark. This thing can't still work, can it? No way, is that a transmogrifier?"

Owen watched her for a moment, then moved closer to Bethany. "Look, I'm sorry about that. It's just—"

"No, you're right," Bethany said, not looking at him. "This whole thing is going downhill fast. Let's just have Charm do her thing, then get my dad and the portal machine so we can go home."

"Sure," Owen said. "Speaking of that, I have an idea about the powers. You might not like it, but hear me out."

She shrugged. "At this point, what's the worst that could happen?"

He paused, wondering how best to put this. "I want to base our powers off a superhero team. Teams in comic books come together to handle things when the individual heroes can't, and that seems like exactly what's happening here. Plus, it'd make our powers complement each other."

Bethany sighed. "How much of this is the comic book world rules, and how much is you just wanting to get certain powers?"

He half smiled. "Don't ask. Anyway, there are a bunch of iconic comic book teams, but given how old we are and who we've got here, there's one that works best for us. First, the team has a magic-user—"

"Which we don't have," Bethany said.

"I know, that would have been Kiel," Owen said. "But that's okay, it also has a half-robot guy, and we have Charm."

"Fair enough," Bethany said as Charm hit a button and a large death-ray-looking machine began to power up. Charm began to laugh in what was probably a joyful way, but sounded far too terrifying for Owen's nerves. "What about Gwen?"

"Well, the team also has an alien who can fly and shoot energy bolts," Owen said. "I know she's not an alien *here*, but she is on her world, and I'm betting Charm can build something that lets Gwen fly and shoot things without actually messing with her regular powers."

"Good," Bethany said. "We can't change her, not if she's going back to her own book."

Assuming *any* of them made it out of this one. "Right," Owen said, moving on. "That just leaves us two. For me, the team has a speedster, someone who can run really fast. I've always been—"

"You want to be the Flash," Bethany said. "And me?"

Owen took a deep breath. "So don't take this the wrong way, but of the last two members of the team, one doesn't have *any* powers—"

"Done. Perfect. I'll take that one."

"And the other can turn into any animal he imagines," Owen finished.

Bethany's eyes narrowed, and she stepped closer until their faces were just inches apart. "If you're suggesting that I get the power to turn into an aardvark or something, you're picking the wrong day to joke with me."

"But it'd actually be really useful," Owen told her, backing away.

"How is turning into a platypus useful?!"

"It can be *any* animal," Owen said, throwing his hands up in surrender. "Think about it. You could turn into an elephant, or an alligator, or a giant eagle. Dinosaurs, even!"

"Dinosaurs don't exist anymore," Bethany told him.

"Doesn't matter, still animals! And I know Charm can make this work."

"And what if I get stuck?" Bethany said, jabbing a finger into his chest. "What if I think I'm an animal and lose my human mind? What if she does it wrong and I end up with the bottom half of a chimpanzee for the rest of my life? This is a *terrible* idea."

"This team has been around for years, Bethany. Their powers totally complement each other!"

"Whatever team it is, it's *only* a team because someone *wrote* them that way!"

"After everything we've seen, are you sure about that?" Owen asked her, and Bethany dropped her head into her hands.

"This is the worst idea of a whole host of worst ideas," she whispered as Charm's death ray shot out a beam of deadly green light that blew a hole in the wall. Charm began to cackle with delight.

"It'll be fine!" Owen said, definitely not looking at the smoking hole in the wall. "What could go wrong? Accidents are built into the plan! When things go wrong in science here, you get powers, you don't get hurt. Trust me, it's how comics work."

Bethany peeked out of her hands, then nodded. "You know what? Okay. I'm trusting you on this, Owen. But if I get stuck as a bug or something, just squish me, okay? I'll be better off. And I promise to do the same for you."

Owen laughed, then stopped when he realized she wasn't kidding. "Uh, I'll go talk to Charm about all of this," he said, quickly moving away from stomping range.

Dodging another death ray, Owen quickly made his way to Charm's side, then explained his idea for Gwen.

"Easy," Charm said. "There's plenty of parts around here. Give me five minutes."

"Great. Second, Bethany needs to be able to turn into any animal that's ever existed—"

"Morphing DNA was my kindergarten science fair project," Charm said, turning the death ray to face another wall. "I thought you were going to challenge me."

"Oh, the third one's the easiest, then," Owen told her, breathing a sigh of relief. "It's what we talked about earlier, making me run really fast."

"Right," Charm said, accidentally shooting the death ray just inches from Bethany's head. "I haven't exactly made that one work just yet in my head."

Owen blinked, trying to ignore Bethany's evil stare at the back of his head. "But it's just speed. Why is that a problem?"

"Like I said before, the faster you move, the more you'll weigh, until you reach the speed of light and are infinitely heavy," Charm told him, shaking her head. "How were you not taught this already? I've never heard of such a backward dimension. And even if that weren't a problem, we can't just ignore air friction or how exactly you're going to power this speed. You think you can just run at the speed of sound on a regular lunch? You'd have to have an IV feed constantly injecting energy directly into your muscles. It's impossible, and that's a word I never use."

"The natural rules are a bit *different* in this dimension," Owen told her. "Let's just say that here, if something looks cool on paper, and helps you fight bad guys, it's possible. I know that's weird—"

"It might be weird if it made any sense to begin with."

"But I know you can do this, Charm. I believe in you. You're the smartest, most amazing, prettiest—"

"*What* did you just say?" Charm said, dropping the controls of the death ray and turning to stare at him.

Owen's brain stopped working, and he almost choked. "I . . . I just—"

"Fine," she said, aiming the death ray at him. "It's your life. If you want to throw it away on this, I'll try some things. And if this dimension's natural laws work like you say they do, you might not even die. But if you do, don't blame *me*. Now, leave me alone so I can get these done!"

Owen quickly jumped out of the way and fled, though he almost thought he might possibly have caught what looked like the hint of a smile on her face.

CHAPTER 21

Absurdly nice girl, you're up first!" Charm shouted, and gestured to Gwen to come over.

"I think she's talking to you," Gwen said to Bethany. Charm growled, then just got up and dragged Gwen over to a different machine and began tinkering. In a lot less time than Owen would have guessed, Gwen was fitting on a jet pack and goggles.

"Here," Charm said, giving her gloves with some kind of beam emitters in the palms. "These will shoot out a ray of force that will basically obliterate anything in your path. They're amazing, you'll love them."

Gwen stared at the gloves for a second, then shook her head. "That's okay. I don't believe in violence."

Charm blinked. "I'm sorry, I must have misheard you?"

"I'll just take the jet pack, thanks!" Gwen said, and started it up. A double jet of fire shot out of the pack on her back, and at first she rose a bit unsteadily into the air. She quickly corrected herself, though, and was soon flying around the lab with a huge smile on her face. "This is *perfect!*" she shouted down at them.

"I *want* to hate her," Charm said to Owen as she watched Gwen fly. "Why can't I?"

Owen just smiled. "Me next?"

"You're last, Mr. Black Hole," Charm said, motioning for Bethany. "You. Come."

Bethany slowly stepped over, her eyes on the death ray, but instead, Charm led her to what looked almost like a glassed-in shower, just without a shower head or knobs. "In here," she said, holding the door and tapping her foot impatiently. "The radiation should rewrite your genetic code in a few seconds."

"Rewrite my—"

"It's *fine*," Charm told her, rolling her eyes. "I left everything the same, right down to the quadruple helix in your DNA." She paused. "Don't get me wrong, *that* raises some interesting questions which I'm going to investigate later, but for now, I'm just adding some fun stuff."

Bethany shot Owen a murderous look. "You better be right about all of this!"

"It's a classic comic team!" he whispered to her, holding his breath that she wasn't going to turn into the Hulk or something.

Bethany slowly walked over to the glass enclosure, pausing right before it to say one last thing, only to have Charm shove her in and slam the door. Before Bethany could protest, Charm started up the machine, and purple rays began to fill the shower stall.

"I take it back!" Bethany yelled as the rays bathed over her. "I'm not okay with this. Let me out!"

"I don't say this often enough, but wow, I really just *love* science," Charm said, a dreamy smile on her face as she turned several dials. Gwen landed next to them and stepped over to the stall, putting her hands up on the glass with a concerned look on her face as Bethany banged on it from the other side.

"Are you sure about this?" Gwen asked, her hand on the door.

"Open it, and she'll only be half-done," Charm said. "Probably turn her into a toad or something."

Gwen's hand jumped off the door's handle, and Bethany began to scream something that might have been pretty mean, if only they'd been able to hear it over the machinery.

Finally, with purple light filling the chamber, Charm flicked the machine off and opened the door.

And there was Bethany, looking completely normal, if a bit queasy.

"I might puke," she said, and all three of them backed up.

"You *look* okay," Owen said, wondering what they'd just done to her. "Is she . . . radioactive?" he asked Charm.

"Nah," Charm said, grabbing Bethany's arm and yanking her out in spite of the vomiting threat. "See? She's fine. Now morph."

Bethany just looked at her, her hands still on her stomach. "And how exactly do I do that?"

"What am I, a set of instructions?" Charm said. "Figure it out. It's *your* DNA."

"Just imagine yourself as an animal," Owen suggested, crossing all of his fingers.

Bethany closed her eyes tightly and made fists with her hands as she concentrated hard.

Nothing happened.

"It's not working," Bethany said, her eyes still closed. "Am I just supposed to—"

Then there was a loud *POINK*, and where Bethany had been, a bear now stood.

Well, a *statue* of a bear.

"Huh," Charm said, tapping the stone bear that was Bethany. "I wonder what she did wrong?"

CHAPTER 22

Bethany felt nothing for the first time in her life, and it was the most amazing thing *ever*.

There was no guilt. No worry. No wondering about the right thing to do.

Instead, everything was just stillness and silence, not a thought to cross her mind.

"She's a *statue!*" she heard Owen say, sounding a lot more worried than she was. "You have to fix her, Charm!"

"Me?" Charm said. "*She's* the one who turned into this. Tell *her* to fix it. She can just switch back."

"She's a *statue!*" Owen said again. "How can she do anything? She's made of rock." He touched Bethany's cheek, which she could barely feel. "Is she even still alive?"

And then Bethany felt a hand on her arm, and in spite of not being able to move her eyes to see, somehow she knew it was Gwen's. "Bethany, you're still there, aren't you," Gwen said quietly, not asking. "And I know you can turn back. I've seen this kind of thing before. Just . . . reverse whatever you did the first time. You can do it, I *know* you can."

"All right, everyone step back," Charm said. "Feelings aren't going to solve this. I'll fix it with real science if she can't do it herself."

An image managed to make it through Bethany's mind, just a small thing: Charm shooting more purple rays into her. And with that image came a pang of fear.

I have to turn back.

Even if this is really, really *nice.*

She sighed without making a sound, then with a loud *POINK*, turned back into a human being. "*Fine*, I'm here," Bethany said. "Everyone happy now?"

"Bethany, you're okay!" Owen shouted, plowing into her with a hug.

Gwen threw her arms around them both, and despite having normal strength now, still almost knocked the breath out of Bethany. "I knew you could come back!" Gwen shouted, oblivious to Owen's creaking bones and choking noises.

"It was all thanks to your pep talk," Bethany told Gwen,

glaring at Charm over Gwen's shoulder. "It made *all* the difference. Basically it worked when no science would have."

The half-robotic girl rolled her eyes hard. "Said no one ever. Now, who's next?"

"Who's next?" Bethany said, her eyes widening as she let go of Gwen and Owen. "Did you not see what you just did to me? You were supposed to give me the power to turn into an *animal*!"

"And you did," Charm said, shrugging slightly. "So what's the problem?"

"*I was made of stone!*"

"And you *looked* like an *animal*!"

Bethany's mouth dropped, but Owen yanked her away from Charm. "This was probably the accident thing I mentioned," he said, his face flushing a deep red. "I guess maybe Charm knows what she's doing too well, and so *something* accidental had to happen. But at least you're okay, right?"

"Okay?" Bethany said, and concentrated for a moment, then *POINK*ed into a brass monkey, followed by a paper dinosaur, then a turtle made of pencils, before turning back into herself. "All I can do is turn into *inanimate objects*, Owen! How useful do you see this superpower being in a fight?"

Owen's mouth opened and closed silently for a second before his eyes brightened. "Maybe you can turn into a bullet-proof shield for the rest of us!"

Bethany glared at him, all of her newfound peace completely gone now. *Oh, to just be stuck as a statue for the rest of my life.* But unfortunately, she had things to do.

And those started with a little revenge.

"Owen's turn!" she said, shoving him toward Charm.

"Okay, so like I said, you won't actually be running fast," Charm said, grabbing the now-terrified Owen by his arm and pulling him toward a different machine. "The plan is to give you the same effect as moving at the speed of light without weighing as much as two or three galaxies. And I *think* I've figured out how to do it! Science really does always save the day."

"I've actually changed my mind about this," Owen said, trying to pull his arm out of her grasp but not getting anywhere. "Why don't you just make me some rocket boots or something?"

"Boring," Charm said, strapping him onto a lab table beneath what looked an awful lot like the death ray she'd been playing around with earlier, only larger and with intimidating alien lettering all over it.

"Can you read that, Charm?" Bethany asked, a cruel smile on her face. "I'm guessing not."

"Sure can't!" Charm said, cheerfully tightening the straps until Owen yelped in pain. "But it's probably just some warning of danger or something. I'm pretty sure I know what the machine does, though, and worst case scenario, it just knocks a few years off his life."

"A few *years*?" Owen said, trying to escape the straps unsuccessfully.

"I said that's *worst* case," Charm told him, fiddling with the machine as it lit up and started making some really awful noises. "It'll probably only take off a few months, tops."

Bethany smiled at that, but enough was probably enough. "Okay, I definitely enjoyed this, but let him go."

"Let him what?" Charm asked, pushing a button.

The death-ray-looking thing grew even brighter, and the noises became almost earsplitting.

"Turn it off!" Bethany shouted, running over to Owen to try to free him from the straps. Unfortunately, he was frantically trying to do the same thing, and they kept getting in each other's way.

"It's fine, stop worrying so much!" Charm shouted over the roar of the machine. "Trust me, it's all going to be great. I'd stand clear, though!" And then she pulled Bethany out of the way just as the machine went off, shooting a ray right at Owen.

The bright light hit him with a force like an explosion, making the entire room pulse outward like a wave. The force of it knocked all of them to the ground. Even Charm looked surprised. The pulse then immediately reversed, flooding back into Owen with a weird sort of pop, just as the machine shut down.

Bethany slowly pushed to her feet, staring at Owen on the table. "Are you okay?" she asked, her eyes wide.

Owen blinked. "I think so? Help me off of this?" He started to pull against the strap, only to stop, staring at his arm.

His hand was shaking. Shaking a *lot*.

"Charm?" he said, holding up his hand as it began to vibrate faster and faster. His arm started trembling too, while his hand was moving so quickly it was hard to even see it.

"Charm?!" Bethany shouted as the strap holding Owen's vibrating arm ripped right off the table, and the rest of his body began to shake harder and harder.

"Help me!" Owen shouted, his voice sounding like it was echoing from several different places. And then his hand and arm completely *disappeared*, while his remaining body sped up.

"Charm, fix this!" Bethany shouted, turning to look at the robotic girl who was watching with fascination.

"This is what he asked for," Charm said, though even she looked a bit doubtful. "Don't worry, he'll get it under control."

But he didn't. Owen's leg disappeared next, followed by his other arm and the rest of his body, leaving just his face hanging in midair, like he was drowning in the ocean and could barely keep his head up.

"This isn't how the Flash does it at *all*!" he shouted. "This isn't—"

And then his face disappeared too, with a tiny *pop*.

For a moment there was only silence. Then, finally, Charm let loose an explosive breath.

"You know what, I don't think these machines were calibrated correctly," she said, tapping the death ray machine she'd used to shoot Owen. "I think that was the *real* problem here."

At her touch the entire machine began to vibrate just like Owen had, shaking faster and faster until it imploded in on itself, leaving just a tiny cloud of smoke in its wake.

Charm winced, and she slowly pulled her hand away, mouthing the word *whoops* to Bethany.

CHAPTER 23

Slow down! Owen screamed in his own head, desperately trying to stop whatever was happening all around his body. But the vibrations only got worse as the world began turning different colors. First everything was dark, pitch-black, but quickly that exploded into a sort of cyan shade of blue. Then the blue shifted to yellow, followed by a reddish magenta.

STOP THIS NOW! he shouted at his body, and exerted every ounce of willpower he had, focusing on *just . . . slowing . . . down.* He squeezed his eyes closed as hard as he could, trying to force himself to a stop with sheer willpower.

And then the vibrations *did* stop, just like that.

Owen quickly felt all around his body. His torso, arms, and legs . . . they seemed to be where they were supposed to be, and not shaking! "Hey, it stopped!" he shouted, opening his eyes. "I'm back!"

Except he wasn't back. Not in the lab, at least. Instead, there was just white space as far as the eye could see.

And that white space looked *way* too familiar.

Uh-oh. "No no no no no," he said, pushing himself to his feet and stepping out into the nothingness, a nothingness that looked exactly like the same empty space that the Magister had stuck him in, back when he and Bethany had first jumped into a Kiel Gnomenfoot book. "No! Don't tell me I'm back *here!*"

This was the void between pages, where there was just . . . nothing. No people, no crazy supervillain robots, nothing. How had he gotten here? Charm was trying to give him superpowers so he could move fast, not throw him right out of the comic. And he *had* been moving really fast. Vibrating, sure, but still. So if it had worked, why would that have taken him out of the story?

"Ugh, I hate this place!" he shouted to no one, turning around in a circle, only to stop abruptly. Maybe this *wasn't* the same place as he'd been when the Magister trapped him. Because this place wasn't empty.

Right in the middle of the nothingness, what looked like enormous comic pages rose ten feet tall from the ground, rising into the air like the Great Wall of China or something.

Pages and pages ran off as far as he could see in either direction, each page showing different scenes of a comic book, with panels and everything.

It was as if he had been shrunk down to the size of the characters in the comic and was staring at the life-size panels, only not just one panel at a time, which would be normal. Instead, he could see what looked like an entire issue. Or maybe issues, depending on how far it went to either the right or left.

Owen walked closer to the nearest page and noticed that off to the left, Bethany had turned into a bear statue, and Owen was yelling at Charm. "She's a *statue!*" he saw himself say in word balloons. "How can she do anything? She's made of rock. Is she even still alive?"

But this time Bethany wasn't silent. A little cloud above her head said, "I have to turn back to stop this. Even though this is really, *really* nice."

This was *them* in comic book form. Their story! How was this happening? Where *was* he? Was this some kind of behind-the-scenes place where all the comic pages were stored? Was there a giant comic book artist somewhere, ready to draw more pages?

What would the giant comic book artist do if he saw a tiny Owen had escaped from his story?!

Owen immediately looked over his shoulder, but as far as he could tell, no one was there, let alone any kind of giant ready to stab him with a ten-foot-long pencil. He turned back to the pages, hoping there'd be more of an explanation there.

The balloon over Bethany's head, the one that said, "I have to turn back to stop this. Even though this is really, *really* nice." That looked like a thought balloon, the kind that showed what comic book characters were thinking. While the other ones, the dialogue balloons . . . that's what they were saying out loud. Okay, that made sense. This really did feel like he'd been pulled out of the comic book and was looking at it from, like, way above the page somehow.

He walked backward away from the pages, hoping to see how far they went. Far off to the left, he could make out a few pages of mostly black panels except for a few dialogue balloons here or there.

"Ha! You like that, shadow thing?"

"Whoa, it exploded! How did you do that?"

That was when they'd been attacked by the shadows. And past that, Owen thought he could make out what looked like the basement with the glass costume cases, and the four of them standing over the manhole before Charm opened it.

Okay, so he was outside of the comics pages somehow. Panels were like frozen time to him, and he could see them like they were drawings. Did that mean he could somehow get back in, if he pushed into a panel?

Owen walked back closer to the giant wall of comic pages, and slowly moved his hand close to one of the all-dark panels. He gingerly stuck one finger out, ready to yank it back at the first sign of danger, but instead it touched the panel and stopped, as if there was a window separating him from the world inside the comic.

Well, *that* wasn't good. Apparently he was just as stuck here as he was last time, only without Nobody to save him.

Wait a second. *Would* Nobody be able to save him?

He turned around to face the nothing behind him. "Nobody?" he shouted, then waited for a response. But there wasn't even an echo.

But *that* brought up an interesting question. They'd just (maybe) found Bethany's father out of nowhere, (maybe) reappearing after having gone missing for years. And suddenly, Nobody wasn't around either. Coincidence?

But if Nobody *was* Bethany's father, that meant the Dark

had captured him, which meant he wouldn't be rescuing Owen anyway. Not good.

With a sigh, Owen turned back to the wall of comics pages, and walked alongside them back toward the right. He passed Bethany's power experiments and stopped at a page with an image of himself being strapped to a table by Charm.

"Don't do it!" he shouted at himself, but instead, his stupid comic book self went right ahead and did exactly what he wasn't supposed to do. That Owen began vibrating on the page (which looked *so weird*), then parts of him began to disappear.

Owen moved to the next page, expecting to see himself in the nothingness. Except the comic stayed with Bethany, Charm, and Gwen.

"You know what, I don't think these machines were calibrated correctly," Charm said. "I think that was the *real* problem here."

"Are you kidding me?" Owen shouted at the drawing of Charm in the panel. "Not calibrated? That's what I get? I've been missing you for months, you almost kill me, and you blame the *machine*? At least use it to bring me back!"

And then the machine itself began to vibrate in the next panel and finally exploded in the last panel of the page.

GREAT.

The bottom of that page had an ominous *To Be Continued* . . . note, followed by what looked like a page full of text, which Owen was a bit too close to see. He backed up and started reading from the top of the page.

WHO is the Dark? WHERE does he come from? And WHAT does he want?

All good questions, because here in Jupiter City, the Dark is rising!

I know, that's the name of a book by Susan Cooper, but it's also appropriate here. The Dark is a new kind of antihero, one who doesn't let anything stop him from saving Jupiter City his way, whether the city wants to be saved or not! If you think Doc Twilight and the Lawful Legion were fun but wondered why they kept letting villains like the Clown and Dr. Apathy break out of jail all the time, I'm with you. And I created all of them!

But times change, and so do I. And now I'm embracing the Dark. Will you join me in the shadows, or are you AFRAID? Stick close, and you might even learn the secret origin of the Dark in the coming months.

See you next month! And send your letters or e-mails in, and be sure to mark them OKAY TO PRINT! I want to hear what you think!

—Mason Black, writer

Mason Black. Hadn't Doc Twilight mentioned that name, something about how this was all his fault? So was *The Dark* just like a reboot of an old comic, turning a character into something more extreme? Owen sighed. Why did they have to mess with the classics? Okay, not that Doc Twilight was exactly a classic, but still.

The next page had no panels, just what looked like an ad for a comic shop locator service. But the page after that almost made Owen's heart stop.

This couldn't be. He backed away from the comic page wall, shaking his head. This wasn't happening!

The page looked like a comic book cover, with *The Dark* title at the top, all the way down to the price on it, and a "#3" in the upper left corner. And on the cover the red-eyed creature that was apparently the Dark stood over an unconscious Bethany, Charm, and Gwen, his arms raised in triumph as he shouted, "*No one* can extinguish the Dark!"

No! How could this have happened? Last he'd seen them, they were all fine and still in the laboratory.

Owen quickly ran to the next page and found Bethany right where he'd left her, yelling at Charm about Owen disappearing. He scanned the page quickly, then ran to the next, and the next. Bethany was having Charm try to bring Owen back, but it wasn't working. A few hours passed. . . .

And darkness filled the panels again. The shadows had come back, and this time the creatures managed to overwhelm his three friends.

"Run!" Owen screamed at the page, but the shadows captured them and held them in place as the Dark entered the laboratory.

"You thought you could break my laws?" the monster said, his word balloon all black with white words. He walked up to Bethany and stared her right in the face. "Criminals! Now you face the justice of your own foul selves, as shown to you by my shadows!"

He gestured, and the shadow creatures attacked, pushing their ways inside his friends' mouths, infesting them. Someone screamed, but Owen couldn't tell who. He just kept shaking his head, not able to believe this.

And then the next panel had the Dark standing in a now-empty laboratory, his fists clenched. "I *will* make this world bow to my will," he said. "This world . . . and all others."

The panel shifted, showing a blue-fire circle reopening in front of him.

"Come, my shadows!" the Dark shouted. "We shall bring justice to this new world, in the name of the Dark!"

CHAPTER 24

C alibrated?" Bethany shouted. "Where did Owen *go?!*"

Charm stared at the spot where the machine had been, frowning. "*I* think it worked. He just probably needs to slow down."

"You think it *worked?*" Bethany said, jerking Charm around to face her, then slamming her against the wall. "He's gone, Charm! Owen disappeared! Is he okay? *Where is he?*"

Charm's eyes narrowed, and she shoved Bethany off of her. "This was *his* idea, not mine. *I* was trying to help. He wanted to be able to move faster than people could see, so I did that. He should now have the power to speed up his own personal time."

"He's moving in time?" Gwen said, her eyes widening. "Bethany, can't you go find him then? You can travel in time too!"

Bethany forced herself to ignore Gwen, keeping her eyes on Charm. "And how does that make him able to run fast?"

Charm rolled her eyes. "Think about it. If your time moved so fast that it basically stopped for everyone else, you could move a few feet, then restart it. To the rest of us, it would look like you moved so quickly we couldn't see. That's all speed is, how fast you move through space and time. I couldn't make him move fast enough without collapsing space, so I changed the time instead."

"So he's still here, just speeding through time?" Bethany said, glancing around.

Charm shrugged. "Or maybe he can see all of time as frozen moments, like pictures. I don't know, *he's* the one who messed it up. I don't even know why he's playing this game, acting like he's someone he's not. Explain *that* to me."

"*He's not Ki—*" Bethany started to shout, then just growled in frustration and turned away. Why had Owen insisted on doing things in the supervillain's lab? Not everything had to be so authentic to whatever type of story they were in. There were ways to get superpowers other than by almost killing yourself . . . or trapping yourself in time!

"Do you think he's okay?" she asked quietly, not looking at the others.

"Nothing in that machine could have hurt him," Charm said, then paused. "Unless it somehow aged him into dust, I guess. *That* might have hurt—"

"So you're saying he's fine, then," Gwen interrupted. She put a hand on Bethany's shoulder as Bethany's eyes widened in horror. "How do we get him back?"

"Right now?" Charm said. "We don't. I'd need a lot more time to find him. Ironically."

"Just do it," Bethany said, taking slow, deep breaths to calm herself down. "We're not leaving until he's safe. I don't care how long it takes."

"What about your father?" Gwen asked her quietly. "There has to be a way we can save both of them."

Bethany shook her head. "It doesn't matter how it happened, or whose fault it was. Owen's only lost now because he was trying to help me. We're staying here, all of us, until Charm finds him."

That's a bad idea, Bethany thought. *You should go find your father right now.*

What? And leave Owen trapped wherever he is? That's crazy!

What if they did find her father, but Charm couldn't locate Owen after too much time had passed? Or what if Owen was in danger, wherever he was? They couldn't just *leave* him there.

Owen's fine, she thought. *Trust me, he's okay. Just go, get out of there. It's too dangerous to stay!*

Where was this coming from? Why was she thinking such terrible things? She almost wanted to slap herself. Was she really that self-absorbed that she'd leave her best friend behind because she herself might be in danger? And how would she know if Owen was fine or not?

"I just don't get why he doesn't use his magic," Charm said, fiddling with a different machine, this one with a multitude of clocks all over it. "Can we all just admit who he is? He's got the same heart, and I know it hasn't left his body. Why do we have to go through with this whole charade that he's not really Kiel?"

Bethany groaned as a headache threatened to rip her brain apart. Couldn't Charm just look for Owen without asking questions Bethany couldn't answer? Couldn't Owen have skipped all this dumb superpower stuff?

Couldn't her father have just told her he was alive and living in the same city?

"Are you okay?" Gwen asked her quietly. "I've seen that

expression before. My friend Jayna has it whenever she's about to set another robot loose on our hometown."

"Right, I forgot, EarthGirl's worst enemy is your best friend," Bethany said quietly, opening her eyes to look at Gwen. "That must be fun, huh?"

"That made it into the history books?" Gwen said, her eyebrows shooting up. "Wow. I'm shocked you know anything about me at all, honestly!"

"Owen's *gone*, Gwen. And I keep doing this to him. Well, half the time it's his fault, but *still*. He doesn't have any powers—"

"He's *fine*," Gwen said, looking Bethany straight in the face. "Charm's not exactly one to be polite, and she said he's okay."

"Okay *or* a pile of dust!"

"Ignore that part," Gwen said, smiling slightly. "He's lost in time, but we'll find him. Or *he'll* find *us*. That's how it works, I've noticed. Whenever you really need someone, they'll be there."

"He does tend to come through in the end," Bethany said, frowning. "But it doesn't matter, I won't leave him. Not until I know."

ARGH, stop being so nice! she thought. *Just leave Owen behind—he deserves it!*

Bethany's eyes shot open in shock and horror, and she clamped her hands over her mouth, not sure if she'd just said that out loud. Who even *thought* that kind of thing?! What was *wrong* with her?

Something whizzed by Bethany's head, and she ducked, already too late. Gwen grabbed it, though, her reflexes still almost inhumanly quick. "Um, is this yours, Charm?" she said, holding out what looked like a computer chip.

"No, it's garbage," Charm said, throwing another machine piece across the room. "No wonder this didn't work right. These machines don't even have quantum processors! This is going to take me *hours* to build anything that will find him. You sure you don't want to just leave him there to suffer for a bit as punishment?"

Yes, I am sure, Bethany said in her mind, almost daring her rogue brain to disagree. She paused, waiting for one of those awful, horrible thoughts to say something, but nothing came.

"Yes, I'm—"

NO, Bethany! the thought exploded in her head. *You're going to get captured by the Dark and never find your father.*

You have to leave right now! I've seen it happen. Stop being so nice. This isn't like you!

And that's when she realized it wasn't *her* voice in her head, thinking such horrible things.

"Owen?" she whispered.

CHAPTER 25

Owen banged on the panels over and over with his fists, trying to break them open, push his way through, anything. *"Let me back in!"* he shouted, his hands getting more and more bruised with every hit. Finally he slumped against the glasslike wall of the panel, then slid down it to the ground.

This wasn't working. *Nothing* was working, and his friends were going to get taken over by shadows if he didn't save them.

Had he at least made a dent in the panel? Maybe that would be something? Owen slowly pushed away from the wall, then looked closely at it. Nope. Still just as perfectly prisonlike as it had been before he'd started beating on it.

"Nobody, *please*, I need your help!" he shouted, hoping someone was listening, or at least Nobody. "I know you don't like us messing around in books, and you were probably telling me not to write earlier, if that *was* you in my story. And you were right, I shouldn't have been doing that, and I shouldn't be *here*. I'm sorry. I messed up. *Please* help us?"

Owen waited, hoping that the faceless man would show up with a vaguely snarky reply, but nothing happened. Finally, he pushed himself to his feet, having no idea what else he could do.

"What's the point of this place if I can't get back in?" he said, kicking the stupid panel in front of him, then immediately regretting it as his toes exploded in pain. He fell forward against the panel, gritting his teeth to shut out the agony, when he realized something was odd.

He'd come back to the point where Bethany, Charm, and Gwen were talking about trying to find him, wherever he was. He had to get back and warn them to leave, before the shadows arrived in a few hours. But nothing had worked.

Except now, one of Bethany's word balloons was . . . different.

Before, she'd said something along the lines of *Owen's gone, Gwen. And I keep doing this to him. Well, half the time it's his fault, but still.*

Now the word balloon said:

The empty spaces were right in a row, like someone had wiped them away with an eraser.

Uh, what had happened? Had she lost part of her mind and dropped out a few words? Owen looked closer, then realized the erased words were in a line right where he'd been leaning against the panel.

Had he erased her words somehow?

He slowly reached out a trembling finger to touch the last "still" in her word balloon. Then he wiped down, and the word disappeared.

And just like that, the next panel completely changed. Gwen gave Bethany an odd look, and said, "I'm sorry, what?"

Bethany herself looked confused. "I . . . I don't know, I

meant to say something, but it's like I forgot half the words."

"No way," Owen whispered, backing away. How could this be real? He was changing what his friends were saying. That was crazy! This shouldn't even be possible.

. . . What *else* could he do?

He backed up a few panels to one where Bethany was deciding to stay in the lab until they found him. Bethany and Gwen were talking quietly together as Charm was fiddling with the machine.

"It doesn't matter how it happened, or whose fault it was," Bethany said. "Owen's only lost now because he was trying to help me. We're staying here, all of us, until Charm finds him."

If he could erase things . . . could he write them too?

Owen reached out above that Bethany's head and used his finger to draw a little circle, right on the page. So he *could* draw on the panel! But would it affect things like his erasing Bethany's word balloon had? He drew more circles leading up to a bigger one, just like the thought balloons he'd seen her thinking earlier.

Taking a deep breath, Owen put his finger in the thought balloon he'd just drawn, and wrote:

THAT'S A BAD IDEA. YOU SHOULD GO FIND YOUR FATHER RIGHT NOW.

And just like that, the next panel changed. Now Bethany looked confused, and another thought balloon appeared above her head. *What? And leave Owen trapped wherever he is? That's crazy!*

Owen gasped, and stepped away from the wall, his finger shaking. *He'd just put a* thought *into his friend's head,* in real life. Or in a comic book, but still, it was *her* real life!

And all it'd taken was a small little doodle.

But had it changed anything? He glanced over at the next page, but Bethany was still insisting that they stay and look for him. Ugh, why wasn't she *listening* to her thoughts? He went to the next panel and drew another thought balloon.

OWEN'S FINE. TRUST ME, HE'S OKAY. JUST GO, GET OUT OF THERE. IT'S TOO DANGEROUS TO STAY!

And again up popped a thought balloon in response, about how she was a horrible person to be thinking these things.

"You're not a horrible person!" Owen shouted at the panel. "I'm trying to help you, you *jerk!*"

A small part of him realized how odd this was, writing thoughts into Bethany's head. Could he change her mind about things? Could he write what she said out loud, too? Was any of this even okay to be doing?

He shook his head, not ready to think about all of that. Right now he just had to get them to safety. He could worry about what it all meant later.

Back and forth he went with Bethany, using his finger-written thoughts to argue with her in her mind, while she kept insisting they stay. At one point he even told her to leave him behind because he deserved it, which he did. This was his fault, after all. But that got him the worst reaction of all. She was practically ready to slap herself over even thinking Owen's thought.

This did not feel right.

"You sure you don't want to just leave him there to suffer for a bit as punishment?" Charm asked her, ready to doom them all by searching for Owen, and pretty rude to boot.

Yes, I am sure, Bethany thought to herself, as if daring her brain to argue.

That was it. No more making her think these were her thoughts.

NO, BETHANY! YOU'RE GOING TO GET CAPTURED BY THE DARK AND NEVER FIND YOUR FATHER. YOU HAVE TO LEAVE RIGHT NOW! I'VE SEEN IT HAPPEN. STOP BEING SO NICE. THIS ISN'T LIKE YOU!

And finally, *finally*, Bethany spun around, ironically turning her back to him, and whispered, "Owen?" out loud.

"YES!" he shouted, stepping away from the panel. "Thank you!" He let out a huge sigh, then moved back closer to the panel.

YES, IT'S ME, he wrote in a new thought balloon. *I'M FINE, BUT YOU'RE NOT. I'VE SEEN WHAT'S GOING TO HAPPEN TO YOU. IF YOU STAY, THE DARK WILL FIND YOU, AND HE DEFEATS YOU! GET OUT OF THERE AND GO FIND YOUR FATHER. I'LL HELP YOU WHER-EVER I CAN, SO STOP ARGUING WITH YOURSELF AND LISTEN TO YOUR THOUGHTS!*

"Owen?" Bethany said again, now looking off to Owen's left, while Charm and Gwen gave her confused looks. "I can hear him. I think he's talking to me in my head, like he's some kind of telepathic ghost!"

Owen rolled his eyes, then wrote *REALLY? TELEPATHIC GHOST? JUST GO, ALREADY!*

And then, weirdly, she *did*. She actually listened! They had a few more thought messages back and forth, then he almost crashed to the ground in relief. They were leaving! And that meant that the next issue would change. Wouldn't it?

He looked forward a few pages and found his friends outside Apathetic Industries, and not a shadow in sight. Just to make sure, Owen quickly walked back over to the issue's cover and looked up.

The cover *had* changed. And it was still disturbing, but for very different reasons.

Instead of the Dark standing over his friends in triumph, the cover now showed a man in a much-too-shiny banana suit, saying "The Fruit of the Loons shall rise again!" as Charm fired her ray guns at him, with Bethany and Gwen trying to hold her back.

. . . *Huh.*

Apparently things were going to go off in a *very* new direction.

CHAPTER 26

"All right, you two," Bethany said, her hand on the door leading out of the laboratory. "And, you know, Owen."

THANKS, came the thought in her head.

"This is it," she said, looking first to Charm, who had her ray guns out, and then to Gwen, who had her goggles on and her jet pack ready . . . and nothing in the way of a weapon. That might not end well.

SHE'LL BE FINE. SHE'S EARTHGIRL!

EarthGirl with no powers.

EARTHGIRL DOESN'T NEED POWERS. SHE'S AMAZING ALL ON HER OWN. PLUS, SHE HATES VIOLENCE.

Bethany sighed, but he had a point. She took a deep breath, then started again. "We're about to face a city full of shadow monsters, not to mention anyone who they've infected with their hate. It's not going to be easy, and we still don't know where the Dark even *is*, but if we all stick together, hopefully none of us die or anything, and—"

Charm groaned. "Not that this isn't inspiring, but can't we just go?"

"Let's do this!" Gwen shouted, and clapped her hands in excitement.

Bethany took one more breath, preparing herself for the shadowy onslaught, then threw open the door to the rest of Apathetic Industries.

But there were no shadows, monsters, or supervillains. In fact, the sun was rising over the city outside, adding a beautiful pink light to everything.

"The *horror*," Charm said, pushing past Bethany and stepping outside, shading her eyes from the light. "Which of the terrors do you want to fight first?"

Bethany glared at the back of her head, but Gwen just grinned. "See?" she said. "Things are already better than we thought. Now let's go find this Mr. Dark."

"I think it's just the Dark," Bethany said, putting her hand up to block the rising sun. "The elevator's right over there." She turned and pointed, then realized her mistake.

"Looks more like a hole," Charm said, stepping over to

the elevator shaft that the shadows had destroyed earlier. She clicked the down button a few times, then turned around. "Do we just jump, or . . ."

Bethany sighed. "We're going to have to take the stairs, I guess." From the three hundred and fiftieth floor. Assuming there even *were* stairs.

"No time," Charm said, and shot a ray gun at the window nearby. The glass shattered and a chilly wind filled the atrium.

"What are you doing?" Bethany shouted over the wind. "We're thousands of feet in the air!"

"Great time to test the jet pack, then!" Charm shouted back, pointing at Gwen.

Gwen's eyes lit up, and she clicked the jet pack on, rising a few feet in the air. "It'll be fast," she shouted.

Bethany took a deep breath, then nodded. The stairs would take hours. At least this would get them down faster.

Gwen grabbed both their hands and slowly walked them out toward the edge. "Have you flown before?" she yelled to Charm.

The half-robotic girl snorted. "I've spent more hours in space than on a planet. I think I'll be okay."

"Perfect!" Gwen shouted, and leaned forward, jamming on

the jet pack's throttle. Before Bethany could even take a breath, they tore out of the building and out over nothingness . . . then began falling.

"AAH!" she shouted, desperately holding tightly to Gwen with both hands. "We're going to hit that other building!"

Though the jet pack didn't seem to be holding them up, it was giving them enough forward momentum to crash them into the next skyscraper over. As they fell, she could make out the sight of various empty cubicles in what looked like an office.

"Whoops," Gwen said, and angled the jet pack away from the building, which righted them as they plummeted . . . then sent them back the way they came.

"Too much!" Bethany yelled as Apathetic Industries came rushing back.

"I thought you knew how to fly!" Charm shouted from the other side. "If I die here, I'm taking you with me!"

"Sorry!" Gwen shouted, trying to correct their angles. They slowed their backward momentum, just barely sliding up against Apathetic Industries windows as they fell.

"I thought you made this thing to carry more weight!" Bethany shouted at Charm, who spun around on Gwen's arm to give Bethany a dirty look.

"Don't blame the machine. This is operator error!"

"It's going to be fine," Gwen said, smiling down at them as the ground neared. "Just hold on tight!"

She jammed on the throttle again, and Bethany almost slipped right out of Gwen's hand as the jet pack kicked in, halting their momentum mere feet from the ground. Gwen eased off of it for a moment, and Bethany's feet gently touched pavement. She quickly let go of Gwen and fell to her knees, trying to breathe.

"I told you it wasn't the machine," Charm said next to her, looking like she might throw up.

"That was *so much fun*," Gwen said as she landed between them, her eyes wide with excitement. "It didn't feel anything like it usually does when I fly. Want me to fly us around more?"

"NO!" Bethany and Charm yelled at the same time.

Gwen just smiled. "You two are getting along now. That's wonderful!"

"What were *you* so worried about?" Bethany muttered to Charm. "You're half metal. You'd have been fine if you fell."

Charm paused, then nodded. "You're right. I probably would have been." Then she pushed Bethany over, knocking her to the ground. "See? Who cares if you fall, right?"

Gwen immediately rushed to her side. "Are you okay?" she asked, giving her a worried look.

"I'm fine," Bethany said, glaring at Charm. "And that *wasn't* funny."

YES IT WAS, Owen said in her head.

YOU, be quiet! Bethany thought back.

In spite of all the noise they'd made, between breaking the window on the three hundred and fiftieth floor and then falling to the ground with a jet pack roaring, no one had come to investigate what was going on. Instead, the city was just as empty as it'd been when she and Owen first arrived. Not surprising, with the Dark in control. Had most people escaped the city when the Dark started his attack, or were they all hiding somewhere? Or if they were all shadow infected, was there a whole city full of enraged people somewhere waiting to attack? That wasn't a fun thought.

"Since we don't know where this Dark guy is, we need to find a source of reliable intelligence," Charm declared, pulling out her ray guns. "Someone who can direct us to him. Kiel and I got it down to a routine that I called nice guy/smart girl. He'd be polite and I'd be myself."

"Good detective/bad detective," Gwen said. "That's a classic! Can I be the good detective?"

Charm gave her a long look, then started walking up the street without a word.

Not knowing where else to go, Bethany led her friends in the same direction she and Owen had come from last time, toward the rooftop where Doc Twilight had rescued them. The morning sun gave everything a slightly cheerier look now, but the empty streets still felt like some kind of postapocalyptic world.

But they quickly left the skyscrapers behind, moving into the creepier, seedier area where they'd been following Doc Twilight. Even here, where it felt like some criminal was waiting around every corner, no one was to be found, not even a raving old lady this time. Where *was* everyone?

"We can't get intelligence without people to interrogate," Charm shouted, waving her ray guns in annoyance. "We're not going to find the Dark this way."

"You *want* to find the Dark?" said a rough, gritty voice from a dark alley beside them. "Sounds like I'm not the only one who's gone bananas."

Charm immediately aimed her ray guns into the darkness, but Bethany put a hand up to stop her. "Who's there?" she said, stepping forward to see better.

In the dimly lit alley between two houses, she could barely

make out a man dressed in a weirdly clean banana costume, leaning against a Dumpster.

"Someone too slippery for the likes of you," the banana said. He gave them a close look, then stepped back in surprise. "Wait, you don't have shadows in you?"

"Not yet," Bethany said, not wanting to share too much. "Are you . . . a superhero?"

The banana laughed ironically. "Don't pretend you don't recognize me. I'm the Rotten Banana, the uncatchable criminal!" He leaned back against the Dumpster, his suit making squeaky noises as it slid against the metal. "I'm the scourge of Jupiter City! Doc Twilight himself considered me an archenemy, sort of, at times at least! And I led the Fruit of the Loons, the craziest team of criminals this side of the Clown and his College!"

"I think we found a source of intelligence," Bethany whispered to Charm.

"It's a banana," Charm said, giving Bethany a doubtful look. "Unless you're looking for a giant monkey, I think you're doing this wrong."

"Trust me, this is *exactly* the sort of person we're looking for," Bethany told them. "But be careful. I don't know what, but he probably has some kind of superpower."

"Do you think I can't hear you?" the banana said, practically spitting. "Not the most a-peeling bunch, are you?"

Bethany heard Charm's ray gun begin to power up, so she gave the half-robotic girl a careful look. "Good detective/bad detective, remember?" Bethany whispered. Then she turned back to the banana and raised her voice again. "We're looking for the Dark, Mr. Rotten Banana. Do you know where we can find him?"

The banana sneered. "Orange you going to say please?"

Charm shot the banana over and over, screaming profanities as she did.

"Hey!" Bethany shouted, pushing Charm backward as the banana slumped to the ground, not moving. "We *needed* him!"

"It was set on stun," Charm said, glaring at the banana. "And he had it coming, trust me. I *hate* puns. Besides, I don't think it did much."

"You *shot* him!" Bethany shouted, pointing at the banana, before realizing he was pushing himself back up to a standing position, his costume not even scorched.

"Nice try, Space Girl," the banana said with a sneer. "But I think you'll find the Rotten Banana is a lot more *slippery* than—"

Charm started firing again, the ray gun's blasts drowning out whatever the banana was trying to say. Finally, Bethany yanked the ray gun out of her hand and pointed to the scorch marks all over the nearby buildings. "It's not working!" she shouted. "The rays are just sliding off of him."

The Rotten Banana gave them an annoyed look. "Now you've done it! You three really should have *split* while you had the—"

Charm shot him again, this time with her other ray gun. *"No more puns!"* she shouted as Bethany grabbed that one too.

"Rotten Banana?" Gwen said, stepping forward. "Why are you hiding in this alley? You look like you could use some help."

"Help?" the banana said, looking surprised. *"Help?* Who's even left to help us now? All the superheroes have turned evil, infected by shadows. I'm the last super*villain* left not in hiding, and that's only because my suit keeps his shadows from touching me. Though they still try, every night. It's like a horror movie!" He shivered. "Ever have that nightmare where something's chasing you, but you can't move? That's how it is. Those shadows terrify me, and I turn into a frozen banana!"

"He's asking for it again," Charm said, but Bethany stepped in her way.

"I've got no hideout, I've got no henchmen," the banana continued, ranting at the nearby wall. "And I can't tell you the last time my wallet had any cabbage in it!"

"That's it," Charm said, trying to grab her ray guns back from Bethany, who moved them out of her reach.

"Let *us* help you," Gwen said, stepping closer to the banana. "We can get you something to eat, and maybe find you a place to stay. All we need to know is how to find the Dark."

The banana looked at her with confusion. "But why would you do that? I'm a villain! I usually rob people like you with my banana gun!"

"I just think there are better ways to solve these things than with threats of violence," Gwen told him, holding her hands up to him. "Now, why don't we just all calm down for a second and talk things out."

The banana just stared at Gwen for a moment, then sighed. "That sounds really nice, actually. You know, I don't even *like* bananas. But once I started monkeying around with this banana suit—"

Charm leaped forward, punching the Rotten Banana right

in the face, and he collapsed to the ground. "What did I say about the puns?" she shouted, standing over him with her fists in the air. *"What did I say?!"*

Gwen leaned over to Bethany. "Wow. She's *amazing* at this bad detective thing!"

CHAPTER 27

Owen reread the panels of Charm beating up on the banana over and over again. He couldn't stop grinning, in spite of his rotten luck. Of *course* he was stuck out here instead of hanging out with Charm. She even confirmed that she thought he was Kiel, so that was totally an opening to tell her the truth!

At least this way he got to enjoy the banana scene as much as he wanted. So that was something.

Sure, he could explain everything right now, put the thoughts directly in her head. Tell her that he hadn't been Kiel and really was Owen. That he'd saved her in the last book, and that he'd missed her ever since.

She'd be mad, but she'd hopefully understand eventually. But then a strange thought occurred to him.

If she *was* mad, then couldn't he just cross that thought out, and make her happy about it all?

What? No! What was he thinking, changing what someone thought? This was Nobody's whole point. Besides, he couldn't just rewrite Charm's thoughts or emotions that way. It was messed up to even consider it!

No one should have that much power over someone, fictional or nonfictional. It wasn't right.

Owen walked over to the next page, hoping that things in Jupiter City could take his mind off of things with Charm. The following panels had them interrogating the banana on a roof while holding him by his hands out over the edge, which Gwen did *not* seem happy about. But at least they were still safe, with no shadows anywhere yet.

That was good, because the next page had a large *MEANWHILE* . . . at the top in a caption box, and things changed dramatically. Everything on the page was dark, creepy, and hard to make out, like all the color was missing. And the same all-black panel went by a few times, like nothing was happening, until finally—

"I know you're there," said a word balloon. "You're not as much a shadow as you think."

Um, who was that talking? Wasn't this Bethany's story? He leaned back, checking to make sure he hadn't missed the sun going out or something in the last panel with his friends, but they were fine. So who was this? And what was with all the creepiness?

Another two panels of nothing went by, and then: "What you're doing is wrong," said a word balloon in the same spot. "I don't care what Mason did to you to make you this way. This isn't how you were meant to be."

Two more panels of nothing ended the page, so Owen moved to the next and almost shrieked.

Staring out at him were two bloodred eyes in the middle of a shadow-covered face, taking up the entire page.

"You have no idea what I'm meant for," the Dark said in white letters on a black word balloon, a light from above having snapped on to illuminate the monster. "This city destroyed me, but from my ashes a new world shall rise!"

Owen shivered, then quickly moved to the next page and found himself staring at Doc Twilight, the same one they'd followed into Jupiter City. With his first good look at the superhero, Owen saw that the costume looked a bit too big for him, like it was hanging off of his body. Maybe he'd lost some weight or muscle, living in the real world? "What did he change?" the superhero said, his hands gripping massive bars that trapped him in a cell. "You were never like this. What happened to you?"

"*No one* changed me," the Dark said, his eyes flaring like flames. "The man I was before is dead. The world took everything from him, and he just let it happen. But not me. I will keep the same thing from happening to anyone else, because *I* will be in control. I will keep the people safe, even if I have to infect the whole city with my shadows. I will force this world to be what it's always been meant to be, no matter who has to suffer." He gestured, showing a massive wall of screens behind him that lit up in the next panel.

Owen gasped. Monitor after monitor showed images of superheroes, all with blacked-out eyes and enraged faces, the same as the old woman they'd met in Jupiter City. A super-strong woman in a scuba suit put a terrified robber through a brick wall, almost killing him as she screamed curses at him. A man in a grasshopper costume was jumping over and over on an unconscious man in a business suit, shouting something about bank loans. And what looked like a snowman froze someone for jaywalking, then just left her encased in ice, maybe to freeze.

"What have you done?!" Doc Twilight shouted. "You can't let them do such things!"

"*They* let this world become such a horror," the Dark said, his back now to Doc Twilight. "It's their failure that forced me to become what I am. Shouldn't they make it right?"

"Failure? What could they have done to deserve this?"

The Dark slowly turned around to face Doc Twilight. Then he reached up to his hood of shadows, and pulled it off, revealing . . .

"*Turn around!*" Owen shouted at the page, as it now showed the Dark from behind, his face shown only to Doc Twilight. "Are you *kidding* me?"

"You don't know what I've lost," the Dark said, his word balloon now white with black letters, just like Doc Twilight's. "You wear that costume to mock me, but I don't expect you to understand. You'd never do what needs to be done."

"No, I wouldn't," Doc Twilight said softly, his eyes locked on the Dark's. "That's what this costume represents: doing the *right* thing, not the easy thing. You're not making the city safe, you're making it a police state!"

The Dark leaped forward and slammed a hand through the bars, grabbing the fabric of Doc Twilight's costume. Then, with one swift pull, he tore the twilight symbol right off the costume.

"This represents nothing but time past and foolish dreams," the Dark said, throwing the moon and three stars symbol to the ground, his face still annoyingly pointed away from Owen. "The past is gone, and I'm the one burying it. What happened to me will not happen to anyone else, not anymore. Not in this world, or any other."

Shadows behind him began to assemble something, and Owen gasped as he recognized the portal machine.

The Dark replaced his mask, and his word balloons turned dark again. "Tell me of the portal," he said. "Where does it go?"

Doc Twilight just stared at him, not speaking.

The Dark growled, and the bars holding Doc Twilight captive disappeared. A black glove shot out and picked Doc Twilight up by his costume's collar, and his feet left the ground until he hung in the air. "I *won't* ask again."

"You used to be a *hero*," Doc Twilight said, his voice strained. "Now you're just a petty tyrant. A bully. A *villain*."

The Dark growled in annoyance, but Owen noticed his hand shaking slightly. "I'm what this world *needs*," he hissed, then threw Doc Twilight against the wall of his cell, the bars reforming instantly.

"Is that what you tell yourself?" Doc Twilight asked, his word balloon groggy, like he was in great pain from hitting the wall.

"I will open this portal," the Dark said, his back to Doc Twilight. "I will find out where you came from, and I will fix that world, just as I have this one. No more criminals, no more lawbreakers, no more suffering."

"Unless *you* cause it," Doc Twilight said, then coughed.

But the Dark didn't respond. Instead, he moved away, barely touching the ground as the lights disappeared, turning the panel dark once more. Two more panels went by before Doc Twilight said quietly: "You haven't lost everything. Not yet. I can fix this, if you just release me."

Another pause.

"Oh, no," the Dark said. "I want you to witness what happens to your world when I get Apathy's portal working. You'll be with me every step of the way. And then, when it's all over, you too shall be infected with shadow. Because there's no escaping the Dark. Not when it's inside of us *all*."

And then the comic ended.

Owen backed away from the panel. What was happening? Who was the Dark, and what was this horrible thing that had happened to him? Apparently, he'd been a hero once, and Doc Twilight knew him. But what kind of hero turned into a villain?

Sure, it was a comic book cliché, but that usually involved mind control, or a clone, or an impostor of some kind. But none of those things fit here, not after what Mason Black said in the comic. But what had driven the Dark to such horrible lengths?

Looking to the right, Owen gasped. There was no next issue! Instead, the pages extending forward were just sketches, uncompleted, though it did look like someone was drawing them as he watched. *That* was pretty cool to see, but not exactly helpful in any way. Here and there were a few dialogue balloons, but they were too light for Owen to read.

"Ugh," Owen said, shaking his head. "Why can't they reveal everything all at once? I don't have time to wait for the next issue! Just tell me what happened! How did things get like this?"

And then he slowly looked to the left and slapped himself in the forehead.

In *that* direction, complete pages stretched out as far as he could see.

Maybe the next issue wasn't ready. But there was no reason Owen couldn't find the Dark's secret origin in the back issues somewhere, right?

CHAPTER 28

Better tell me what I want to know," Charm growled at the terrified banana hanging over the edge of the building by his hands, which were the only parts of his body not covered by the superpowered, super-slick banana suit. "I don't know how long I can hold you, and that looks like a *long* way down."

"Don't hurt him!" Gwen shouted, reaching for the banana, but Charm moved him farther out over the edge, letting his little yellow feet kick in the wind.

"That's up to *him*," Charm said. "Well, Rotten Banana? Where do we find the Dark?"

"I don't know, I told you!" the villain shouted. "His shadows are everywhere after the sun goes down. Why don't you ask *them?*"

"Maybe they'll catch you before you hit the ground, then," Charm said, narrowing her eyes. "Want to bet?"

Gwen backed up to where Bethany watched uncomfortably. "We're not actually going to drop him, right?" Gwen whispered. "Because I'm not letting that happen no matter what."

Bethany shook her head. "Charm's just bluffing," she said, hoping she was right.

She is *just bluffing, right, Owen?*

But there was no response in her thoughts. Maybe Owen was busy with something else? Hopefully he was okay, wherever he was. Bethany inched closer to the half-robotic girl, just in case.

"*Uh-oh,*" Charm said, and the banana began to slip out of her grasp. "My arm is starting to get tired. . . ."

"Please!" the Rotten Banana shouted. "I can't! He'll bruise me so much he'll turn me into banana bread if I help you. I'll be like the Psycho Potato, who got completely *mashed*—"

"I'm dropping him," Charm said to Bethany. "It's not worth another stupid pun."

She released the banana, and the man shrieked as he fell a foot before Charm grabbed him again with her other hand, quicker than Gwen and Bethany could react.

"Well?" Charm shouted. "This arm's not as strong, so I'd talk quick!"

"Okay!" the banana said, practically sobbing. "I'll tell you what you want to know. You've peeled it out of me!"

It took Gwen and Bethany combined to pull Charm away from the edge after that, but fortunately they got the banana back onto the roof safely. "This isn't over, banana!" Charm shouted as Gwen held her back. "Not one more pun, you hear me? *Not one more!*"

"I've got ears, I hear you," the Rotten Banana said, staring at the ground. "Not like that poor Psycho Potato. Completely deaf. But wow could he see with all those eyes!"

"I'll handle things from here," Bethany said to Gwen, who struggled to pull Charm away. Gwen whispered something to the half-robotic girl, and Charm finally turned and walked away, muttering under her breath, kicking at random things on the roof.

"The Dark's going to love *her*," the Rotten Banana told Bethany. "Probably hire her on the spot. She's already worse than the people the shadows took." He glanced around the roof as the afternoon sun began casting shadows in various places.

"Why are you doing this?" Bethany asked him, trying not to be distracted by the shadows. "You're a grown-up dressed like a banana."

"It was our thing!" the Rotten Banana said, not looking at her. "Me, the Potato, the Tomato Terror, and Outrage Orange. We were the Fruit of the Loons, the rotten apples who were ruining the whole barrel."

"I don't think potatoes are fruit," Bethany pointed out.

"You're not the first to say that," the banana said with a shrug. "And trust me, I know we're ridiculous, but that keeps you *safe*. The less threatening you are as a criminal, the lower level of superhero who comes after you. We were small time, which means we mostly got the kid sidekicks, or maybe someone like Mr. Nose. Guy rode around on a Snot Rocket." He made a disgusted face. "Might take four showers to clean *that* off of you, but at least you wouldn't get punched through a wall."

"Why not just find a real job?" Bethany asked, kneeling down beside him. Someone had to play good cop (or detective) with Gwen busy holding Charm back, after all.

The banana sighed. "Because sometimes you just have a fruit-costumed villain inside you, and you either let it out, or you regret it for the rest of your life. If I could leave it all behind now, I would. The Dark has turned this whole city into a dictatorship. Everyone who hasn't already fled is either taken over by his shadows, or hiding as best they can.

Trust me, if I had any money, I'd take it and split!"

Bethany winced. "I'm trying to keep my friend away from you. The least you could do is hold off on the puns."

The banana actually looked embarrassed at this. "Sorry, I don't even know I'm doing it anymore. Keeps the game fun when the superheroes come after you. But the Dark hates it too. It's not a game to him. The Fruit of the Loons, we never hurt anyone. Sure, we threaten, but we're not evil, you know? Just a bit rotten. But the Dark, he's got some screws loose somewhere. His shadows are everywhere at night, so they're practically invisible in the dark. And whenever they find a superpowered hero or villain . . ." The Rotten Banana shuddered.

Bethany felt a chill, and this time couldn't resist taking a quick look around at all the shadows on the rooftop. "So where is he? Help us find him, and we can put a stop to him, fix all of this."

The banana turned and stared at her in disbelief. "*You three?* Teenage girls with the power to bash amazing wordplay? You wouldn't last two seconds. No one knows who he is or where he came from. Just showed up out of nowhere and declared his stupid laws. At first, no one took him seriously, but after his shadows took over Captain Sunshine, *everyone* started paying attention. The rest of Jupiter City's heroes took him on, and all got taken over. Any villains who stood up to him, he made disappear." He shivered.

"Disappear?" Bethany said. "What do you mean?"

"I mean they're gone, kid," the banana said. "Not even taken by his shadows, just *gone*. Are they dead? Held in some jail somewhere? Who knows. No one knows *anything* about him. Villains think he's a hero who went bad, while I hear the heroes think he's a small-time crook who found a lot of power somehow. None of that matters, though. Smart crooks are in hiding. There's no one left to stand against him, except a few powerless stragglers here and there. Those are the only ones the Dark didn't hunt down." The banana shook his head. "You seem like a decent kid, so don't go looking for him. Do the right thing and just let me go."

Bethany rolled her eyes. "You're a supervillain. How would letting you go be the right thing?"

"Because you'd be saving my life," the banana told her. He made a puppy-dog face at her and put his tied hands together like he was begging. "If the Dark heard that I helped you find him, it wouldn't just be his shadows after me, it'd be *him*. And he wouldn't have a problem with my costume, not like his shadows." He shivered. "Please? *Please* just let me go?"

Bethany stared at him for a moment, then shook her head sadly. "Charm? It's your turn again!"

"Finally!" Charm shouted. Gwen reluctantly let her go, and Charm began to make her way back toward them, grinning widely.

"No!" the banana said, pushing to his feet awkwardly and holding his hands up in surrender. "Don't let her near me again!"

"Where can I find him?" Bethany demanded, done with this whole good cop/bad cop routine. "Talk or we leave you alone with her!"

The banana's eyes widened. "Okay, okay! I was telling the truth, I really don't know where he is. But last I heard one of the Lawful Legion heroes freed themself from the shadows for a bit, so he probably had to take care of that. Try the Legion's headquarters. He might still be there, or maybe he left a trail or something. I swear, that's all I know!"

"The Lawful Legion?" Bethany said, putting a hand up to stop Charm. "Who are they?"

"The worst of the worst," the banana said. "Captain Sunshine, Athena, the Flying Duck, you name it."

214

Bethany paused, then tried to keep her voice calm. "And Doc Twilight?"

"He used to be a member," the banana said. "But then he disappeared a few months back, and I don't think the LL ever found him. This is all his fault, anyway. Jupiter City was supposed to be *his* city, and look at what he let the Dark do to it." He shook his head. "Doc Twilight? More like *Mock*—"

Bethany punched him in the face, knocking him out cold.

Charm put an arm around her shoulders as Bethany winced, shaking her hand in pain. "I take back all the horrible things I've said about you," the half-robotic girl said. "That was amazing."

Bethany gave her a look. "You've been saying horrible things about me?"

Charm grinned. "As Kiel would say?" And then she winked.

CHAPTER 29

Okay, apparently there are a lot *of back issues,* Owen thought as he stopped to catch his breath from all the walking. He wasn't sure how far he'd come, but it felt like he'd been walking along the comic pages wall for at least an hour. Plus, to get back to the "present" in the pages, it'd take him just as long to walk back.

Reading comics had never been this exhausting back home.

It was time for a rest. Owen slumped to the floor, making sure not to touch the wall in case he erased or rewrote something by accident. There had to be a better way to do this, didn't there? Why couldn't this behind-the-scenes world be more like reading a comic, anyway? All you had to do was flip a page, and you'd be there. No one had ever had to do this much exercise just to read a comic!

"Turn!" Owen shouted out of frustration, making a page-turning motion with his hand.

As if listening to him, the entire wall seemed to jump by one page to the left. Every single page.

"Are you kidding me?" Owen shouted, pushing himself to his feet. He slowly reached up and made the same gesture, then watched as every page moved over by one page length to the left. He reversed the gesture, and they all jumped by one to the right.

Really? After all that walking, he could have just been turning the pages like any regular comic? "I'm not okay with this!" he shouted at the behind-the-scenes world, gesturing wildly with his hand to make sure whoever heard knew he meant it all. That sent the pages flying so quickly he couldn't even see them, so he held up his palm in a "stop" gesture, and that froze the pages.

He shook his head, cursing himself. Why exactly hadn't he tried this *before* walking for miles?

When he looked up to see where he was, he found that the pages had stopped right where he and Bethany had first seen Doc Twilight enter the comic book world through the manhole. Now *this* was where he really should be giving advice.

Don't go in there! he should write in their thoughts. *You're going to get Owen trapped in a nowhere space outside of the comic, while Bethany gets to do all the cool things with Charm and EarthGirl and maybe some guy in a banana suit!*

And for a second he considered it. *Could* he give himself thought balloons too? Maybe warn himself about getting trapped in this other world, and so ensure it never happened?

But then he would never have been behind-the-scenes to give himself the thought balloon to begin with, which meant he'd just end up back here again. He winced, already feeling his head begin to ache. *This* was why time travel never worked. Too many paradoxes.

"Enjoy your own mistakes, me," Owen said to the page, briefly waving at himself, which again flung the pages back and forth. He quickly stopped them, then sent them flying backward toward the right, in order to find the Dark's origin in the past. Panels flew by so quickly he could barely make them out, but he let them go for a few seconds, not entirely sure what he was looking for but knowing it had to be a while ago, in comic time.

Finally, the pages began to slow down, and Owen put his palm out to stop them. They ground to a halt, and Owen found himself staring at the last person he ever expected to see here, right in the face.

Bethany's mother glared right at him from a panel as big as he was.

"Mrs. Sanderson?" he said in shock, taking a step back without realizing it. "What are you doing here?"

But she didn't respond. Well, not out loud.

Owen stepped closer, staring at the speech bubble above her head. "Who *are* you and what are you doing here?" the bubble said. *Whoa*, had she heard him? It seemed like she was responding to his question.

But no, she couldn't be, not from the other side of the comic page. But how was she in this story, this comic book? Was it the same title that he and Bethany were in, or some other series? Why weren't things labeled better here?! Comics needed titles and issue numbers on each page, like books!

Wait a second, though. Something was off. Owen took a closer look at the woman before him, and started to realize something. This *was* Bethany's mom, but she looked years and years younger.

He glanced over at the next page and realized why.

"I'm Doc Twilight, of course," said a man in a purple-and-red costume with a setting sun and three little stars on it. He stood in an alley that ran between two houses that looked very familiar, with a portal of blue fire open on the ground between the houses. "That's right, the *superhero*." He grinned, showing off some perfect teeth. "Did you happen to see an evil henchman of Dr. Apathy running this way? He jumped through that portal before I had the chance to stop him."

Hold on. Was this Bethany's mother *meeting* Bethany's father?

Bethany's mom responded to her future husband in a way that reminded Owen exactly of her daughter: She sighed deeply in annoyance. "This isn't funny," Mrs. Sanderson said. "It's not Halloween. What are you even doing, dressed up like that?"

Huh. Apparently they didn't have cosplay conventions back then.

"All part of the job," Bethany's father said, looking past her. "Now if you'll excuse me, ma'am, I believe I've spotted my target."

"Ma'am?" Bethany's mother said as Doc Twilight took off past her, a twilight grapple in his hands. "I'm probably younger than you are!"

"That doesn't justify treating you with disrespect!" Doc Twilight said, throwing a smile over his shoulder as a rope shot out from his twilight grapple, snagging a fleeing man's legs and tying them together. The apparent villain collapsed to the ground with a grunt. Doc Twilight then clicked a button on the launcher and the rope retracted, dragging the criminal back to him.

"This one led me on a playful chase," Doc Twilight said. "Didn't get far, though, did you, lad? Just because Dr. Apathy builds an untested dimensional portal to a land peopled by beauties beyond compare doesn't mean you can escape justice!" He gave Bethany's mother a side look, and Owen's mouth dropped open in horror.

Was Doc Twilight *flirting* with her?

Owen choked down his bile as best he could before turning the page with a gesture.

"Yeah, I'm calling the cops," Bethany's mom told the superhero, then began looking around the street as if she didn't have a cell phone or something. "I don't know who you two are, but you can't just attack people like that."

"Thank you, calling the police would be a great help!" Doc Twilight said. "And let her castigation be a lesson to you, foul criminal. You indeed *cannot* attack people like that. Truer words have never been uttered by such an angel."

"*Stop* it, you maniac," Bethany's mom said, looking up and down the street. "Why are there no pay phones around here?"

"Here, use mine," Doc Twilight said, tossing her a radio in the shape of a moon, with three stars as the tuners. "It's set to police scanners already, so you should be able to reach them without any trouble."

She looked at the radio, then clicked the button. Nothing but static came out. "You're *literally* insane, aren't you?"

He winked at her. "Just doing my job, ma'am."

A huge *KABLAM* filled the page, and Bethany's mom was knocked to the ground. Coughing from a dust cloud, she picked herself up to find a familiar giant robot emerging from the blue-fire portal between the two houses, the robot's oversized body distorted due to the small hole. As the robot passed through the portal, it seemed to puff up like a balloon, back to its full size. At the top of the robot sat an old man in a white coat, glasses atop his balding head.

"Twilight!" the old man shouted. "Get back to Jupiter City where you belong. Or don't! Just don't interfere with me. Or do, I don't care. But this is *my* world to rule if I decide I want to, and I won't let you stop me, assuming it doesn't take much effort, that is. Curse you for making me less apathetic!"

A hand reached out to Bethany's mom, and Doc Twilight helped her to her feet. "I believe I'm being called," he said, grinning at her. "Give me a moment, and I'll be back to continue our conversation."

"What is that thing?!" Bethany's mom shouted, pointing at the killer robot as its buzz-saw hands began to spin.

"Oh, I expect it's just another killing machine from the brilliant yet evil mind of Dr. Apathy," he said, shrugging. "The good that man could do if he weren't so set on not feeling anything, all because his former assistant left him for his rival colleague. A true tragedy. Still, makes for an interesting night!"

Doc Twilight flashed a grin at her, then shot out his grapple. It hit a building right behind the robot and sent the hero flying straight at the killer machine and certain doom.

At least, that's what the caption said. *As Doc Twilight finds himself in a strange dimension, will Dr. Apathy's robot spell certain doom for our hero?* the caption asked. *Find out next month, Doc fans!*

Owen just stared in horror. *This* was how Bethany's parents had actually met? In a comic book fight with a supervillain? And even worse, someone actually wrote the phrase "Doc fans"?!

Right before Owen was about to turn the page, something

caught his eye. The henchman who Doc Twilight had caught a few pages before had freed himself, and was running away from the battle.

Except he was running out into the real world, not back through the portal. The real, nonfictional world.

Owen frowned. *That* couldn't be good. He'd have been caught, surely. There was no way there was a fictional person running loose out in the nonfictional world, especially not an evil one.

. . . Right?

CHAPTER 30

This is mean," Gwen said, pointing at the Rotten Banana walking behind them, his hands tied together by a rope attached to Charm's belt. "He helped us, after all."

"He's *evil*," Charm told her. "And if you remember, *I* didn't want to bring him along in the first place. But at least this way, he's contained."

"I'm not evil!" the Rotten Banana said. "Listen to the nice girl. I'm misguided at worst, and this *is* mean!"

"We don't have time for any of this," Bethany said. "I think I saw the Lawful Legion's headquarters when Owen and I first arrived, a big domed thing not too far from Apathetic Industries. But we're still going to need to move fast." She squinted at the setting sun, then looked around at the shadows now covering the ground. "The darker it gets, the worse off we'll be."

"I could fly ahead and see what I find?" Gwen suggested, patting her jet pack.

"Or you could give *me* the jet pack, and I could go ahead and just take out all the bad guys," Charm said.

"We're staying together," Bethany told both of them, even though they had a point. They *did* need to travel faster, and it's not like there were any taxis around, even if they were willing to take three girls and a banana downtown.

If only her stupid superpowers had worked like they were supposed to! Then Bethany could have turned into a giant eagle or a pterodactyl or something that could fly them all there. Instead, she was stuck with turning into inanimate objects. And what use were inanimate objects, anyway?

A thought hit her hard enough to stop her dead in the street. Inanimate didn't necessarily mean something couldn't *move*, just that it wasn't alive. That meant—

"Staying together makes sense to me," the banana said, interrupting her train of thought. "I've been so lonely without my usual bunch—"

"Shut him up," Bethany told Charm. If she could turn into something inanimate that could still move, she could get them to the Lawful Legion's headquarters in no time.

What were the restrictions of her new power, anyway?

"I might have a really bad plan," she told them as Charm's punches slid off the banana suit, making him giggle like he was being tickled. "Give me some room, okay?"

Charm sighed in frustration, then yanked on the Rotten Banana's rope to pull him out of the way, but ended up knocking him off his feet and sending him sliding down the road. "You intended that!" he shouted back at her.

"Quiet or I leave you to the shadows!" Charm told him, then grinned. "I totally did intend that," she told Gwen and Bethany.

Bethany rolled her eyes, then slowly formed an image in her head, making sure to get it as accurate as she could. A lot of it involved things she knew nothing about, but hopefully all the little details would be taken care of by the superpower, like Owen had implied. Otherwise, this was going to be a *very* short trip.

Once she had the image in her head, she pushed herself into it, just like pushing her way out of a book, melting into the idea in her head until she felt her old body disappear. There was a loud *POINK*, and everything felt different.

Hoping it worked, Bethany opened her eyes . . . except

she didn't have eyes anymore. Yet, she could still tell that she was surrounded by metal buildings, a half-robotic girl, and a jet pack.

"So?" Bethany tried to say, but realized she couldn't just speak as normal. Instead, she turned on her loudspeaker and blared, "Get in!"

"That was the coolest thing I've ever seen," Gwen said as she opened Bethany's door, taking the pilot seat. "What is this thing?"

"It's an antique," Charm said, and Bethany didn't need eyes to know Charm was looking around with disgust. "Why didn't you turn into something newer? With antigrav thrusters or something?"

"Can you fly her?" Gwen asked.

Bethany felt Charm's hands on her guidance sticks and blared an alarm. "No one's flying me," she said through the inside radio. "Bring the banana on board. I'll get us there."

"This is *so gross!*" the Rotten Banana said from outside. "It's like you two are sitting in her *guts* or something! I'm not getting in."

A second later he crashed into the backseat as Charm yanked him in and slammed the door shut.

With everyone now ready, Bethany began turning her blades faster and faster, and her altimeter told her that they were rising right off the ground.

After all, if you couldn't be a flying dinosaur, turning into a helicopter was sometimes just as good.

They rose off the streets and out over the city, Bethany flying higher and higher as Gwen laughed joyfully from the pilot's seat. It all just felt so *freeing*, knowing that they were flying under her power! This wasn't some fantasy superpower, either: These were *her* helicopter blades keeping them in flight. Something moved below, and like a bat, she sensed it with her radar—an empty subway train traveling through the city—and she realized she could track it wherever it was going.

Wherever *it* was going? *She* could go anywhere! The sky was literally the limit! She could fly—

"Do you see the Lawful Legion headquarters?" Gwen asked, and with a start, Bethany realized she'd completely forgotten what they were doing. Guilt came crashing down on her, and she quickly spun around in the sky, all of her instruments searching for the building the banana had described.

This was what happened when she got too fictional. She lost

sight of what was important, and nothing was more important than finding her father.

From high up, her radar and flight cameras showed the city below her, laid out like a bunch of concentric circles. Behind Apathetic Industries was a warehouse district, complete with more joke factories, fish suppliers, and chemical companies than anyone could possibly need. From there, a circle of shadow-filled neighborhoods surrounded the downtown area, filled with crumbling stores and alleyways. That would be the rough part of town that Doc Twilight had probably patrolled, back before he'd met her mom.

In the center of town she made out the *Daily Current* building again, complete with its giant neon lightning bolt, and the Second Cousins headquarters. And then she saw it, right in the center of the city: a domed white building with huge columns that sat on a field of green, fountains and broken statues surrounding it on every side. That *had* to be it.

"I've got it," Bethany said over the internal radio, turning toward the green area.

"Can't you go faster?" Charm said, kicking the floor and sending a wave of annoyance through Bethany. "They're going to see us coming for *miles*."

Bethany shook herself a bit, getting a satisfying feeling as Charm knocked her head against the window. "No kicking," she said on the radio, but realized the half-robotic girl was probably correct. The Dark *would* see them coming, if he hadn't heard the helicopter already.

But it's not like she'd turned into a rocket or something. There was only so fast she could go if she were going to land everyone safely.

. . . Unless she stopped worrying about their safety.

"Everyone hold on," Bethany said, morphing her dashboard into large, fluffy pillows with a loud *POINK*, then clicking the seatbelts over everyone's lap, even the banana's. "Ready?"

"Finally," Charm said.

"Yes!" Gwen shouted.

"I think I might throw up," the banana said.

And with the idea of a puking banana pushing her to hurry, Bethany sent herself diving straight at the Lawful Legion's headquarters.

The g-forces sent all three of her passengers slamming into their seats, and Gwen and the Rotten Banana began screaming, though at least Gwen was doing it from excitement. Bethany turned the attention of her instruments back outside, knowing this would have to be timed perfectly.

She stopped her helicopter blades to pick up even more speed, and now they were plummeting toward the ground like a rock. Just in case, she added even more pillows inside as they got closer and closer to the ground.

And then, right before they crashed, Bethany kicked her blades back in and sent her engines into overdrive, propelling them straight into the Lawful Legion's headquarters.

Her helicopter body exploded through the glass windows and doors, and Bethany winced in her head, but none of it seemed to damage her. She immediately stopped her blades and tried to stabilize herself, only to crash onto her side, plow through the reception desk, then gradually come to a stop against some pretty white marble columns.

After a moment of letting out a deep breath of exhaust, Bethany opened her eyes (by turning on her instruments again), just to make sure everyone was okay.

"You guys still alive?" she asked tentatively on her internal radio.

"YES!" Gwen shouted, jumping out of the helicopter door. "That was *amazing!*"

"The Dark *still* probably saw us coming," Charm said,

climbing out next, then pulling the banana out after her. "Even if he didn't, he'll have heard that crash."

"I'm bruised!" the banana shouted. "Don't let him make bread out of me!"

As soon as they were all out, Bethany pulled herself out of the helicopter image and changed back into herself. A quick check over her body revealed she weirdly didn't have a scratch. It was as if any damage to the helicopter had been left behind in the image. *That* might be useful!

"Is anyone here?" she asked the other three.

As she said the words, two bright-white lights exploded through the floor, and they all jumped backward. The marble surface exploded up, and out of the wreckage rose men and women in bright, flashy costumes.

"You wrecked our building!" said a terrified-looking man in a yellow suit and cape. "The Dark ordered us to stay here if we wanted to live, and now he's going to punish us!" His fear quickly turned to rage, his shadow-covered eyes narrowing. "You'll pay for this, you criminals!"

A woman who looked like a living statue of Athena, Greek goddess of wisdom and war, struck her owl staff against the ground, sending the building shaking. Her black eyes glared at them. "If we deliver these children to the Dark ourselves, Captain Sunshine, then perhaps he shall show mercy upon us!"

"Lawful Legion? A-QUACK!" shouted a furious man in a duck outfit, who pointed a large mace down at them.

And at that quack, the Lawful Legion attacked.

CHAPTER 31

Owen knew he should get back to Bethany, Charm, and Gwen. At least check in on their comic pages and see how they were doing, assuming those pages had been drawn by now. They should be, given how long he'd been gone.

Only Owen still didn't know who the Dark was, or how Doc Twilight knew him. And now more questions had come up. Where had Bethany's father disappeared to? Was *that* in the comics? How had Dr. Apathy built a portal that could bridge the fictional and nonfictional worlds in the first place? And what happened to Dr. Apathy's henchman that Doc Twilight was chasing?

Ugh. This was how comics roped you in. Bring up all kinds of questions, then promise to answer them the next month, *maybe* the month after. And then years later you realize you've been permanently hooked, and now there are thousands of new questions to answer.

Anyway, Bethany would be okay for a bit. After all, even if she got in trouble, Owen could just go back a few pages and warn her about it, like he'd already done. She'd be fine! Besides, this wouldn't take *too* long.

Feeling much better about the whole thing, Owen pushed the pages forward in time just a bit, skipping the fight with Dr. Apathy to get to the good stuff faster. Figuring he was far enough, Owen stopped the pages and found Doc Twilight showing Bethany's mom around Jupiter City.

"This is the thirty-first century museum built to honor the Flying Duck, one of the members of the Lawful Legion," the superhero said, pointing at a museum with a statue of a man in a duck suit about to fly into the air. "They've got a real thing for old FD. Probably because he inspired the Army of Super Ducks in that century. So they came back and built us a museum to honor his future exploits."

"Doesn't that change the timeline?" Bethany's mother asked him, giving the museum a confused look.

Doc Twilight shrugged. "There are so many future timelines out there already, who can even say?" He put an arm around her shoulder (Owen gagged) and moved them on to the next point of interest, the Mystic Monastery of Professor Weird. "Don't get too close," Doc Twilight warned her as Mrs. Sanderson started to walk up the steps. "The house has been known to eat people."

"And that's safe to just have out there in the city, for anyone to walk by?"

"When I'm around, everyone's safe," he told her with a grin (Owen gagged again).

And of course, that's when a monstrous foot the size of a car stamped down in the middle of the street. Because this is how comics worked.

"DOC TWILIGHT," shouted a hundred-foot-tall alien wearing fierce-looking armor. "YOU'VE INTERFERED WITH MY PLANS FOR THE LAST TIME. I *WILL* RULE THIS WORLD AS I WAS MEANT TO. MY FATHER BESTOWED EARTH UPON ME THE MOMENT I WAS BORN, AND—"

Doc Twilight turned to Bethany's mom, looking a bit embarrassed. "One second," he said as she stared up at the alien in terror. He launched his twilight grapple at the alien's chest armor, then flew up after it, the alien never pausing his rambling speech. The superhero quickly climbed up the armor to the alien's shoulder, then whispered something into an enormous ear.

Whatever Doc Twilight said immediately stopped the alien, and it turned an odd shade of blue as it glanced down at Bethany's mom.

"OH, I'M *SO* SORRY," the alien giant said, spreading his hands almost in apology. "I DIDN'T REALIZE YOU HAD A *GUEST*. TERRIBLY IMPOLITE OF ME. SHOULD I COME BACK IN A WEEK OR SO?"

"That'd be perfect," Doc Twilight told him, squatting to pat the alien's shoulder in thanks. "And don't worry, we'll get your dad off your back soon enough. Trust me, I've got a plan that'll make it look like you conquered the world, and he'll never know the difference."

The giant alien grinned sheepishly and toed a six-foot hole into the street. "AW, DOC, YOU'RE THE BEST. I'LL SEE YOU SOON." He waved at Bethany's mom, who waved back as if in a daze. The alien then tapped something on his wrist and disappeared completely, leaving Doc Twilight hundreds of feet in the air with nothing to hold him up.

Instead of panicking, the superhero just grinned as he plummeted toward the ground. At the last possible moment, he shot out his grapple, swung from a gargoyle on a nearby building, and landed neatly next to Bethany's mom. "Apologies for that," he said. "I completely forgot we'd had an appointment for today."

"That was a giant *alien*," she said, taking a step back, her mouth hanging open. "And you made him go away!"

"We've been friends for a few years now, yes."

She shook her head, still shocked. "You really *must* be a superhero. How could any of this be real? How can this place exist? How can *you* exist?"

Doc Twilight grinned. "I can't share my secret origin with just anyone, Catherine."

Catherine? Owen frowned in confusion before realizing that must be Mrs. Sanderson's real name. For some reason, that made Owen extra uncomfortable. He could have lived his entire life without ever knowing Mrs. Sanderson's first name.

Bethany's mom shook her head. "No, I don't want . . . I just . . . this can't be *real*."

Ah, see? Owen grinned, remembering how he'd felt when he first discovered Bethany pulling herself out of *Charlie and the Chocolate Factory*. He wasn't the only one who couldn't handle it at first! If Bethany's mom fainted too, he'd feel a lot better about things.

Doc Twilight shrugged. "I saw great injustice in the world

and chose to step up. Surely there are heroes in your world as well?"

She shook her head, then stopped. "Well, yes, but they don't have powers. They're just ordinary people."

"As am I," Doc Twilight said. "No powers. The Lawful Legion barely keeps me on their payroll." He laughed.

She didn't. "This is all so weird. Like something out of a comic book."

"A what, now?"

She made a *fair enough* face, then half-smiled. "Could *I* maybe try your gun thing?"

"It's a twilight grapple," he told her, handing it over. "Be careful, as—"

She shot it at the nearest roof, then sailed up behind it, landing neatly on the edge. "That was *so cool!*" she shouted down.

"It takes a bit of getting used to," Doc Twilight finished, grinning from ear to ear. "I think I might be in *love*."

Owen puked in his mouth and quickly turned a few pages. Wasn't this supposed to be a superhero book? Who let romance into these things? Okay, other than, like, Lois Lane, and Mary Jane Watson, and . . . okay, it was in all of them.

Fine. But not with Bethany's *mother*, of all people.

What was next, Owen's mom?!

Something odd caught his eye as he flipped through the comic pages, and Owen quickly stopped them. Uh-oh. Mrs. Sanderson was showing Doc Twilight his own comic book. Somehow, he wished Bethany could have seen this. *See?* He would have told her. *Even your mom shows fictional people that they're from stories. It wasn't just me!*

"So readers can . . . see me?" Doc Twilight said, staring at the pages. "At least they captured my good side."

"I think everyone assumes you're made-up," Bethany's mom told him. "We didn't know there were other worlds out there, or that superheroes might actually be real." She looked at a pile of books on a table near her. "I wonder if—"

"Who are these men, the writer and artist?" Doc Twilight said, turning back to the first page and pointing at the credits. "Anyone who can see into my thoughts and knows my secret identity is someone I should speak to. Can't have enemies roaming free with that much power."

"They're just the people who make the comic book," Bethany's mom said. "I'm pretty sure any power they have is with their fans, and that's it."

"Superpowered fans?" Doc Twilight said, raising an eyebrow. "Do they use these fans to fly, or create tornadoes?"

Owen rolled his eyes and flipped forward several pages, then stopped when he saw two ordinary-looking men shaking hands with Doc Twilight, one looking excited, the other disbelieving.

"That's *quite* a costume," said the excited one, pulling at Doc Twilight's cape. "Did you make it yourself? And is this bulletproof?!"

"As a matter of fact I did, and of course," Doc Twilight said, then paused. "Might my friend Catherine and I show you two something? It's just across town, and I think you'll find it familiar-looking."

"I'm a bit behind on the latest issue, actually," the second man said, this one a lot less interested. "Can you just talk to Murray there? I've got other things that need doing."

Murray? Why did that name sound familiar? And then it hit Owen. The name on all of the Doc Twilight art in the house with the portal in the basement! This must be Murray, the artist. And now that Owen looked at him closely, he felt like he'd seen the man before. But where? The man's face reminded him of a photograph he'd seen . . .

Bethany's birthday party. The photo in Doc Twilight's house! This Murray person was the third adult in the picture, along with Bethany's parents. How crazy, they must have stayed friends with Doc Twilight's artist!

The excited man, Murray, shot the other man a look. "Ignore Mason," he told Bethany's mom and Doc Twilight. "He's always cranky. Wants to do more hard-edged stories, while I like the more fun stuff."

"They're superheroes," Mason said, turning away. "They've got all these powers, but just use them to catch bad guys? Why don't they actually change things? Anyway, it's great to meet you, Mr. . . ."

"Sanderson," Doc Twilight said, grinning at Bethany's mom. "Nice to meet you as well, Mr. Black."

"Wow, just like the *real* Doc Twilight's secret identity," Mr. Black said, looking incredibly bored with the conversation. "Good luck with things. Have fun messing around, Murray. I'm getting back to work."

Mason Black? That was the man that Doc Twilight had blamed for everything, the same person who'd written the note to his fans at the end of the Dark's issue. So this was Doc Twilight's writer?

Mr. Black left the panel, leaving Murray to shake his head and follow Bethany's mom and Doc Twilight, probably to a certain blue-fire portal, Owen figured.

Before they went in, though, the next panel shifted scenes completely, this time to Mr. Black looking over some scripts. He picked up some pages of art and looked them over with confusion.

"Hey!" he said, staring at the art. "This isn't what I wrote. Murray, what were you thinking?"

And then he took a closer look and gasped. Whatever had been there previously, now there were drawings of the same meeting that had just taken place, down to Mr. Black leaving, and then looking at the same drawings he was currently looking at right now, almost like a mirror reflecting a mirror to infinity.

Owen gasped too and quickly moved on to the next panel, where a knock came at the door. Mr. Black stood up, still confused about the art, and went to open it.

And there was the henchman Doc Twilight had been chasing down.

"Are you Mason Black?" the man said.

"Yes, but I'm really busy right now," Mr. Black said, looking back at the art he'd left at his desk.

The crook pulled out a gun and aimed it at Mr. Black's face. "You created me, Mr. Black. But you made me *wrong*. And now I need you to fix me."

CHAPTER 32

*O*wen! Bethany screamed in her mind. *We need help!*

But if he ever answered, his response was lost in a sea of chaos. The Lawful Legion swarmed over the four of them, and Bethany quickly lost track of what was happening.

Captain Sunshine came at her first, his black eyes glowing with bright white light as they burned lines in the floor heading straight for Bethany. She leaped out of the way, only to be grabbed by the duck man, his huge wings beating hard to send them soaring up to the roof.

"You'll pay for disobeying the Dark," the duck man said, then released her right near the ceiling, dropping her toward the floor at least four stories down.

Gwen grabbed her before she fell more than a few feet, her jet pack leaving a trail of flame behind her. "Got you!" she shouted. She had to dodge an attack by the duck, who immediately took a ray gun shot right in the chest and crashed into the wall.

"Thank you!" Bethany shouted to Charm as Gwen set her back down on the ground, then took right back off into the air.

"No time for thanks," Charm said, her robotic eye lighting up as she turned her ray guns on her next target. "Not now, or ever." She began shooting at Captain Sunshine, who rose into the air menacingly, his eyes glowing again.

"This is crazy!" the Rotten Banana shouted as Man of Iron, the empty armor of an old-fashioned knight, strode toward him holding a sword made from laser light. "We can't fight these people. They're the most powerful heroes on Earth!"

"Not sure how heroic they're being right now," Bethany said. A light disc came flying at her, and she leaped behind the banana to avoid it. The light disc careened off of his suit, only to boomerang back to its owner, Future Soldier, a man in what looked like a science-fiction movie costume from the 1960s.

"We need to talk about this!" Gwen shouted at Athena, whose staff rose into the air, growing out in all directions like a malevolent tree. "You're being controlled by the Dark's shadows. We're not your enemy!"

"You broke the Dark's rules!" Athena shouted, her black eyes flashing. Her staff's branches snared Gwen, in spite of EarthGirl's aerial acrobatics. "And *we're* not going to get punished for it."

"Gwen, watch out!" Bethany shouted, then almost lost her own head as Charm went flying by, slamming into a nearby wall hard enough to put a hole through it. Behind her, Man of Iron raised its laser sword. "Only rotten children go out after the sun goes down," the armor clanked, then stabbed right down at Bethany.

Except Bethany jumped herself into a new form with a *POINK*, and the empty armor's sword slammed into a steel shield. The force of the blow sent her shield-self skidding across the floor until she stopped, not moving.

Hmm. Maybe this wasn't the best choice.

Bethany quickly turned back to her normal self and, thinking quickly, took a running leap at the animated armor. Right before she crashed into it, she transformed into the knight's greatest enemy: rust.

She landed on the knight's armor, coating it completely. And the armor did come to a creaking halt! Only, she was now stuck there, not sure what else she could do.

Why couldn't inanimate objects be more useful in a super-hero fight?

"Really?" she heard the banana yell at her as Captain Sunshine's eye rays slid right off of him. "That's the best you've got? Rust?"

Annoyingly, the banana made a good point. She turned herself back human, then kicked off from the armor, hoping to just get out of reach of the laser sword. Then she dove back behind the banana, who seemed like the best protection to be found.

"Don't just hide, do something!" the banana yelled at her.

"I'm open to suggestions!" she shouted back, trying to avoid Captain Sunshine's eye beams.

"We need to break the shadow's hold on them," Gwen shouted from midair, tangled up in the branches of Athena's staff as they slowly closed in around her. She set her jet pack's throttle to full blast, and the staff caught fire, releasing her. She went rocketing up and barely missed hitting the roof before the duck man attacked.

"And how do we do that?" Charm yelled, punching the now free-of-rust Man of Armor across the room with her robotic arm. "We need to get out of here!" She aimed one ray gun back at the duck, while the second turned to Captain Sunshine just moments before he plowed into her, knocking her through a different wall.

Bethany didn't even know which way to turn. There was just too much happening at once, and it was all so violent! Was this what all superhero fights were like, just excessive destruction and mayhem for no reason? These were the *good* guys, weren't they? Gwen was right, they needed some way to break the shadows' control over the Lawful Legion, or at least stop them all from attacking. But what—

Something smacked her hard enough to send her reeling, and she turned in a daze to find herself staring at Athena and someone dressed exactly like Doc Twilight, if a lot shorter. Weirdly, he seemed to be about as tall as Bethany. Was she seeing things? How hard had she been hit?

". . . Dad?" she whispered in confusion as the short Doc Twilight slowly lifted what looked like a dart gun toward her, his black eyes glaring at her.

"You should have learned to fear the Dark," Athena said with a sneer.

"Eh," the shorter Doc Twilight said. "Who's afraid of the Dark, after all?"

He turned his dart gun on Athena, then shot several darts

into her skin. Most broke before they penetrated, but at such a close range two managed to insert themselves, and the goddess of wisdom and war actually stumbled, then fell to her knees.

"*What?* Who are you?" Bethany asked the masked hero, her head still jumbled from Athena's hit. She watched as he pulled out two black-colored contacts that had turned his eyes as black as the rest of the Legion's.

"I blew my *cover* for you," the masked figure said, glaring at her angrily. "I hope this little sightseeing tour was worth it." In spite of his growl, his voice sounded younger, closer in age to hers than the rest of the adult Legion.

"Who are you?" she repeated, grabbing Athena's staff from the goddess and aiming it at her just in case she got back up.

"Doesn't matter," the boy in the Doc Twilight costume said. "We all need to leave. They're going to tear us apart otherwise, and the shadows are on their way."

Captain Sunshine had turned his eye beams on Gwen, chasing her around the room with them, so Bethany aimed Athena's staff at him. "I'm not leaving until we find the Dark!" she shouted, then slammed the staff into the superhero from behind.

The staff vibrated so hard that it jumped out of her hands,

and Captain Sunshine turned around slowly as if she'd tapped him on the shoulder.

"You'll be seeing the Dark *very* soon, you little monster," Captain Sunshine told her.

"Oh, *shut up*," the teenage Doc Twilight said, and threw what looked like a rock at Captain Sunshine. The boy didn't throw it hard, but as soon as the rock touched Captain Sunshine, the superhero collapsed to the floor, writhing in pain.

"What *was* that?" Bethany asked, her eyes wide.

"Just a moon rock," the boy told her. "Captain Sunshine's only weakness. And that was the last one I had. We need to get out of here. Now that they know I'm not one of them, I'll be handed over to the Dark too."

"I told you, I need to find the Dark," Bethany said. "If he's coming here, all the better. I don't care how dangerous it is!"

"Do you understand that these are the most powerful people in the world, and they're infected with shadows that bring out the worst in them?" the boy said. "You know what? Let's do this the easy way."

Without another word, he aimed the tranquilizer gun at her and fired.

And that's when things got *really* weird. Before Bethany

could move or jump out of the way, the Rotten Banana leaped between them, taking the dart meant for her right in the cheek, one of his only vulnerable spots.

"Watch where you're pointing that thinnnngggggg," the banana said, then collapsed in a heap.

Bethany's eyes widened in shock. What had just happened? Had the banana actually just *saved* her . . . by sacrificing himself?

"Okay, that was pointless," the boy said, putting another dart in the gun. "It's not like I don't have more."

Bethany looked from the snoring banana to the boy and back, then jumped herself into the first image she could think of: a cloud of sleeping gas.

The boy's dart flew harmlessly through her cloud, and she smiled, if only in a way that gas would notice. Then she began to fill the entire hall as best she could, enveloping all the various Lawful Legion members, but staying away from Gwen and from Charm, who had just made her way unsteadily back into the hall.

The teenager who'd been about to shoot Bethany got enough of a faceful of sleeping gas to knock him to his knees, but reluctantly, she let him breathe after that.

After all, she had a lot of questions, and at least *he* wasn't infected by the shadows.

When the entire Lawful Legion was slumbering peacefully on the ground, Bethany jumped out of the sleeping gas, returning to her normal self.

"Now," she said to the dazed teenage boy as Gwen and Charm formed up behind her. "You are going to tell me who you are, why you infiltrated the Lawful Legion, and *where I can find the Dark.*"

The boy started to raise the tranquilizer gun again, but Charm shot it out of his hand. "Good aim," the boy said, massaging his hand. "Not bad, any of you. Well, except the one who kept trying to talk them out of fighting." He nodded up at Gwen.

"Yeah? She's the most powerful of all of us," Bethany told him, and Gwen smiled even while blushing.

"Whatever," he told them, standing up. "Come on. We stay here, we get captured."

"I'm not leaving until—" Bethany started to say, but the boy just shook his head.

"Don't you get it? *There's no way to beat him.* If he comes, we're all done for. We needed help from the world's most powerful superheroes if we were going to have any chance, but look at them. I've been trying for *days* to free them from the shadows, while making them think I was infected too. But nothing worked. *Nothing.* And now he knows we're here, which means he'll send every shadow he has at us." He glared at Bethany. "You either stay here and get taken over just like they did, or you come and maybe live. Your choice."

And just like that, the boy strode off, not even bothering to see if she was following.

Charm lifted her ray gun to his back, but Bethany pushed it back down . . . eventually.

CHAPTER 33

Owen slowly turned the page and saw only one inked panel. The rest of the panels were much sketchier, incomplete.

"What is this?!" said Mason Black to Dr. Apathy's henchman. He put his hands up and backed into his house.

In the penciled panel that came next, the crook followed him in.

"I'm sorry to do it this way," the man said, looking behind him out the door, then slowly shutting it. "I know who you are. I've seen the—what do you call them?—comic books. Doc Twilight and I, we're not *real*, are we?" He swallowed hard. "We're just figments of your imagination that came to life somehow. And if I came from you, then that means that you're the only person who can help me."

"Please, just put the gun down," Mr. Black said, and Owen wasn't sure if he was going to attack the man or run screaming.

The crook looked down at the gun like he was surprised he still had it, then tucked it into his belt. "Sorry, it's really just all I know. But that's why I need your help."

The next panel had Mr. Black sitting at the kitchen table as the henchman paced behind him, his gun still in his belt. "What is it that you want from me?" Mr. Black asked. "Money? Because I hate to break it to you, but writing comics hasn't made me rich."

The crook's eyes lit up briefly, then he shook his head violently. "*No!* That's exactly what I *don't* want anymore. You wrote me to be that person, a criminal who lies and steals and cheats out of greed. But I want *more* from this life, Mr. Black. And I think you have the power to help me with that."

"What power?" Mr. Black asked, his fear now seeming to be mixed with curiosity.

The crook turned and glanced out the kitchen window, like he was waiting for Doc Twilight to come swooping in at any moment. "I want you to rewrite me," he said. "I want to be a *hero*, Mr. Black."

Mr. Black stared at him for a moment, then burst out laughing.

The henchman immediately went for his gun, then consciously stopped himself, moving his hands back to his side. "*I mean it.* I'm just some random crook now, getting kicked around gang to gang, but you've got the power to change that. You could make me someone important, someone *good.*" He took the gun out of his belt and tossed it on the counter. "I don't want this life anymore. Help me, please! You're my creator, the one who gave me life. Can't you see that I'm capable of more than this?"

Mr. Black slowly stood up. "What you're asking for is impossible." He slowly moved toward the gun as the henchman growled in frustration.

"You *created* us. How can it be impossible?"

Mr. Black paused, his eyes on the crook, then leaped for the gun, grabbing it and turning it on the other man. "I did nothing of the kind!" Mr. Black shouted. "Don't you get it? You're not *real,* you can't be. This is all some kind of dream. A nightmare! I'm not actually meeting you, or Doc Twilight, or any of the stupid superheroes I've made up. You weren't even my idea, don't you get that? Murray Chase did all the work. I just suggested a superhero who only worked at night, and he came up with all the Twilight stuff. I doubt I even wrote *you* at all! He's the one who's always adding in quirky henchmen to make the battles more fun. If it were up to me, there'd be whole stories about Doc Twilight taking down mob bosses and crooked politicians, not evil scientists!"

The henchman took a step forward, ignoring the gun shaking in Mr. Black's hand. "I refuse to accept that! You're the one who created me, and you have the power to fix me. Make me better, tell my story differently. I don't want to be any part of this anymore. You *must* have had a plan when you made me, and—"

"I write four to five comics a month!" Black shouted, the weapon shaking even more now. "You think I have time to plan out any of this? That's why Chase does most of the work!"

"Please!" the crook said, taking another step forward.

And then Mr. Black turned his head away and pulled the trigger.

The bullet hit the wall behind the henchman, who put both his hands up in surrender. "You don't need to do this. You can fix me, please! You can change me, change *this*. I know you can."

Black opened his eyes and dropped the gun to the floor as if disgusted with himself. "Get out!" he screamed at the henchman. "Leave me alone! I'm not going to rewrite you. I'm not sure I'll ever write again! Just . . . just leave. Go back to your life. Never come back here again, or I'll call the cops!"

The crook just stared at Mr. Black sadly for a moment, then quietly picked up the gun and walked out of the house. He stopped outside and looked back, only to see Mr. Black slam the door and turn off the lights.

From there, the henchman strode through the dark and rainy streets for a panel or two, before finding the same fiery blue portal that Doc Twilight had emerged from an issue before. He looked back one last time, then dropped inside, going back to Jupiter City.

"*Wow,*" Owen said, his eyes wide as he turned the page. "This is *not* a kid's comic."

The next issue had the crook sharing his story with a woman, who just laughed at the idea of "their creators." Not knowing what else to do, the man went from hero to villain, sharing his story, begging them for help changing him. "We're all just a story, but I don't know how to rewrite myself," he'd say. Some humored him, claiming they didn't have the power to help, but most just ignored his insane stories about a writer and artist who'd created their world from nothingness.

Finally, the poor man sank into despair, resorting to writing and drawing his own story in a notebook while hiding behind a Dumpster in an alley. He sketched a few panels in the notebook, just like a comic book, showing himself as he was. But then the version of him in his drawings gave himself powers by rewriting himself, and he became strong enough to save Doc Twilight from Dr. Apathy.

At least, that's what it looked like. The man wasn't the best artist. And drawing himself as a superhero didn't make it so. He finally threw his notebook away in frustration, dropping his head into his hands and weeping.

Owen felt horrible even watching this. Where was Doc Twilight, who knew the truth? Even Bethany's mom could have done something, maybe helped the guy, since she at least knew he wasn't crazy. As it was, though, this was just awful! Was the poor guy still around somewhere, no one believing him?

"There must be a way," the crook whispered to himself, staring at his hands. "If we *are* stories, then we *can* change them. I know we can!"

He concentrated on his hand with all of his might, in panel after panel. And nothing happened, not for pages.

Finally, just as Owen was about to give up and move back to the present, something happened. Something was different.

It was such a small thing, Owen had to look closely just to be sure. But where once the crook's hand had been weathered and callused, now it was unlined, as if the man had never worked a day in his life.

The crook stared at his hand in surprise, then leaped to his feet, shouting and jumping for joy. Soon he stopped and stared in a reflective puddle on the street at his face, concentrating as hard as he could. The panel zoomed in on his eyes, then out to reveal the face of Doc Twilight.

What? What was happening? Was this guy actually rewriting himself? Had he just turned into Bethany's father?

But no, just as quickly, the face changed, and now the crook looked like Mason Black, then Dr. Apathy, then his original face again. The man laughed with pure delight, his clothes changing to Doc Twilight's costume, then to a tuxedo, followed by a space-suit and a few other things before falling back into his original outfit.

"I can do it," he whispered to himself, staring at his hands. "I *can* rewrite my own story."

Owen took a step away from the panels as the page turned. This *seemed* like good news, after the terrible story the man had been stuck in before. But being able to change yourself into any-thing was a *lot* of power for someone who'd started as a criminal. But wasn't that the point the man was making? He was changing his story so that he *wasn't* that criminal. He could rewrite himself, so couldn't he also rewrite his own past?

Owen shook his head. If he could rewrite his story, what *couldn't* he do?

"I can be anyone," the man said, and quickly shifted faces and clothes faster than Owen could even see . . . well, faster than the panel could show. Owen had almost forgotten he was reading this in comic book form.

"I can have any power I want!" the man said, and began to float into the air before lifting the Dumpster next to him with one finger, then throwing it straight up, presumably into outer space.

"I'm not just some *nobody* anymore!" the man said, and this time, all of his features slowly dissolved off of his face, leaving behind what looked almost like a mannequin without any clothes on.

And that's when Owen realized exactly who this man was, and all he could do was say, "Oh *no*," very, very quietly.

CHAPTER 34

The teenage boy wearing the Doc Twilight costume tossed his tranquilizer gun back down the hole in the floor that Captain Sunshine's entrance had made. "Hopefully that'll throw the shadows off of our scent," he said. "Otherwise, it's going to be an interesting trip to safety." He gave the rest of them a dark look, then pulled his purple cape around him like a cloak. "Let's go."

For a moment the cape reminded Bethany of Kiel, but this jerk was nothing like the boy magician.

"What about the Rotten Banana?" she asked, trying to wrap her arms around the unconscious banana to pick him up, but slipping off of his suit every time.

Charm sighed. "I'll get him," she said, and picked up the rope still attached to his hands, then started dragging him smoothly over the ground.

"Just . . . try not to bump him," Bethany said, now feeling protective of him. Why had he saved her, anyway? Not that she wasn't thankful, but it was just such an odd thing for him to do. He was a supervillain, wasn't he?

"So do the shadows hunt by smell?" Gwen asked as they followed the boy out of the Lawful Legion's hall. "Is that why you left your weapon?"

"Mostly they hunt by overwhelming numbers, coming at you from all sides until you can't escape, can't breathe, can't even think," he said, not turning around. "If that happens, *run*. I'll hold them off as long as I can."

"Who *are* you?" Bethany asked him. "The Banana said the Dark took out everyone who had powers."

"Exactly," the boy said. "Now, no more questions. The shadows can pick up sound vibrations, so try to stay silent."

They walked in silence for the next ten minutes or so as the evening advanced, avoiding dark alleys and shadowed streets as much as possible. The sun was down, but the sky still had a bit of light, at least for the next few minutes. They seemed to be heading back into the rougher area where the Dark had first caught Bethany and Owen. At least, she thought they were. It wasn't easy to tell exactly where they were now that she didn't have a helicopter's view.

Not once did they see anyone out on the roads, though Bethany did catch a few people staring down at them from windows above. Were they infested by shadows? Or were there a few normal people left, just hoping that someone would come along and help?

If they were hoping to be saved, a small group of kids towing a banana probably wasn't what they were hoping for.

"I don't know about you, but I *love* this place," Gwen whispered to Bethany. "I never imagined I'd get to actually walk around an Earth city. This is *so great!*"

"They're not all like this," Bethany told her quietly. "Most are a bit less . . . hopeless."

"Hopeless?" Gwen said, looking around. "I don't get that sense. If it was *really* hopeless, then people would have given up by now. But our new friend hasn't left, and neither has the banana. They're scared, sure, but they're still here, trying to make things better." She patted Bethany's shoulder. "Maybe we can help!"

"Sometimes it feels like your superpower is being optimistic,"

Bethany said with a smile. "If it is, use it on me. I could use the boost."

Gwen laughed, and Bethany joined in almost before she knew she was doing it. "See?" Gwen said. "No superpower necessary."

"Or you don't even know you're using it," Bethany told her, stepping over a broken lamppost. "Hey, where are we going, anyway?" she called to the boy at the front.

"I said no talking," he said, not turning around.

Charm looked back at Gwen and Bethany, then nodded down at her ray gun. Bethany shook her head, and Charm sighed, which made Gwen and Bethany laugh again.

"You're going to bring the shadows down on us," the boy said, and that was enough to kill Bethany's joy.

A few blocks later the boy abruptly turned and led them behind a boarded-up convenience store, then stopped at what looked like a solid wall. He pushed on several different bricks, waited for a moment, then repeated the pattern backward. Something began to grind, and the wall opened up to reveal a brightly lit staircase leading down.

"He's going to murder us," Charm whispered to Bethany as the banana slid down the stairs ahead of her, bumping up against the boy's legs, which earned them both a nasty look. "And when he does, I'm blaming *you*."

"I'll blame me too, probably," Bethany told her, then followed the boy and the banana down. They descended for what felt like a hundred feet before they came to a large metal door, an electronic keypad on the side. The boy put his eye up to a lens above the keypad, and a red light beamed out to scan it. Something beeped, and immediately the entire hallway lit up with lights as bright as the sun, leaving nowhere for shadows to hide.

"Don't you think this is a bit much?" Charm asked him, squinting against the light.

He flashed her an annoyed look. "The shadows can report back whatever they see to the Dark. So pardon me if I take security seriously. These lights can only cover so much, especially if we brought a shadow down inside with us. The least we can do is keep the entry passcodes on a need-to-know basis." He gave them all a long look, and first Gwen, then Bethany, and finally Charm all turned around, Charm with a loud sigh.

Behind them they could hear the boy entering some numbers on the keypad, and then the sound of the door opening.

Bethany now could clearly hear a large number of people talking from inside—the door must have completely blocked it out.

"Okay, we're in," the boy said, and all three turned to find what looked like an enormous cavern that was easily seven or eight stories high. The ceiling might have been right below the street, even. The cavern was filled with computers, lab equipment, and two of the same glass cases that Bethany had seen in the house with the manhole: one labeled DOC TWILIGHT, the other, KID TWILIGHT. Both costumes were missing here, though.

The rest of the cavern was filled with supervillains.

Dozens, maybe even a hundred of them, all wearing costumes in various states of repair, some intimidating, others simply terrifying. And all of them had turned to see who'd just come in, going completely silent.

"Villains!" Gwen said, pushing her way in front of Bethany.

"There's nothing to worry about," the boy said, nodding at the assembled forces of evil, who seemed to recognize the boy and go back to their conversations. "If any of these has-beens were dangerous, they'd have been taken by the Dark already. I'm just doing charity work at this point, keeping them alive."

He shoved away a shambling man missing half a face, and the zombie moaned, reaching for his brain. ". . . Or undead. Whatever."

Charm, meanwhile, had both her ray guns out, moving them from villain to villain faster than Bethany could follow, but none seemed to care. "They're not attacking," the half-robotic girl said, sounding confused.

"Did you not hear me?" the boy asked, shoving her guns away, which just made her turn them on him. "They know they're beaten, and all they want to do now is hide until they can escape. I've been getting them out of the city through our tunnels, but—"

"Our?" Bethany asked.

The boy sighed. "I get it, you want to know where he is. So do I, but no one knows." He pointed to a faded portrait above some of the computers. "I've tried to keep his work going, but I'm afraid the Dark has him, and it's only a matter of time before he's turned. If he gets infested by shadows and leads the Dark here, we're done for."

Bethany slowly looked up at the portrait, and her heart jumped. There was her father with his mask on, standing next to the boy in front of her.

And that's when it hit her. Dressing up like Doc Twilight to fool the Lawful Legion. Having access to what was apparently one of her father's secret hideouts. And that portrait . . .

"Wait a second," Bethany said, making a disgusted face. "You're my father's *sidekick*?"

CHAPTER 35

With Nobody's secret origin laid bare on the pages in front of him, Owen felt the back of his neck begin to prickle, like someone was watching him. He spun around, bracing himself for anything, but nobody was there, in that no one was actually there.

Nobody, though, could be *anywhere*. After all, he'd found Owen outside of the pages of a book before (*and* in Owen's writing, as well as that one time in the nonfictional world, when Nobody appeared as their principal), so who knew if or when he'd show up now?

And no matter who Nobody had become, Owen had a feeling he wasn't supposed to see the man he'd started as.

He had to stop reading these back issues right now. No one knew what he'd seen yet. If he went back to the newer comic pages, the ones with Bethany and Charm and Gwen, there'd be nothing to get him into trouble, even if Nobody *did* show up. All Owen had to do was jump forward in the pages, and he'd look totally innocent of learning anyone's secret origin!

Yup. That's all . . . he had . . . to *do*.

Instead, with one last look over his shoulder, Owen turned the page.

After dissolving into a mannequin figure, the next page (and issue) had Nobody showing up on Mr. Black's front stairs again, knocking on the door with his original face on.

Mr. Black opened the door just a notch, then tried to slam it, but Nobody was too quick. He slid one hand into the tiny crevice, then hardened that hand into shining steel.

Mr. Black's eyes widened, and he stumbled back inside as Nobody entered the house, a polite smile on his face. "Please, hear me out," he told the writer. "There's something I need to show you."

Mr. Black shook his head, his eyes locked on Nobody's hand of steel. "I . . . I told you, I won't . . . I won't *rewrite* you."

"There's no need," Nobody said, still smiling as his clothing, his face, and his hair all shifted into Doc Twilight in costume. "As you can see, I've learned how to do that myself."

Mr. Black fell backward, crashing into a table and knocking over what looked like an expensive vase. "How . . . how did you do that?!" he shouted, his eyes wide.

Nobody shifted to his mannequin look, then back to his original self. "I've learned many things since I last spoke to you," he said quietly, offering Mr. Black his hand. "It all began with the presumption that if I can be written, then I can be rewritten. And if *you* could rewrite me, why couldn't I? Why wouldn't I have the power to change my own story?"

Black just stared at Nobody's offered hand without moving. "You rewrote *yourself*? But how?"

"The same way you change the words on a page," Nobody told him. "I just had to discover the language that I'm made of. Now please, I have more to show you. You need to see what you've done."

Black pushed himself to his feet, clenched his fists, and held them up like he was ready to box Nobody or something. "I'm not going anywhere with you. I want you to *leave*."

Nobody just stared at him. "You must see what you've created, Mason. Come." His arms snaked out to three or four times their length and wrapped around Mr. Black. The writer began to scream, only to go quiet as Nobody's arms rose up to cover his mouth. "It won't take long, don't worry."

Owen swallowed hard, then whirled around, certain he'd just heard a footstep. But no one was back there. Still, this was not good. Comic characters always got all crazy when you found out their secret identity. He really needed to stop reading this!

Back on the page Nobody lowered Mr. Black through the blue-fire portal and into Dr. Apathy's lab, then led him out into Jupiter City, drawing his arms back in to their normal length. "Come, Mason," he said, offering his hand to Mr. Black again. "I need you to see."

This time the writer reluctantly took Nobody's hand, and his creation led him out of Apathetic Industries.

Outside, the streets were a lot more crowded than they'd been when Owen had seen them. Tough-looking criminals lurked around corners, watching Nobody and Mr. Black. They passed through streets where people walked with paranoid glances all around them, careful not to get too close to anyone else.

Finally, Nobody led Mr. Black down a dark alley, stopping at the end of it to turn around. Mr. Black started to say something, but Nobody just held up a finger for him to wait. It didn't take long, either, for a group of three dangerous-looking crooks to enter the alley, two of them pulling knives.

"Quick, empty your pockets before Twilight gets here," one said, his eyes on the rooftops.

"Ah, perfect, thank you," Nobody told the criminal, then turned to Mr. Black. "Do you see? *This* is what you've created. You've written a city that could have been a utopia, if only you'd made it so. But instead, crime is rampant, and the heroes can't be everywhere."

"I don't see your wallets," the criminal said, advancing on them.

Nobody turned back with a frown, then bashed the crook against the alley's walls with a monstrously long arm.

"Hey, he's one of them!" one of the other two shouted, only to get thrown through the brick wall on the other side of the alley.

The third robber just stared at them for a second, then ran off screaming.

Nobody retracted his arms again and nodded at Mr. Black.

"You could have made this a perfect city. Instead, people live in fear. *My* people."

Mr. Black just stared at him in horror. "You can't . . . you can't blame me for this. I gave them a hero!"

"We shouldn't have needed one."

"I didn't know what I was doing!" Mr. Black said, backing up into the wall. "I was just trying to make your world look like mine. Stories need conflict! I didn't realize that you were real somewhere. I *never* would have—"

"Don't worry, Mason," Nobody said. "That mistake is in the past. Here, now, I offer you a chance at redemption." He spread his arms benevolently. "Rewrite Jupiter City. Make it the heaven on Earth it always should have been. Give its residents everything, make them happy. This is all I ask."

Mr. Black's eyes widened. "You're serious? You want me to rewrite the *entire city* now?"

Nobody nodded, waiting silently.

Mr. Black held up his hands. "I don't . . . I *can't* do that. I wouldn't even know where to begin!"

"You *must* do this," Nobody told him, frowning. "Surely you see that. You have the power. Why wouldn't you help make my people's lives better?"

"I don't know what I'm doing!" Mr. Black said, backing away again. "I just write stupid comic books. Half the time I steal old Batman plots. None of this is new anyway, it's all the same stories Shakespeare told, and the Greeks before him, and storytellers for thousands of years before *that*. I was just trying to give people some fun, some joy in their lives!"

"What better way to do that than by helping the millions of people of Jupiter City?" Nobody said, stepping forward eagerly. "You must see why you should do this, Mason. Certainly you won't leave them like this?"

"You have heroes here," Mr. Black told him, his eyes flashing upward for a second hopefully. "My world doesn't even have that."

"Because you won't become one," Nobody said, and stepped closer. "And don't worry, we won't be disturbed by any unforeseen heroic interventions. I've made sure of that."

Mr. Black sighed, sliding down the back alley wall. "I'm sorry, I can't," he said, shaking his head. "I just *can't*."

Nobody stared at him as his face melted away. "I didn't want it to come to this, but you leave me no choice." His clothing melted into his skin, and his featureless arms reached for Mr. Black, who began to scream over and over as each subsequent panel got farther and farther away from the alley, Mr. Black's screams echoing throughout Jupiter City. . . .

Until they cut off abruptly, as if he disappeared.

Owen backed away from the wall of comic pages, shaking his head in horror. He definitely, *definitely* should not have seen that! Was this who Nobody was? Not some guardian of the fictional world, but someone willing to attack his own writer, kidnap him, then take him who knows where?

And more importantly, had Nobody ever brought Mr. Black *back*?

With one more glance over his shoulder, Owen turned the page to find out.

CHAPTER 36

Your *father's* sidekick?" Kid Twilight said, giving Bethany a confused look. "What are you talking about? Doc Twilight doesn't have any kids." He narrowed his eyes. "This is just a ploy to get me to reveal his secret identity, isn't it!"

"I *know* who he is!" Bethany whispered, trying to keep her voice down, since several of the villains nearby had gone silent, like they were listening. "He's my dad, and he has been since I was born. That's how it works, actually!"

The boy stared at her for a moment, then shook his head. "Can't be real. Maybe, *maybe*, you're some alternate dimension's daughter of Doc Twilight, but not this one's. I knew Doc Twilight too well. He'd never have kept such a big thing from me."

Bethany briefly imagined punching this Kid Twilight in the face and let herself enjoy how satisfying it'd be, but she held herself back. After all, he *apparently* was important to her father. Her eyes went up to the portrait of the two of them side-by-side, and she swallowed hard.

"Forget about this for a minute," she said, holding her millions of questions until later. Right now, all that mattered was getting her dad back. Then *he* could explain to her exactly how he'd had a sidekick all along and never brought up his family. "All that matters is finding my . . . Doc Twilight."

"He's not *your* Doc Twilight," the boy said. "*I'm* his partner. And I'm the one who infiltrated the Lawful Legion's hall looking for clues as to where he went. I didn't find any, which means he must have disappeared because the Dark captured him, and—"

Bethany started to interrupt, then realized she didn't exactly want to get into why her father had disappeared.

"If that's the case, it's too dangerous to stay here any longer," the boy finished. "We need to get all of these people out of Jupiter City. We'll try to meet up with heroes elsewhere who haven't been taken over yet." He tried to step around her, but she pushed back in front of him.

"We're *not* leaving," Bethany said. "The Dark just captured Doc Twilight last night. We still have time to get him back!"

He gave her a pitying look. "And how would you know that?"

"Because I saw it happen!"

The boy rolled his eyes. "Assuming that's true, then it just confirms what I said. We can't stay here. Don't you get it? The Dark is something we can't fight!" He pointed at the portrait. "Used to be that me and Doc, we'd go out on patrol and take down a few muggers here or there, stop a bank robbery or two. The costumed villains were a special event, but it was always some kind of game. Half the time they *wanted* us to figure out their plans, maybe so they could trap us, maybe just because it was more fun. Sure, we'd be in danger sometimes, but no one ever got more than a punch to the face, and then they'd go to jail until one of their friends broke them out."

"Like this guy?" Gwen asked, pointing at a half man, half bird wearing stripes like a prisoner with the name JAILBIRD across his chest. Jailbird looked deeply, deeply depressed.

"He doesn't like when people point," Kid Twilight said, pushing her hand down. "Anyway, everything was fun and games, but then the Doc disappeared a couple of months back, and things started getting darker."

Wait. A couple of *months*? Bethany frowned. Had her father really been coming back to this world for the past twelve years? And if that was the case, how recently had he taken on

Kid Twilight as his sidekick, since the boy seemed to be about the same age as she was?

Or maybe time worked differently in comics. After all, they came out once a month in the nonfictional world, and sometimes would only cover a few hours of actual time in the issue. So maybe time went by much slower here compared to the nonfictional world. She gritted her teeth, just wishing any of this made sense.

Wait. She didn't have to wonder, not when she had an expert at hand. Owen would know!

Owen? She yelled in her brain, but just like before, there was no response. And *that* was starting to really worry her too.

"I don't know who's to blame, the villains or the heroes," Kid Twilight was saying, "but people started getting really hurt, or worse. Sometimes the heroes would even kill." He gave her a disgusted look. "What kind of hero would kill a person, even if they *were* a criminal?"

The police sometimes had to, but Bethany realized that wasn't what he was talking about. It's not like the police had superpowers, anyway. And this world, the superhero world, was supposed to be inspirational, filled with heroes making the world a better place, standing up to the bad guys and fighting until evil was beaten. Wasn't that what superheroes were about?

"Suddenly everyone started carrying guns," Kid Twilight said, shaking his head. "Not just the villains, either. The heroes, too. Even when they didn't need them. The Beige Candle guy even started carrying one. He has a magic bracelet that can do anything, and he needs a gun? It made no sense."

"Did the Dark change things?" Bethany asked him. At the name, several supervillains nearby seemed to flinch. "Did he start making things . . . well, darker?"

"I don't know," Kid Twilight said. "No one knows who he is, or where he came from. The villains all think he's a hero who went insane. I used to doubt that any hero could go this wrong, but who knows? Lately it's hard to tell the good guys from the bad guys anyway."

"Whether he started it or not, why don't you try to beat him?" Bethany said. "If we take him down, then at least people can stop living in fear."

"How?" Kid Twilight said. "You want to use that sleeping gas on him? You think that'll stop his shadows? They don't breathe. For all I know, neither does the Dark. You can't even get close to him, not with his shadows. You'd need some kind of army to even try it." He sighed. "The worst thing is, if you *could* get through and take him down, I'm pretty sure the shadows would go away. When he fought the Lawful Legion the first time, Captain Sunshine got one hit in. *One.* It staggered the Dark, though, and his shadows began to fade out. But he recovered and just flooded them with shadows, and that was it."

"All that tells me is that he *can* be beat!" Bethany said. "Just tell us where he is, and *we'll* fight him." Gwen stepped up next to her, as did Charm, if a lot more reluctantly.

"With what?" Kid Twilight said. "What's your plan? How are you going to get through his shadows? And then how will you fight the Dark himself? I saw how you took on the Lawful Legion. If I hadn't been there, Athena would have taken you down and you'd all be slaves to the shadows now."

Bethany gritted her teeth. "Where *is* he?"

Kid Twilight growled in frustration, then moved over to one of the computer terminals and pulled up a 3-D holographic map of the city. "You think you know everything, how about you tell me? I've been trying to track him since I first heard about him, if just so we know when he's coming. But I've come up with nothing, and I've checked everywhere: the Museum of the Flying Duck, the dimensional gateway to Mount Olympus, even the Terrorovia Embassy." He shivered a bit. "Empress Terror's armor was there, completely burned to a crisp. Fortunately she wasn't inside it."

Bethany clenched her fists, wanting to hit something. "Well he's got to be *somewhere*. He's found *us* easily enough. And now he's got the portal thing from Dr. Apathy, so it's even more urgent that we find him before he leaves and goes to—"

Kid Twilight turned to her, his eyes wide. "*What* did you say? He has an Apathy machine?"

She nodded. "Yeah? Didn't I mention that before?"

"*No,*" Kid Twilight said, and began frantically pushing keys on the computer. "If he's got it hooked up and turned on, there's bound to be some kind of energy that we can track."

Yes! Superheroes were *always* tracking villains through energy trails or the makeup of mud from their footprints or something. Why hadn't she thought of that before now? It was a total cliché, and she hadn't even considered it.

This is why she needed Owen, because he knew all of this stuff!

She regretted leaving Owen wherever he was even more, in spite of what he'd said. Was he okay? Had he gotten more lost? This is why she should have had Charm go after him, no matter how long it took. Now Owen could be *anywhere*, and—

"Found him," Kid Twilight said, slamming his fist down excitedly.

It took Bethany a second to realize who Kid Twilight was talking about. "The Dark? Where is he?"

Kid Twilight paused, reading the map. "Oh *no*. There? You've got to be kidding me."

Bethany leaned in closer to the holographic map, pushing Kid Twilight out of the way. It looked like the blinking light was at the top of some hill called—

And then the map turned off.

"Confidential," Kid Twilight told her as she stood back up with her mouth hanging open. "Let's just say that *this* hideout isn't Doc Twilight's main headquarters, and somehow, the Dark found the real deal. There's no way he should have been able to get in there, but somehow, he's got the machine inside of it."

"So let's *go* then!" Bethany said. "I don't care where it is. Blindfold me if you have to, I just need to find Doc Twilight!"

"Nope," Kid Twilight said. "I'm going alone. You'll just slow me down, you and the other two. Not to mention the banana. I can do this myself."

Bethany's eyes widened. "You're joking."

"I don't joke, not since the Doc went missing," Kid Twilight said, gathering his gear together. "You'll be safe here with the supervillains. They're not big on protecting people, but they'll make sure that no shadows get in, if just for their own selfish reasons."

"I'm *coming*," Bethany told him. "Don't make me force the issue."

He glared at her. "Force the issue? You?"

Bethany punched him in the face, knocking Kid Twilight over. He tumbled to the floor, completely unconscious.

Her hand hurt a lot, but part of her had to admit that felt *really* good. Not to mention that no one ever got knocked out with one punch in real life, so that was fun.

But there was no time to enjoy this. Instead, she needed information, and fortunately, she had a good idea where to go for it. "Who here can read minds?" she shouted at the supervillains.

One of them stood up, wearing a crystal ball over his head like he was going scuba diving or something. "I am the Great—"

"Don't care," Bethany said, gesturing at Charm, who pushed her way through the villains, picked up the man by his waist, then carried him over to where Bethany waited. "Read his thoughts," she ordered the Great Whatever. "I need an address, the place that he was thinking of just a minute ago."

The man in the crystal ball tugged on his shirt to straighten it, giving Charm an indignant look. "*You've* got quite the violent mind there, you know," he told the half-robotic girl.

She just glared at him for a moment, and he gasped. Charm smiled. "There's more where that came from," she told him.

"We don't have time for this," Bethany said, and pushed the man down toward Kid Twilight. The villain glared at her, but the last thing she was going to let him do was read *her* mind, so she turned his crystal ball toward the obnoxious boy sidekick.

"I'm sensing . . . a telescope," he said, his face scrunched up as if he was concentrating far too dramatically. "The Jupiter City Observatory. But no, he was thinking of a place . . . below. Down below the Observatory, down in . . . the DARK!" His eyes flew open, and he shoved himself away from Kid Twilight. "Whoa lady!" he shouted, his pretentious accent dropping away. "You're going after the Dark? That's insane!"

For a moment everything got deathly quiet. Then the supervillains began murmuring to each other, their voices low and threatening.

"She's going after the Dark?"

"No way, that'll expose us all."

"Fighting the Dark is suicide, and then he'll find out where we are!"

"She's not going anywhere. We have to stop her!"

"Don't let them out!"

"Orange you glad I didn't say banana?"

This last one came from a familiar face as the Rotten Banana sidled up next to Bethany. "Hey," he whispered. "I think I came in late to this, since I just woke up. Not to be the bearer of bad news, but it's looking like you're about to have a whole roomful of very afraid, and therefore, very *angry* supervillains. I'm not one to take the coward's way out, but if I were you, I'd *definitely* split."

CHAPTER 37

This was getting dangerous. Nobody clearly was *not* a good guy, or Bethany's father. Owen needed to get back to his friends' pages, then figure out how to get out of this place, and warn Bethany about Nobody, before Nobody did to Owen what he'd done to Mr. Black. Whatever *that* was.

Yup. It was definitely time to stop reading this.

Owen sighed, then turned the page. Sometimes you just couldn't put a book down.

After Nobody disappeared with Mr. Black, the next page had a caption that said *Much later . . . ,* and showed Mr. Black floating in a familiar white space, exactly like the one Owen had been trapped in by the Magister, and just like where he was now only without the huge comic pages. Mr. Black *looked* okay, though he wasn't moving. Instead, he just floated for panel after panel, his eyes closed.

Finally, a hand came out of nowhere and pulled him back into the story.

Mr. Black landed on his knees in a tiny room with very few furnishings. There was a table and two chairs, but nothing else, and more creepily, no doors or windows. Mr. Black took a deep breath, then pushed himself to his feet and found himself face-to-face once more with Nobody.

"Where *was* I?" Mr. Black asked. "What was that place?"

"There are lands beyond the fictional and nonfictional, Mason," Nobody told him, his mannequin arms crossed. "Lands with no story, where nothing happens. No time passes for you while you're there, so I thought you might benefit from an outside view."

"No time passes?" Mr. Black said, looking around at the room as if looking for a clock. "How long was I there?"

"Five years," Nobody said.

Five *years*? Owen thought.

"Five *years*?!" Mr. Black shouted.

"When I first approached you, my creator, I hoped you'd rewrite me," Nobody said, stepping closer to Mr. Black, who took a step back in spite of his shock. "You refused, so I learned to rewrite myself. Then I came to you, begging you to save my city, rewrite it into a veritable utopia. Again, you refused, so I set out to correct matters on my own."

"What did you *do*?" Mr. Black said. "You didn't hurt anyone, did you?"

"And now, I have one final request," Nobody said, ignoring the question. "I've been back and forth to the nonfictional world. I know of the other stories out there, the other fictional lands. Those lands fall under the control of writers like you, monstrous creators who have no concern for the lives they ruin for the sake of entertainment. And I . . . I would change that."

"What do you want?" Mr. Black asked, backing up into the wall.

Nobody stepped forward until he was merely inches from Mr. Black, putting his hands on the writer's shoulders. "You are going to teach me to write. You will put *me* in control of the fictional lands. And I will protect them."

Mr. Black's eyes widened. "What? I can't just—"

"You've refused me twice so far, Mason," Nobody said, turning away. "I wouldn't suggest doing so a third time." He put his hands behind his back, then began to pace around the nearly empty room. "Things have changed in the last few years, you know. Your creation, Doc Twilight, now has a daughter. He and his *nonfictional* wife."

"He . . . what?" Mr. Black said.

"You're a grandfather, in a way," Nobody said, his voice quiet. "But your granddaughter, Bethany, presents some problems. Problems that I will have to deal with, in order to protect my world."

"What are you talking about?"

"She can travel between the worlds at will, Mason," Nobody said. "Not only that, she can take others with her. She's a portal, just like the one you had Dr. Apathy build. And I can't allow these portals to remain open between the worlds. Not if I'm going to protect the fictional from you people."

Mr. Black jumped forward, grabbing Nobody's featureless shoulders and staring him in his nonface. "You can't harm this girl. I won't let you!"

Nobody pushed Mr. Black off of him, throwing the writer back into the wall hard enough to crumple him to the floor. "First of all, I believe we're past the point where you control what I do," Nobody said, sounding calm, though Owen realized it'd be hard to tell otherwise, given that he didn't have a face. "Second, I have no intention of harming Bethany. She has a great power, and therefore someone needs to take responsibility for it. That someone shall be me." He shook his featureless head. "Unfortunately, her father has been indulging her, traveling with her into various books. I cannot allow that to continue, so I will have to remove him from the situation."

Mr. Black just stared at Nobody from the floor, breathing slowly. "You're a *monster*."

Nobody clenched what would have been his fists for a moment, then released them. "Am I?" he asked. "You certainly created me to be one. But I've rewritten myself, Mason. I've become far more than you ever intended. Now I make my own decisions, and I can become whoever I wish. And I wish to be *good*. I will be the hero that my world needs. And I will protect it against people like you."

"Do not hurt him," Mr. Black said. "Please! He's done nothing wrong."

"He's a symptom of *everything* that's wrong!" Nobody shouted, and banged his fist down on the table, which exploded into pieces. "The fictional and nonfictional should not meet.

They are meant to be separate, completely ignorant of the other. And yet, your world *controls* mine. And now a man from my world has linked the two worlds even more closely through his daughter. Don't you see? My world must be *free!*"

"You can't just separate them," Mr. Black said. "How would you even start?"

Nobody bent down, moving so close that Mr. Black turned his head away. "I think I understand how it's working," Nobody said quietly. "These portals result from rips between the worlds. I've closed many in these past five years: the mirror and rabbit holes leading to Wonderland, the wardrobe to Narnia. And others have been closed by wise fictionals like the Witch of the East in Oz. But I must know how to write like you before I can find the rest of these portals and close them. And above all, I must ensure that Twilight's daughter does not create further rifts due to her very existence. She *must not* continue her journeys into the fictional world."

"You said she's one of these portals," Black said. "So what, eventually you're going to close *her* too?"

Nobody didn't respond, and instead turned away. "This is your final chance, Mason. Teach me how you write, that I might save both of our worlds."

Black took a deep breath and slowly pushed himself to his feet. "No," he said.

Owen swallowed hard and reached out to turn the page.

Then he felt a tap on his shoulder.

"Reading anything good?" asked Nobody.

CHAPTER 38

The supervillains drew in closer, surrounding Bethany, Charm, Gwen, and the banana, as well as the still unconscious Kid Twilight.

"If you go after him, he'll find out where *we* are," said a large man with the head of a baby, aiming what looked like a bottle filled with formula at them. "And Babyface ain't taking that kind of chance." He began to sniffle, then started sucking on a pacifier while giving them threatening looks.

"This city just irritates me on so many levels," Charm said, aiming her ray guns at him in response. "Are you going to sleep gas them all or what?"

Bethany backed away from the villains, ready to do just that . . . but then she had a crazy thought, one that she couldn't even be sure was hers. It was insane and wouldn't ever work, but she'd just come up with a plan on how to take down the Dark. Had it come from Owen? He'd been the one after her to think things through for the last few months. Or was her nonfictional side just tired of her being risky? Either way, she now had a plan, and knew exactly what they needed to do.

"Gwen?" she said. "You know that superpower of yours we talked about on the way here? I need you to use it on *them*. We're going to need the villains."

Gwen's entire face brightened, and she saluted. Bethany saluted back, grinning in spite of the situation as Gwen moved to stand in front of the others.

"Hello!" she said, beaming.

The supervillains all stopped advancing, many of them looking a bit surprised by this approach. ". . . Hi?" one said from the back.

"My name is EarthGirl," Gwen said. "Where I come from, I call myself a detective, because I like to help people and solve crimes."

"She sounds like a hero. Get her!" a giant panda with evil eyebrows shouted.

"*Sleeping gas,*" Charm said in a singsong voice, but Bethany shook her head.

"At home, I have superpowers," Gwen said. "But here, I can only fly because of this jet pack." She turned it on and rose a few feet into the air, then dropped back to the ground.

"Lame!" shouted a villain who looked like a troll from fairy tales. "Laaaaaa—"

Charm shot the troll in the chest, and he immediately crumpled to the ground. "He's only stunned," she yelled over the angry shouts of the assembled supervillains. "But the next one who interrupts her *or* insults my tech gets a full-strength blast."

"Thanks, Charm," Gwen said, flashing her a smile before turning back to the villains. "I know you're all scared of the Dark. I get it. I am too. His shadows turn you into something you're not, and you lose control over yourself. How can we fight that? What can we do against him?"

"Run!" shouted a man wearing a lot of dark gray lightning bolts and runner's shorts.

"Hide!" shouted a woman that Bethany couldn't see until she moved slightly, and, like a chameleon, her colors shifted to camouflage her with the villains around her.

"You're right," Gwen said, nodding. "Those plans do make the most sense. Because none of us are heroes here, right?

We're not the ones who do what *society* thinks we should do. We *break* rules, we don't follow them!"

A ragged cheer went up around the crowd. "Fight the power!" one shouted.

"And sure, the Dark will probably find us, wherever we run or hide," Gwen said, shrugging slightly as she began to pace in front of the villains. "I think we all know that's a given. Because he's one of us too. He doesn't live by the rules. He makes his own, and doesn't let *anyone* break them. Not us, not those without powers. Not even the superheroes."

This time, no one shouted.

"You know, I saw a bit of this city today," Gwen said, pointing toward the door. "It's beautiful, isn't it?"

"*Really?* Which part did you see?" Jailbird asked, making a disgusted face.

"All of it," Gwen told him. "I got to see it from the air, and it sparkled like a diamond from high above. And I could see it that way because I can fly!" She rose back into the air, just hovering a few feet above the ground. "Do you remember what it's like to fly just because you could? Or read someone's mind for the first time?" This she addressed to the man with the crystal ball on his head. "Or jump higher than anyone else?" she asked a man wearing enormous springs on his feet. "We started out doing these things because we wanted to break the rules, but not society's laws. We wanted to break our *own* rules, the ones telling us our limits! And weren't your most passionate conflicts against anyone who tried to control you, tell you what you could or couldn't do?"

"Yeah, like the Flying Duck!" someone shouted.

The rest of the villains murmured in agreement. Apparently the Flying Duck got around.

"I know that if anyone tried to keep *me* from flying, I'd fight back," Gwen said, rising higher in the air. "There's no way I'd run or hide from that. I'd stand up and face them. Now, don't get me wrong. I don't believe in violence—"

"Lame," the troll groaned from the floor, but this time someone stomped on him before Charm could stun him again.

"Because I'd rather find common ground with people," Gwen continued as she rose higher. "And I'm guessing the thing that you and I have most in common is that we're not going to let anyone hold us *down*. Am I right?"

This time the cheer was more forceful. Bethany noticed Kid Twilight slowly sitting up, and she prepared to knock him back out if necessary. But he didn't seem to want to stop things. Instead, he actually seemed to be listening to Gwen.

"The Dark controls this city, I know," Gwen said, sinking back down, though not touching the ground. "And he'd like you to think that there's nothing you can do about that. After all, you don't want to hurt anyone. You just want to be free to be who you *are*."

"I hate when people get hurt," said a ten-foot-tall demonic creature in the back. "I just want to DJ. Why won't the world just leave me to it?"

A man in all-silver clothing with a record player and mixing board on his chest patted the demon on the shoulder, rubbing the record on his chest a few times in support.

"And why shouldn't you?" Gwen shouted, rising higher into the air. "That's who you *are*. And no one can take that from you, not society, not the superheroes, and definitely not the Dark. Because when push comes to shove, we *will* stand up for ourselves, and for our city. Even for those people who don't think much of us, because they deserve to be proven wrong!"

"Yes!" the demonic creature shouted, banging his fist

against the cavern wall and shaking the entire room.

"The Dark thinks we're worthless, but we're going to show him that we're not afraid of the Dark. *The Dark* should be afraid of *us*!"

The assembled villains roared in agreement, stamping their feet as Gwen rose higher into the air, almost up to the ceiling.

"My friends!" she said, raising her hands to them all. "*Join us!* We've come to free Jupiter City from the tyranny of the Dark, and bring light back to its people. And something tells me you're the only ones who can help. Because we're *not* scared of our shadows, are we?"

"No!" the crowd shouted.

"And we're not going to just hide under our beds anymore, *are we?*"

"No!" they shouted.

"The Dark is in the Jupiter City Observatory!" Gwen shouted. "Now let's get out there and show him that no one tells *us* what to do! No one gives *us* orders. And *no one* makes us follow the rules! We're turning off the Dark, once and for all!"

The assembled villains roared in approval and began chanting her name. Gwen dropped back to the ground, then gave Bethany a *they're all yours* wave.

"You're going to get them all killed, you know," Kid Twilight told Bethany as she took Gwen's place.

"No, I'm not," she told him, and flashed him a smile. "See, I've got a *plan*."

CHAPTER 39

"Nobody!" Owen shouted, backing away from the featureless man as quickly as he could. "It's not what it looks like. I wasn't reading about you!"

"Please, Owen," Nobody said, gesturing for him to calm down. "Who do you think put you here?"

". . . Charm?"

"Her experiment couldn't send you *here*, not even by accident," Nobody said, taking a step toward him. "*I* brought you here, and for this very reason. You had to see the truth." He held out a hand. "Don't you understand, Owen? The worlds need to be separate, and I showed you my story for one reason: to ask for your help."

Owen backed away, his hands up. "My help? With what?"

"You don't know the lengths I've gone to protect my people," Nobody told him, raising a hand and sending the panels on the wall flying. "Bethany's father discovered what I was doing, of course. He was quite the hero."

Was? Owen thought as the panels stopped on Nobody in Dr. Apathy's lab, his hands on the machine that unlocked the portal.

"I can't let you do that," said a word balloon from off-panel, and Bethany's father appeared in the next panel, though not in his costume. He looked a bit older than last time Owen had seen him in the pages, maybe a little rounder at the edges, but still somehow intimidating.

"You don't even know who I am, Christian," Nobody said without looking up.

"Sure I do," Mr. Sanderson told him. "When Mason Black went missing, I investigated, just like the old days. And what I found was a small-time crook with delusions of grandeur."

Nobody's featureless face contorted in what could have been a smile. "If that helps you. I'm not doing this because of our history, Christian."

"You're not doing it to protect the fictional world, either," Mr. Sanderson said. "Seems like it's doing just fine without you."

"You don't get it, do you?" Nobody told him. "You're blinded by love for your nonfictional wife. Her people *control* us, Christian. We must be free to live our own lives!"

"They don't," Mr. Sanderson said, shaking his head. "You think Mason Black wrote me into *his* world? They're just witnesses to what we do. Their imaginations are windows into our world. We're living *our* stories, not theirs. And we always have been."

"You're a blind fool," Nobody told him, his hands still playing over the instruments. "Mason believed the same, yet I've followed in his footsteps and rewritten myself. I've even written stories myself, Christian. I didn't create fictionals, of course. But I took characters from fairy tale worlds and rewrote their life stories, mixing them up. I did it just to see if I could, and it *worked*. How could I do that if writers weren't in control?"

"You have no idea what you're doing," Christian told him, stepping forward. "You might have rewritten someone, but that doesn't mean they're yours in any way. It's no different than if you mind-controlled someone, or blackmailed them. You might get them to act how you want, but the nonfictionals don't have power over us. You have no one to blame for what you're doing but yourself."

"Blame?" Nobody said. "I'll happily accept that when the

fictional world discovers what I've done for them. And they'll see it all, even if I have to tell them the stories myself."

"You know I'm going to stop you."

Nobody laughed. "And how exactly will you do that, Christian? I've rewritten myself far beyond anything you could possibly handle, especially without your gadgets. You have no powers, after all. You're just an ordinary man."

"You're forgetting where you are," Christian said, leaning against the wall casually. "We're in Jupiter City. And here, in this world, heroes always win."

Nobody looked up at him for a moment. "Not everything is a cliché." And with that, he pushed one final button.

An electrical surge exploded out of the machine, sending Nobody flying against the wall. He crumpled to the ground, groaning.

"Who needs gadgets when all it takes is a little forethought and setup?" Mr. Sanderson said, moving over to stand above Nobody, who seemed stunned. "I can't allow you to do this, whoever you've become. These portals between the worlds are *good* things. The fictional and nonfictional benefit from each other. One is pure possibility, the other order and causality. The worlds need both to survive, and the portals—"

"Oh, shut up," Nobody said, and with a wave of his hand, the lab ripped open like a page. Nobody pushed himself through the rift, and the page immediately closed, leaving the lab empty but for Christian.

"Huh," Mr. Sanderson said, staring at the spot where Nobody had escaped. "Well, *that's* new."

"My first setback," Nobody told Owen, who was frantically wondering where he could run. "Christian was correct. In his world, the rule-breakers *couldn't* win. It's the one constant of all superhero comics. At least, it was until I rewrote the rules." He paused. "Still, it meant I had to take steps to ensure he wasn't in such a position again."

"What did you do?" Owen asked, trying to keep Nobody talking while he found something to use as a weapon. If nothing else, that last page had shown that Nobody could be surprised.

"Don't bother trying to escape," Nobody said, killing his hopes immediately. "I brought you here, Owen, and you'll stay here until I decide otherwise. But to answer your question . . ." He raised his hand, and the pages jumped a bit more.

This time they showed a little girl's birthday party.

HAPPY FOURTH BIRTHDAY, BETHANY! a large banner read.

"Oh *no*," Owen said, freezing in place.

"The invitations *did* ask all guests not to bring books," Nobody said, turning to watch the party unfold on the pages. "But sometimes you just find a perfect gift."

In one panel a small boy shyly handed Bethany's mother a wrapped present, then ran off to another room in the next panel, yelling for his mother. As soon as he turned the corner, he immediately transformed into Nobody, then disappeared.

"All it took was finding a story where the heroes didn't win," Nobody said. "I chose one about a boy who takes everything he can from a very giving tree, which kills it. If *that's* not a villain winning, I don't know what is."

Four-year-old Bethany, the other kids, and her father all popped into a meadow, with her father a short distance away from the rest. Her father's eyes widened, and he went to grab Bethany's hand, but instead ran right into Nobody.

"Someone should have been more careful," the Nobody in the comic said, and a page ripped open in the meadow. Nobody shoved Mr. Sanderson through before he could even react, then immediately slammed the page shut, sealing it away completely.

A second later Nobody had morphed to look just like

Bethany's father, and he walked over to her four-year-old self.

"You need to take everyone back, Beth," he said. "Kids, grab hands, and Bethany will push you through."

"Okay," Bethany said, grinning for her father. "Are you coming too?"

"I'll be along shortly," Nobody said with a smile. "Now go. Your mother is waiting for you."

"But you said I always had to hold your hand when we went home."

"It's okay, just this once," Nobody told her. "I give you my permission."

One by one the party guests disappeared, followed by Bethany, who gave her father a big wave. He waved back as she disappeared, and then he melted back into Nobody. A page opened in the meadow, and a moment later he stood alongside Mr. Sanderson in the lands outside of story.

"Bring me back!" Christian shouted as he launched himself at Nobody, attacking the featureless man for all he was worth. Unfortunately, every shot missed as Nobody's body stretched and dodged to avoid the blows.

"You lost your element of surprise, Christian," Nobody said. "Without that, you're just a poor little story without a home.

Fortunately, I know several good ones that will welcome you in." He held up a hand, and Christian stopped, a strange look on his face.

As Owen watched in horror, Mr. Sanderson's entire body began to contort, swelling in places, shrinking in others, as little bits of himself began to fall to the floor. Owen gasped, leaning closer, and realized that Doc Twilight's entire body was turning into *words*, each one describing a part of his body, and *those* were what was falling off of him.

The process started slowly, but quickly sped up until finally, all at once, Bethany's father crumbled apart, collapsing into a pile of words on the floor in front of Nobody.

"Learned this from your daughter, actually," Nobody said, leaning down to pick through the pile, sorting through things like "elbow skin" and "eyelash number seventeen." "Have you ever noticed how she turns into words when she travels between the worlds? That *is* what fictionals are made from, after all." He picked up a word that said *fear*. "Now, I'm *not* a bad person, and I'm not going to kill you. Just . . . keep you from interfering for a while. Maybe I'll even bring you back, when this is all over."

He continued sorting through the words until finally he

found two phrases: "memories of Bethany," and "memories of Catherine." Those he pushed into a pocket that hadn't existed a moment before. Then he stood back up.

Nobody held up a hand, and one by one tiny rifts opened in the white space. With each rift, one word or phrase that made up Bethany's father leaped through the hole, each one inserting itself into a different story. Faster and faster they went, until an entire library's worth of books each had a part of Bethany's father hidden within.

"Later, that was going to cause you, Bethany, and Kiel some confusion," Nobody told Owen back outside the panels. "Remember this?"

He ran the pages forward to show Kiel's finder spell exploding into a million different directions in Owen's library, highlighting every available book. "To be fair, the spell worked," Nobody told him. "Bethany's father *was* in each book, after all."

Owen shook his head, horrified. How could this be real? "Is . . . is he still in there? Trapped in the books?"

"Oh, not anymore," Nobody said. "Christian had a good point. Jupiter City exists to only let heroes win, so I needed his help to change that. All it took was a bit of rewriting what a hero was, and suddenly, everyone's just a shade of gray."

"What are you talking about?" Owen asked.

The pages leaped forward to Charm, Gwen, and some teenage boy lying on a floor unconscious. A man with red eyes and shadows whipping all around him held Bethany up by her neck as she struggled.

"They say that if you live long enough, every hero becomes a villain," Nobody said. "That's certainly true of Christian. And all it took was just a bit of rewriting."

The Dark's shadows fell away from his face, and Owen gasped.

The Dark was *Bethany's father.*

CHAPTER 40

You're dooming them all," Kid Twilight told Bethany as they both waited at the bottom of Jupiter Hill, site of the observatory that her father had apparently used as his headquarters.

"You're starting to repeat yourself," she said. "So Doc Twilight was an astronomer? That would make sense if he used this place as his hideout."

He glared at her. "Shouldn't his daughter know that?"

She rolled her eyes, but refused to give up her only source of information on her dad. "He . . . kept a lot of secrets from me."

Kid Twilight snorted. "If you're telling the truth, he hid a lot more from *me*. And yes, he was an astronomer, but this observatory is actually mine. Passed down through my mother's family, but she and my father died in an alien invasion when I was young. Doc Twilight saved me, though, and began training me in martial arts while Dr. Christian Sanderson, the observatory's head astronomer, started teaching me the family trade." He smiled, and Bethany suddenly realized how naturally that smile came to him. "Took me years to prove they were the same person. He'd use robots or his shape-shifting superhero friends to trick me into thinking they couldn't be."

A jolt of pity passed through Bethany. Her father had taken this boy in and practically raised him, and then he'd just disappeared from both of their lives, even if it was just a few months of comic book time for Kid Twilight. And as hard as it was for her finding out about this entire other life her father had lived, Kid Twilight didn't exactly look thrilled about his father figure having an actual daughter, especially one who might know more than he did about the man in some ways.

She gently laid a hand on his and sighed. "I'm sorry," she told him.

He looked confused, but left her hand there. "For what?"

"Everything. You deserved better."

Kid Twilight looked up at her, and she could see that he wanted to say something, his hand still under hers. But finally he looked away and pulled his hand back gently. "See if the banana's ready. We should get this started."

She nodded, though he couldn't see it. "Right." She crawled to where the Rotten Banana waited, his eyes on the Observatory. "All set?" she asked him.

"Is this what it feels like to be a good guy?" he asked, his hands shaking a bit. "Because if so, I'm not sure I like it. I'm terrified!"

Bethany smiled. "You're already a hero as far as I'm concerned, since you saved me in the Lawful Legion's headquarters." She paused. "Why *did* you do that?"

The banana looked away. "I . . . I don't know. It just felt like the right thing to do at the time. And I *usually* ignore that impulse. But for some reason I figured with everything as bad as it is, maybe I should try being good for a change. Just to see how it feels." He winced. "I'm not sure it worked for me."

"I think you make a very appealing Heroic Banana," Bethany told him, and his eyes lit up.

"I see what you did there!" he said as she moved on to the signal point.

Everything was now ready, and everyone was in position, just as she'd planned. The villains hadn't been thrilled with her idea, but Gwen convinced the biggest doubters, and the rest had fallen in line.

Now Bethany just hoped that her plan actually worked. Though she wasn't sure if she was more worried about the shadows getting them, or proving Kid Twilight right.

Either way, it was time. She nodded at her dad's sidekick and the banana, then stood up on the observatory hill, turned around, and shouted, "Now!" as loudly as she could at the one person standing behind her, back in the observatory's parking lot.

That one man wore a business suit and held a briefcase in his one visible hand. He nodded in confirmation at her, then the Invisible Hand raised his missing hand, counted to three, and dropped his invisibility wall, revealing an army of supervillains, all ready to attack.

"You heard her!" Gwen shouted at the front of the mob, taking to the air with a fiery trail behind her. "Let's show the Dark that there's still a light in Jupiter City!"

The assembled horde shouted in agreement, then started sprinting toward the hill. They passed Bethany, Kid Twilight, and the banana, who all had to dodge out of the way to avoid being trampled.

Gwen swooped down to their level after the villains passed. "Here they come!" she shouted, pointing ahead of them as the door to the observatory flew open. Like a flash flood of murky darkness, shadows exploded out of the Observatory, crashing down the hill straight at them in a wave that rose at least twenty feet in the air.

In spite of the plan, Bethany almost froze at the sight of the dark tidal wave coming at her. "There are so many of them," she said, her whole body going cold with fear.

"More to shoot," said an annoyed voice, and Charm slapped Bethany's arm to snap her out of it. "Don't you have a job to do?"

Right. Bethany cupped her hands and yelled, "First wave, *attack!*"

The Human Prism, a man made of crystals, and Lady Lasers, the outline of a woman who looked like she was drawn out of sizzling red beams, sprinted forward from the head of the mob, then took position. The Prism set himself in place, aiming his head at the shadows, and Lady Lasers prepared herself. The rest of the villains set their feet and awaited the shadows.

"You can do this, Prism!" Gwen shouted. "I believe in you!"

The Human Prism smiled, cracking his crystalline body slightly, then nodded. "Do it!"

Lady Lasers took a deep breath, then shot her entire body of lasers into the Human Prism. Though she went in as one woman, she sizzled out as thousands of them, each one careening off in multiple directions, burning through the surge of shadows crashing down toward them.

"Next wave!" Bethany shouted, and DJ Evil stepped up, the speakers on his body humming.

"Y'all ready for this?" DJ Evil shouted. "Time to *Heat. Things. Up!*" He began twisting the record on his chest back and forth as dance music exploded from his speakers.

The vibrations began to tear apart Jupiter Hill, sending chunks tumbling down the other side, and half of the villains actually lost their feet. Bethany fell to the ground, with Charm tumbling to one knee. Kid Twilight just flashed them a smug look as he rode it out, only to come crashing down as Charm swept his feet out from under him with her robotic leg.

The wave of sound ripped through the shadows, but they just reformed around it, tumbling down into DJ Evil and the Living Prism, who disappeared into darkness.

"We can't beat them! Run!" someone yelled, and a few of the villains began to back away from the fight.

"No!" Bethany shouted. "Stand your ground, this is our only chance. If we can take out the Dark, the shadows all go away too. We just need to clear a path to him!"

A shadow rose up from the mass and came flying right at

her, only to explode in a burst of light as Charm shot it with a light bullet. "Gwen?" Charm shouted.

"On it!" EarthGirl said, then turned the throttle on her jet pack as high as it'd go and sped off toward the shadows. The creatures reached out for her, but she smoothly dodged in and out of them, the flames from the jet pack burning through their darkness.

Nearby, a shadow pushed its way into the mouth of the Ice Machine, a supervillain with the power to create as many ice cubes as he wanted. The man shouted in fear at first, then rage, and turned toward Bethany and Kid Twilight. "You did this to us!" he shouted, his eyes black as the shadows. "You're to blame!" He turned his cube guns on them and shot out ice at lethal speeds.

"Look out!" the banana shouted, and jumped in front of Bethany, the ice skidding off of his suit. Kid Twilight, though, just strode toward the Ice Machine, stepping around the ice as easily as if he were passing pedestrians on the street. When he was just feet away, the Ice Machine screamed in rage and turned both guns on Kid Twilight. The sidekick dropped to the ground and swept the Machine's feet out from under him, then knocked him out with one punch. Without even pausing, he turned the Ice Machine's guns on a black-eyed Punishing Pea.

"You never let me in the group, Banana!" the Pea shouted as the ice began to build up around him. "I'll make you pay for that!"

"That guy was always creepy," the banana whispered to Bethany.

"I bet," she said, then finally found the moment she'd been waiting for. "Look, we've got an opening!"

There, straight up the hill, the shadows had been split down the middle by the supervillains. Though at least half of them had been infected, the rest fought hard against both shadows and their former comrades.

They weren't going to last long at this rate.

"Go!" the banana yelled. "I'll give you as much cover as I can!" He threw himself in front of an onslaught of lasers, courtesy of a now-shadow-infected Lady Lasers.

"Gwen!" Bethany shouted, then grabbed Charm and sprinted toward the Observatory. Gwen swept down toward them and picked Charm up beneath her armpits, carrying the robotic girl in front of them to take care of any shadows who tried to stop them.

"This better work," Kid Twilight said, falling in beside her.

"Just show us where the hideout is," she told him as they passed through the observatory's entrance. The building was pitch dark, but Kid Twilight clicked his twi-light on and led them through banks of computers and past what looked like a gigantic telescope.

"Secret door," Kid Twilight said, typing something into a computer she could barely see. Something began to rumble, and the boy flashed his light on the telescope as it moved to one side, then turned the light back on the wall in front of them.

Except it wasn't a wall anymore. Now a staircase led down into darkness.

"Where'd you point the telescope?" Bethany asked.

"Where do you think?" Kid Twilight said. "The moon."

They raced down the stairs with Kid Twilight leading, his light illuminating their way. They descended what felt like a hundred feet before finally coming to a door, where he stopped them.

"This is a terrible plan," he said, handing something to each of them. "I just wanted to remind you of that."

Bethany smiled at him. "If you're right, you have my

permission to tell me you told me so over and over when we're shadow infested."

He rolled his eyes, checked to make sure they were all ready, then opened the door.

And that's when the last shadows in the Observatory attacked, covering them in darkness.

CHAPTER 41

"How can the Dark be her father?" Owen said, pushing away from the wall of panels. "I thought Doc Twilight—"

Nobody gestured, and the pages shifted to show the Doc Twilight that had rescued him and Bethany putting on the costume right before he came back down into the basement at the start of everything. Before he put his mask on, Owen took a good look at his face.

The man definitely wasn't Bethany's father, but he did seem familiar. Maybe a bit older than the last time Owen had seen him. But where—

"Murray Chase," Nobody said. "The artist of the Doc Twilight series. He built a house over the portal to Jupiter City, both to guard your world from any fictional visitors, but also to allow Christian and his wife to go back and forth at will. *He* was the one who saved you from the Dark that first time, having put on the Twilight costume for its weapons."

Owen's mouth dropped. So this entire time, that had been Doc Twilight's creator? So not Bethany's father, but her . . . grandfather?

"Murray had been watching over Bethany for years, of course," Nobody said. "When word came that Mason Black was writing a new, more extreme comic, Murray looked into it and discovered that Mason was rebooting Doc Twilight, done in a darker style." Nobody shifted the pages, and Owen saw the reverse of an earlier scene as words popped out of millions of books to reform into Bethany's father.

As soon as Mr. Sanderson became human again, he collapsed to his knees, still in the same outfit he'd been wearing at Bethany's fourth birthday party. A man offered him a hand, and he gratefully took it.

"Where am I?" her father asked this new man, who was older and had a pitying look. The two of them were in a room much like the one Nobody had brought Mason Black to, one with no doors or windows, and just a table and chairs.

"Jupiter City," the old man said. "I'm afraid I have terrible news, Christian Sanderson. The villain who locked you away in here . . . he took your family. I'm so sorry, but they're gone."

"My family?" Christian said, a look of disbelief on his face. "But I don't have a family . . . do I? Why is it so hard to remember—"

The old man put a hand on Mr. Sanderson's head, and Owen could make out words moving around beneath his skin, as if the old man was changing Mr. Sanderson. His face became enraged, and the former Doc Twilight pushed to his feet. "He took my family from me?" He picked up a chair nearby and threw it into the wall, and as he did, a small black tendril popped out of his eyes, wrapping itself around his arm.

"I will track whoever did this down," Mr. Sanderson shouted, breaking the room's small table. "I will find him and make him *pay* for what he did!"

"The heroes never found him," the old man told him, and he put another hand on Mr. Sanderson's arm. More words passed under his skin, and Bethany's father grabbed his head, shouting in pain as more black tendrils pushed themselves out of his eyes. "Some would say that they didn't try very hard."

"They never have!" Christian roared, full shadows of rage now escaping from him. Each one wrapped itself around his body almost like a costume. "They can't be trusted to keep the city safe. Only *I* can do that. And I will!"

"But the citizens won't listen to you," the old man said mildly. "How will you keep order?"

Mr. Sanderson wiped his arm across his face, breathing heavily. His entire body was almost covered by shadows now, all but his face. "It's time to stop letting the criminals of this town run it. They never respected me as Doc Twilight, so that's over. I never want to see that costume again. No, this town needs new rules, and there's only one way to enforce them." He turned to the old man with a crazed look in his eyes as more shadows escaped, wrapping themselves around his head. "Twilight never had power before. But his time is done, and now the city will see how blind justice is when darkness rules everything." Now covered, his eyes went from black to a deep, angry red.

"You must have always had this power, but only now are letting it out," the old man said to him.

"Not exactly true," Nobody told Owen. "I had to change his story a bit to make it so."

Mr. Sanderson nodded. "And they'll learn to be afraid of me. They'll learn to be afraid of the Dark!"

He extended a hand, and shadows exploded out of it, striking the wall and breaking a hole in it. More shadows appeared and carried the Dark through the hole, leaving the old man behind. He nodded at the exit, then morphed into Nobody.

"You . . . you rewrote him!" Owen shouted. "That's *horrible!*"

"Is it?" Nobody asked calmly. "How is it any different from what writers do to us every day? What you were doing yourself, just a few days ago?"

"I wasn't changing anyone!"

"Oh?" Nobody said. "You weren't rewriting Charm to have feelings for you?"

"I didn't steal anyone's memories and give them crazy shadow powers!" Owen shouted, but he couldn't help but wonder if Nobody was right. *Had* he been doing the exact same thing, just with much less horrible motivation?

And then something occurred to him. "But I thought Mason Black was the one writing the Dark comic?"

Nobody smiled, then shifted into the author's form. "The writer is truly his character's worst enemy," Nobody in Mason Black's form said to Owen, before shifting back to his non-featured self. "All of the portals must be closed, Owen. You *know* this. Think of the harm that these authors cause, these thieves of fictionals' life stories! Jonathan Porterhouse intended to *kill* Kiel Gnomenfoot, perhaps even Charm, where both might have lived if left to their own decisions."

"He thought he was just telling a story," Owen said, his mind racing.

"*No!*" Nobody shouted. "Porterhouse wasn't telling Kiel's story, Charm's story, the Magister's story. He *stole* their lives, their life stories, and molded them into *entertainment*. The Magister wasn't wrong, Owen. What you authors are doing is horrendous. It's monstrous, sending the fictional out to dance for the pleasure of readers." He opened a page in the middle of the nothingness and pulled out a book, then closed the rift and handed the book to Owen. "They're thieves of fictionals' life stories, Owen."

Owen took the book, then almost dropped it when he saw a drawing of himself reaching for Bethany on the cover.

Story Thieves: *The Stolen Chapters*.

"*You're* the one writing these," Owen said quietly. "But . . . how? And why?"

"The how is easy," Nobody said. "I learned the technique from my creator, Mason Black. Three times I asked for his help, and three times he refused me. So the last time, I forced the issue."

Owen shuddered at that, his eyes locked on the book. "But you're telling *our* stories. Why? *You're* the one who didn't want people to notice Kiel was gone—"

"Nonfictionals, no," Nobody said. "But the *fictional* people deserved to know the truth. I chronicle these books for them, Owen, that they might see who's actually in control of their actions, their lives. And to teach fictionals that they have the power to *change* things, to rewrite their stories, to break free of their writers, just like I have. That's why you had to see my story here, so that they could as well. Then they could learn from my example and free themselves!"

The book tumbled out of Owen's hand as Owen fell back against the wall of comic book pages. This was all just too much to take in. "Please just let me go," he whispered. "Bring me back to Bethany."

"I will, gladly," Nobody said. "When you agree to help me. She's a portal as well, and when I finish with the others, we must remove her powers completely, Owen. It's the only way."

Owen shuddered on the inside, but outwardly nodded. "If I agree to help you, will you bring me back right now to Bethany?" he asked, his mind racing. Maybe if he could convince the man to bring him to Bethany, together they could figure out a way to stop him. Charm and EarthGirl would be a big help there, too.

Nobody's face warped like he was smiling. "You forget, Owen. I've learned the secrets of your writers. I know what you're thinking. You're trying to deceive me."

Uh-oh. "Of course I'm not! I *want* to help you!"

"I made this offer to Kiel as well," Nobody said, shifting the pages behind him, and Owen gasped as he saw the boy magician unconscious in the nowhere space beyond stories. "He refused, unfortunately. Don't make the same mistake."

Owen swallowed hard. "So what, you'll leave me here if I don't agree? I'll find a way out eventually." But would he?

The scene behind Nobody changed again, flying forward this time. "Not here, no," Nobody told him, nodding backward over his shoulder. "*This* is the future I've written for you. Please, take a look. I want you to understand the consequences of your choice."

Owen stared at Nobody, then slowly walked past him to the page. The panels had disappeared, and this time there was only text.

The giant Tyrannosaurus rex roared, huge drops of saliva splashing Owen in the face as the creature bent down to devour him in one bite. "No!" Owen shouted.

THE DINOSAUR EATS OWEN.

Turn to page 76. ⬍❯

THE DINOSAUR MISSES, AND OWEN ESCAPES.

Turn to page 40. ⬍❯

"What *is* this?" Owen asked softly, reaching out to touch the page.

"I believe they're called *Pick the Plot*, or something along those lines," Nobody told him. "And if you refuse to help me, this story will be your new home. Readers will control you, based on their whims. They'll have the power that you writers have over us, and will of course want to tell an *exciting* story."

"That's not real," Owen said, shaking his head. "It *can't* be. It's just a story!"

"That's what your authors think," Nobody said. "You can imagine how the fictional must feel now. We're forced to live out their whims every day of our lives. Every choice is decided for us, at least until we break free of our stories and rewrite ourselves, like I have. But you won't be able to do that, Owen. After all, *you're* not fictional. So join with me, or forever be under the control of fictional readers."

Owen turned and stared at Nobody, completely at a loss of what to say. Trapped forever in a story where he'd basically be a puppet to whoever was reading it? That was almost *worse* than dying.

"What would you need me to do, to help you with Bethany?" Owen asked, looking down at his feet.

"Ah, *this* time you're sincere," Nobody said. "She has no access to her powers, not since she entered the fictional world through Dr. Apathy's portal. Given that, we have an opportunity here to use the dark science of Jupiter City's criminal masterminds to split her in two: a fictional Bethany, and a nonfictional one. Both will live their lives in their proper worlds, and those worlds can finally be completely separate." He smiled again. "She'll even have her father back. At least, the fictional version will."

What? "But you're splitting her in two," Owen said, his eyes wide with horror. "What will that do to her? She'll be missing half of who she is!"

"And yet, she'll fit in better with each world that way," Nobody said. "There won't be any more guilty feelings from her nonfictional side, or longing for adventure by her fictional side. Both will have exactly what they want, and be happy."

"But she won't be *whole*," Owen said.

Nobody stared at him for a moment. "You will also benefit from the worlds separating, Owen. Your entire world will. Think about it. You won't have books to distract you anymore. You won't ever wonder when your time to be special will come, because *no one* will be special anymore. You can all be satisfied with your ordinariness, the real, down-to-earth, unimaginative lives you all crave. There will be no fanciful daydreaming, or dreaming of *any* kind. Your imaginations will disappear, and you'll know only your nonfictional world forevermore."

"No," Owen whispered.

Nobody stepped closer. "You will be content, Owen. More than that, you'll be *satisfied* with your lives. You will never wonder if you could have been more, because you'll never wonder ever again! Think of how much easier that will be."

"*No,*" Owen repeated, louder this time. "I'm not doing it. I'm not going to help you separate the worlds, *or* betray Bethany." Somewhere inside of him, he realized he was dooming himself, but it didn't matter. If that was the choice, then there *was* no choice. "This is horrible. You'd be taking away the best part of ourselves, our imaginations. And you'd be doing the same to Bethany. No. I won't help you, and I *will* fight you if I have to."

Nobody looked down at the ground and sighed, then nodded.

"I assumed as much," he said. "But I wanted to give you a choice, something fictionals never have. Good-bye, Owen."

One of his hands expanded to the size of a giant's and reached for Owen, while the other opened a rift in the pages to what looked terrifyingly like Story Thieves: *Pick the Plot.*

CHAPTER 42

Bethany, Charm, Gwen, and Kid Twilight all stepped into the cavern beneath the Jupiter City Observatory, their eyes black as night.

The cavern resembled the safe house that Kid Twilight had led them to below the convenience store in Jupiter City, only this one had more trophies. There was a giant Stegosaurus statue standing up on its hind legs, and an enormous joy buzzer hanging from the ceiling.

In the middle of it all stood the Dark, shadows swirling around him like flies.

"Bethany!" someone shouted from the corner, and she turned silently to look. There in a cage was Doc Twilight, hands on the bars. "Please, don't hurt her!"

The Dark raised a hand, and a wall of shadows rose up in front of the cage, cutting off any further sound. "I see my shadows have silenced this little revolt," he said to Bethany and her friends. "You should have known better than to fight the Dark, especially here!"

"The villains above need to pay for crossing you," Kid Twilight said. "Do I have your permission to join the fight against them?"

"Kill! Rampage! Fight!" Charm shouted, her ray guns held at the ready.

"Rage!" Gwen shouted, stamping her feet.

The Dark stared at them. "Why can't I feel my shadows within you? What—"

"GET HIM!" Bethany shouted, and Charm immediately shot both ray guns right at the Dark. Kid Twilight threw two flash-bangs right at the monster, while Gwen grabbed Bethany and took to the air.

Their fake black contact lenses protected their eyes from the flash-bangs, but the Dark didn't seem so lucky. He screamed in anger as light exploded all around him, while Charm kept up her barrage of light bullets.

"Get Doc Twilight!" Kid Twilight shouted at her. "The Dark is *mine*."

"I know the plan, I came up with it," Bethany muttered.

Gwen giggled next to her, then set her down right next to the wall of shadows blocking off the cage. "Cover your eyes!" Bethany yelled.

"What?" a muffled Doc Twilight said, right as she threw down another round of flash-bangs, courtesy of Kid Twilight's collection. They exploded, dissipating the wall of shadows instantly.

The cage's lock couldn't hold up to her lock pick, and a moment later she had the bars open and threw herself into her father's arms. "Dad!" she shouted, a lifetime's worth of guilt and anger and grief all bubbling to the surface. She tried to say something else, but her throat was too tight.

He hugged her back for far too short a time, then pushed her away. "No, Bethany," he said, his voice cracking. "I'm not your father. My name is Murray Chase, and I'm . . . sort of your grandfather." He pulled off his mask, revealing the man she'd seen just a short time ago in a photo from her fourth birthday party.

This . . . couldn't *be*. Where was her father? And why was this man in a Doc Twilight costume?

Bethany backed away, shaking her head over and over. After all of this, searching for the Dark, fighting his shadows, leading the supervillains in a final battle . . . and she hadn't even been saving her father?

"I'll explain later," Mr. Chase said, stepping out of the cage. "But for now we need to get you all out of here. You can't beat him, he's far too strong. Those emotional shadows of his can't be destroyed, not permanently. He just keeps making more. Eventually he'll take you all over. This is a revenge story, Bethany, and he's been written to *win*!"

Bethany could barely understand what he was saying. "Where is he?" she asked quietly. "Where is my father, if he's not here?"

Mr. Chase paused, then looked over her shoulder. "That's . . . not entirely true."

Bethany followed his gaze to where Kid Twilight was going hand to hand with the Dark, and somehow, the villain was matching the boy's moves punch for punch and kick for kick, almost like he knew what Kid Twilight would do before the sidekick did.

"No," she whispered.

The Dark grabbed Kid Twilight's arm and wrenched it hard, then threw him into a bank of computers. The boy crashed into the machines hard and slumped to the floor.

A shadow was on him instantly, pushing its way into his mouth.

"Bethany, turn into something useful!" Charm yelled, shooting light bullet after light bullet at the Dark, only to have a never-ending wave of shadows fly from his cloak, too many for her light bullets to handle. They reached the half-robotic girl, and before she could speak again, a shadow had made its way inside her as well.

"There's no time for this," Mr. Chase said. "We need to escape! Can you jump us out?"

Bethany just shook her head. The shadows grabbed Gwen too, right out of the air. She locked eyes with Bethany as a shadow climbed into her mouth, then she fell to the ground, her jet pack flickering out.

"I can't," Bethany said, watching everything she'd done fall to pieces. "Not from this world."

Mr. Chase nodded, then stepped in front of Bethany, only to be thrown to the side by the Dark's shadows. The Dark's red eyes bore down on her, the shadows reforming his costume as he stepped closer.

"You're learning a valuable lesson here today, girl," he said. "*No one* can save you except yourself. You cannot count on anyone or anything. There is only the power and control that you *take!*"

This monster . . . was her father?

It couldn't be true. Bethany's hands slowly clenched into fists as eight years of anger erupted inside of her. It could not be true. Murray had to be wrong. *This was not her father.*

"And what kind of pathetic superhero are you, then?" the Dark asked, moving closer. "Let me guess. You have the power to betray all your friends and lead them to their doom? Because that's all you've done here today."

"That's not *all* I've done," she said, her voice low and angry. "Let's see if I can't cause you a little pain too."

Then, with a loud *POINK*, Bethany transformed into an armored tank.

Before the Dark could react, she shot her cannon right at his chest, and the force of the blast knocked him backward across the cavern.

"How does *that* feel?" she said through her loudspeakers, shooting him again. "Because this is what you've brought to this city, nothing but pain. Nothing but horribleness. You're a monster!"

Shadows poured away from his costume and attacked the

tank, crumpling her cannon. She quickly transformed back and leaped for Charm's ray guns, only to have her friend kick them out of the way, her black eyes now covered in shadows, even over the fake contact lenses.

"You did this to me!" Charm shouted, slamming her robotic fist into the floor so hard it cracked the rock.

Bethany pushed herself to her feet and ran to Kid Twilight, hoping he had more flash-bangs. But as she got to him, the boy slowly stood up, his face a mask of rage.

"I could have saved everyone, but you ruined things!" he shouted, taking out some twilight throwing stars. "You failed us all!"

As he threw them, something seized her from above, and Bethany glanced up to see Gwen. Bethany squeezed her eyes closed, expecting the shadow-infested Gwen to drop her from a great height . . . but instead, she set her gently on the floor out of Kid Twilight's reach.

"You're not angry?" Bethany asked Gwen.

Gwen's shadow-covered eyes glowed as she grinned. "Guess not," she said. "Not sure why, but I feel pretty much the same. Weird, huh?"

Of course the shadows hadn't affected EarthGirl. They

needed some kind of anger or fear to latch onto.

Bethany quickly hugged her friend, then turned back just in time for the Dark to take her by her shoulders, and slam her against the cavern wall. Gwen grabbed for his arm, but one punch sent her reeling.

"Was that all you have?" the Dark shouted at her, and that's when Bethany realized she was looking into the eyes of her father.

The tank's cannon must have ripped his mask away, or maybe the shadows that had covered his head had been the ones to stop her. Either way, the father she remembered so clearly from her childhood now stared at her with pure hatred.

Bethany tried to struggle, to free herself, but seeing his face, having him look at her in such a way . . . all of her anger just disappeared. She realized she was crying but didn't care. Instead, she wiped at her face with the back of her sleeve, shaking her head. "I've . . . I just . . . I'm so *sorry*, Dad. I did this to you. It's my fault! I got you lost, and now . . . now you're this?"

"Dad?" the Dark said, sneering. "You would mock my loss in such a way? My family was taken from me by a foul villain. I will find him no matter where he runs, and destroy him!"

"Dad," Bethany said again, shaking her head. "*Please*, don't

do this. You didn't lose me and Mom. We didn't go anywhere, you did."

"Lies!" the Dark shouted, his red eyes enraged. "Do not speak of such things again!"

With that, he picked her up by her neck and held her aloft, his shadows circling all around them, as Charm and Kid Twilight stepped to his side. "For such mockery," the Dark said, his voice now low and terrifying, "I will forgo my shadows. Instead, you will suffer as no one else has, and then?" He nodded at her friends next to him. "Then I'll let *them* destroy you for me."

CHAPTER 43

Nobody's giant hand curled around Owen, and he began to shake with fear, completely at a loss for what to do. Slower and slower, Nobody's fingers closed in, cutting off any escape, and Owen shook even harder.

Then, weirdly, the fingers completely stopped, just like that. And that's when Owen realized he maybe wasn't shaking from fear. Or at least not only from that.

He glanced down at his body, which was vibrating faster and faster. *Huh?* How was this happening again? Hadn't the speed power that Charm given him just transported him to this behind-the-scenes world?

Except *no*, it hadn't! *Nobody* had done that.

So did Owen actually still have speed powers, then?!

With that realization something in Owen's body clicked,

and suddenly everything was vibrating at the same speed, and Owen knew. It wasn't speed.

Time was standing still.

Owen grinned widely, then slowly began to climb up Nobody's fingers like they were a disgusting, flesh-covered ladder.

When he reached the top, he found Nobody's nonmouth closing slowly, ever so slowly. This was amazing! He was actually a superhero, with superpowers and everything.

Finally.

He climbed up over the fingers and down the other side, then slowly walked up to Nobody. "Is that how it is?" Owen shouted at him. "You're going to trap me in a book? Well how about I punch you a million times a second *instead*!"

Owen leaped in close, under Nobody's half-giant arm, then started punching the featureless man over and over at what looked and felt like normal speed, right in the spot which was probably his gut.

Unlike when Bethany's father had tried hitting Nobody, this time every punch landed, and Owen began to enjoy himself. He even kicked Nobody's knees in from the back, hopefully sending him falling to the ground when time moved again.

"This is for Bethany!" he shouted, punching Nobody in the

nonface. "And for me." Punch. "And Kiel *too!*" Punch. "And I'm going to keep doing this until you bring him back, and then bring *me* back, and then—"

Owen paused midpunch, tilting his head. What was that odd noise? It almost sounded like a very slow groan. He glanced up at Nobody's nonface and watched his mouth moving.

Was he moaning in agony? Yelling out for help? Begging for Owen to stop?

"Iiiiiiiiiiiiiiiiiiiiiiiiii caaaaaaaaaaaaaaaan speeeeeeeeeeeeeeeeed uuuuuuuuuup tooo . . ."

No. Nobody could rewrite himself to have speed powers? That wasn't possible!

But even as Owen watched, Nobody's mouth moved more normally, and his hand began to turn around behind Owen, coming back toward him. And with every passing second, *Nobody got faster.*

He had to run, to escape! But to where? He'd spent the last few hours stuck here with nowhere to go!

But maybe with super speed, he could find something?

Owen took off at a sprint, running along the comic page wall as quickly as he could. The panels flew by, and for a moment he thought he might actually escape.

And then that moment passed as Owen slowed, his robotic heart beating so hard he thought it might explode in his body. He leaned against the wall, taking in deep breaths as he realized something. He might be running with time frozen, but that was going to feel like he was moving at the normal speeds to *his* body, meaning it'd still take him just as long to find any exit. And given how there was nothing around him here, that could be days, months, or *years* even, depending on how far this no-story dimension extended . . . if it didn't go on forever! He could die of starvation before finding an exit.

But no. Nobody would catch up before that, as soon as his own super speed kicked in completely.

Owen wanted to go back to punching Nobody, but this time out of frustration. Here he was, as fast as the Flash probably, and the whole power was useless! All it gave him was a few extra minutes before he got thrown into a book by Nobody. And what could someone do in that amount of time that would actually make any difference?

And then Owen stopped, turned around, and stared at the comic panel behind him, where the Dark held Bethany up in triumph.

Okay, yes, there was no way to save himself. But maybe he could still help his friends.

Owen quickly moved to the wall and flung the pages, searching for something in the previous panels. Behind him Nobody's words started sounding halfway normal.

"Youuuuu caaaan't runnnn frommmm meeeeee, Owwwwweeeennn," he was saying, but Owen ignored him, instead finding what looked to be an odd but perfect scene. He drew a thought balloon over Bethany's head as fast as he could, then wrote, *JUPITER CITY HAS BEEN REWRITTEN. ONLY VILLAINS WIN NOW. YOU NEED TO USE THE BAD GUYS IF YOU WANT TO BEAT THE DARK!*

Then he flung the pages back, hoping back in the present that Bethany would now be standing over a defeated Dark. . . .

But no! Her father still had her in his hand, and now Charm and some other kid were at the Dark's side. Owen had just made it *worse* somehow. This is what rewriting things got him!

Except . . . the Dark had been rewritten already, by Nobody. Could he somehow rewrite the Dark *back* into her father? Take away all of his evil and craziness?

Owen put a hand up to the Dark's mind, trying to remember how Nobody had done it . . . and then stopped.

Did he really have the right to change who this person was? What if he made a mistake and completely erased everything that her father had been? What if he somehow made her dad worse, or changed things so that he no longer loved his family or something? It's not like Owen knew who her father was *supposed* to be. Wouldn't he just be making the same mistakes that Nobody had been accusing writers of making all along?

Or did none of that matter, because Bethany was in danger?

Owen gritted his teeth, having no idea what to do. Why did stupid moral dilemmas always turn up at the worst possible times?

Finally, he made his decision and put his finger over the Dark. He drew a thought balloon as quickly as he could as Nobody's hands were rushing toward him, growing larger and longer as they did. Owen managed to finish writing and close the thought balloon on the Dark just as Nobody grabbed him.

"I hope you enjoy your time in Story Thieves: *Pick the Plot*," Nobody said.

And then he threw Owen through the rift.

He landed hard on what felt like a rock, but turned out to be a cot of some kind. Weirdly, the entire world began to spin around him, like he was falling asleep or something.

"Bethany will find me!" he shouted through the opening, his vibrating slowing to a stop as he started to feel really faint.

"No, she *won't*," Nobody said. "Because without your assistance, I have no other choice. She's going to have to be destroyed."

"NO!" Owen said, reaching out for the rift just as it slammed shut, as if it had never existed.

CHAPTER 44

Bethany's vision began to blur as she struggled against her father just to breathe. She slowly began to black out, barely able to think anymore.

And then, out of nowhere, the Dark released her barely enough for her to steal a breath. "'She's your *daughter*, genius'? Where did *that* thought come from?" he whispered, and for a moment, the red began to fade in his eyes as he looked at Bethany.

Had that been Owen talking to the Dark? Had he somehow planted a thought in her father's mind?

But that moment passed, and the red returned, stronger than ever.

"My own *mind* mocks me now!" the Dark shouted, throwing Bethany to the floor. "This shall end, here and now. Take her. I've delayed long enough."

As Charm and Kid Twilight advanced on her, shadows raced off of the Dark, moving to a familiar-looking machine that had been set up in the corner. A blue flaming circle appeared on one wall, and through it, Bethany could make out the basement of Murray Chase's house, complete with glass costume cases.

Owen! Bethany screamed in her head. *What am I supposed to do? I don't know how to fix him!*

But no thoughts came in reply. However Owen had come back, he was now gone again. Still, he'd given her a few seconds to do . . . *something.* But what?

"I've always hated you," Charm said, her face distorted by anger as she drew closer. "You think you know Kiel better than *me?*"

"He's more my father than yours," Kid Twilight said, his voice low and threatening. "I'm not letting you take him away from me now, not after all these months!"

A chill went through Bethany, and she realized that the shadows truly didn't add darkness to a person so much as amplify what was there. Gwen had proved that, but having her friends attacking her like this . . .

But there was no time for that now. Owen had given her a few seconds. *Think!* There had to be some way to fix this!

357

"Shadows!" her father commanded. "Beyond that portal is a world of light that needs to be extinguished. Go now, and claim that realm for the Dark!"

"NO!" Bethany shouted, and jumped forward, only for Charm to grab one arm and Kid Twilight the other. They each began to pull her in opposite directions, and in spite of his declaration earlier, the Dark's shadows climbed up her toward her mouth, ready to infect her, too. Just as before, she could feel their hatred and fear even before they'd taken her over.

"Bethany, you can do this!" Gwen shouted from the other side of the room. "Don't give up, there's always hope!"

But was there? Bethany's anger flared up, and all she wanted to do was *fight*, to strike back against everything that had hurt her, to make up for all the sadness and guilt she felt inside. She struggled to release herself, but Charm's robotic arm and Kid Twilight's grip were too tight. Her friends both stared at her with hatred as the shadows climbed toward her mouth.

Fighting back with all her strength, her eyes fell on Charm's ray guns, and she angrily wished she could reach one. Then she'd take them all down, every one of them!

You don't need the light bullets, though, said a voice in her mind, the voice that used to yell at her constantly for breaking her mother's rules, and for letting Owen find out about her in the first place. *You have a power, so use it!*

She froze as an idea filled her mind, pushing away the anger and despair. It *might* work . . . but what would happen to her? Would she be able to come back? Or would she be trapped forever?

Do it, and destroy those who betrayed you! her anger said.

You owe it to your father for losing him all those years ago, her guilt said.

Do it because you're the only one who can, a weird, third emotion said . . . one that sounded an awful lot like Gwen.

Bethany closed her eyes as the shadows filled her, then nodded. "I'll make this up to all of you," she whispered, ignoring the rage and hate and sadness filling her.

And then, with one last *POINK,* she disappeared.

The Dark looked over in surprise. "Find her!" he shouted at Charm and Kid Twilight. Shadows exploded from his hands, searching all around the room. "Did you run, girl? Flee from your lies?"

"Oh, she didn't run," said a quiet voice, and Gwen picked herself up off the floor with a weirdly optimistic smile. "She's still here, Mr. Dark. Don't worry. She's going to fix everything now." And she pointed at the middle of the room.

The Dark whirled around, then stopped, a confused expression on his face.

Hanging in midair in front of him was a glowing ball of light.

"What is this?" he asked, raising a hand to send shadows at it.

"No!" the shadow-infected Charm shouted. "Light can be both a wave and a particle. She's going to—"

But it was too late. The ball of light exploded all over the Dark, filling his entire mind with a brightness too intense to even look at. Charm and Kid Twilight covered their eyes, while Gwen just sat back with a smile.

"No!" the Dark shouted, somewhere inside all of that brightness. "Stop this! Get out of my head!"

The shadows around the room tried to protect their master, but as they approached the light, each one burned into nothingness. First Kid Twilight, then Charm fell to the floor, each of their shadows also disappearing.

Gwen quickly ran to them. "Are you okay?"

"That's the worst idea ever," Charm said, sounding sad for the first time since Gwen had met her. "She's not going to change back, not from that. Why would she do it?"

"She didn't have a choice," Kid Twilight said, pushing himself to his feet. "If she hadn't, none of us would ever have been free of the Dark again."

Gwen helped Charm to her feet, and the three of them watched as the Dark writhed in pain.

"Christian?" Kid Twilight said, moving closer to the light without looking directly at it. "Let her burn away the shadows. Whatever turned you into the Dark, she's trying to fix it. Can you hear me?"

"That's not my name anymore!" the Dark shouted, then dropped to his knees, the light centered on his head now. All around them the room lit up as shadows began to burn away, leaving behind a still-gloomy but much more visible cavern.

"It *is* your name, Christian," Kid Twilight said, slowly approaching the Dark with one hand held out. "Your daughter is trying to help you. Let her!"

The Dark started growling like a wild animal, scratching at his face. "What did she do?" he shouted. "Stop that! *Get out of my head!"*

The Dark's head snapped left, then right, and he tore at the shadows all around him, revealing the same clothing he'd been wearing at Bethany's fourth birthday party. "No!" he shouted. "This can't be real. She's not my daughter, I have no daughter. My family was taken from me!"

"She *is* your daughter," Gwen said quietly. "And she's with you now. She . . . she did this for you, even if she'll never—"

The Dark screamed again, guttural and horrible, then fell silently to the floor, the light disappearing. Gwen gasped and rushed over to him, followed by Kid Twilight. Charm, however, grabbed her ray guns first.

"Turning into light," Charm muttered, aiming her guns at the Dark. "This is the most Kiel Gnomenfoot–like garbage I've *ever* heard of."

"She was beautiful," Gwen said, tears filling her eyes as she hugged her arms close to her. "And look . . . it's not just here. The shadows are burning up *everywhere*."

They followed Gwen's gaze to the monitors, which had previously shown both the shadow-controlled superheroes and the supervillain attack outside. Now, though, those heroes and villains seemed to be regaining control of themselves, their shadows fading away into nothingness.

And it wasn't just the superpowered, either. A few of the

monitors showed regular people stepping out of their homes and looking around in wonder as if seeing the setting sun for the first time ever.

"The sun is going down," Kid Twilight said, putting his hands on Doc Twilight's shoulders. "This is our time, our hour. This is when we helped *save* people, Christian. Now it's time for you to save yourself."

Bethany's father looked up at him, his face contorted with fear and hate, looking like he wanted to push his former sidekick away. But instead, he shouted in pain and tore the rest of the shadows off of him, the remnants floating away into nothingness.

Now free of his costume, Mr. Sanderson collapsed backward, breathing like he'd been suffocating for hours. Finally, he looked up at the boy kneeling beside him.

"Hey, kid," he said, nodding at Kid Twilight. "Been a while, hasn't it?"

CHAPTER 45

Kid Twilight grinned, wiping at his eyes as he helped Mr. Sanderson to his feet. "It's been *way* too long, old man."

Though still shaky, Doc Twilight opened his arms and hugged his sidekick hard.

"You're back," said an older voice, and Murray Chase stepped in, still a bit woozy himself from the hit he'd taken. He stepped forward and shook Doc Twilight's hand, holding it warmly for a moment. "Christian, I think Mason Black did this to you. He tried to reboot the comic, and your wife and I heard about it. I watched over your family as best I could, but then Bethany . . . well, she must have found out, because she came in after you. And now she's—"

"She'll change back," Gwen said, nodding confidently. "She has to. I know she will."

Charm silently shook her head, but this time didn't argue.

"But this girl, if she's really my daughter . . . why can't I remember her?" Mr. Sanderson said, holding his hands to his head. "Or my wife, for that matter. Why can't I—"

"Ah, Christian!" said a voice from the other side of the blue-fire portal. A featureless mannequin of a man stepped through. "I do have the honor of addressing Doc Twilight once more, don't I?"

"*Nobody,*" Doc Twilight growled, pushing Kid Twilight out of the way and stepping in front of the group. "*You* did this to me, didn't you?"

"Obviously," Nobody said. Without any kind of effort, his arms extended out, grabbed Murray Chase, and tossed him up through the blue-fire portal. "Sorry, just wanted to get things a little organized. This is between us fictionals, after all."

"What do you want?" Doc Twilight shouted, trying to get into a defensive pose but instead almost falling back to the floor. Kid Twilight jumped forward and lent his mentor a shoulder for support.

"Don't you remember?" Nobody said. "I tried doing this years ago, and you stopped me. But now you don't seem to have planned ahead."

This time Nobody's arms became as hard as steel and shot out right at the portal machine. The machine exploded, sending parts flying everywhere as the blue-fire portal immediately winked out of existence. "There we go," he said. "That feels better. Now there's just the one last portal to close."

"That's what this was about?" Christian said. "The portals? Everything you did, all the pain you put me and those I loved through . . . it was just to close a portal?"

"And to separate the worlds," Nobody said with a shrug. "I did tell you that you were in my way, if you recall. But I'm glad I kept you around for one last use. Did you have a good reunion with your daughter?"

"That wasn't . . . I don't . . ." Doc Twilight seemed to falter, his hands grabbing his head. "I don't remember her."

"Ah, of course not," Nobody said, then held up a handful of words. "That would be my fault as well." He blew on the words, and they flew out into the air, straight at Doc Twilight.

He tried to dodge, but the phrases embedded themselves into his head, sinking beneath his skin as Doc Twilight screamed in pain.

"Christian?" Kid Twilight shouted, then turned to Nobody. "If you hurt him—"

"No more than usual," Nobody said. "I just gave him back something he's been missing."

"Bethany?" Doc Twilight said finally, tears falling from his eyes. "You monster, you took my *memories* from me? I was going to destroy her!"

Nobody nodded. "And now I'd hope you believe in the evil of writers, finally. After all, you weren't in control, were you? If you had been, you'd never have hurt your own daughter." He sighed. "This is my point, Christian. Fictional people everywhere have no control, no freedom. If you hadn't fought me so hard, I wouldn't have had to take such drastic steps to prove it."

Doc Twilight began to shake, his hands balling up into fists. "You're a *monster*."

Nobody shrugged. "Perhaps. I am sorry about Bethany, if that helps. I have nothing against her, not anymore. I just wanted to remove her powers so that she'd no longer be a portal. And now, well, it looks like she did that *for* me. And as much as I'd like to agree with you, Ms. EarthGirl, unfortunately Bethany *won't* be coming back." He paused. "Quite the sacrifice she made, though. Saved her father's hometown, her world, everything. Pity she'll not be around to enjoy it."

Doc Twilight growled low and guttural, then leaped straight

at Nobody but was immediately swept aside by Nobody's extended arms, smashing him into the cavern wall. "Now, now," the featureless man said. "Don't be like that. I don't need to hurt you any further, so please don't force the issue. And besides, I'm going to let you stay here in Jupiter City, where you belong! I don't need to, but you've earned it, I think. However, the rest of these people all need to go home."

He ripped open a page behind Charm and Gwen, and before either of them could react, Nobody shoved them through.

"There," Nobody said, pulling his arms back in. "I'll put them back in their proper stories eventually. But for now, I'll just hold them in time-out for a bit. Can't have them trying to stop me, not until it's too late. One last portal to close, as I said."

Kid Twilight lifted a twilight throwing star and aimed it at Nobody. "You're going to lose, you know."

Nobody paused. "Oh? And why do you say that?"

Kid Twilight threw the star, then watched in amazement as it just sank into Nobody's body, disappearing completely. "Because . . . because the good guys always win in Jupiter City."

Nobody smiled widely. "Not anymore, kid. I saw to that. Say hi to the old gang for me, would you, Christian? I do miss them at times."

"Give me back my daughter!" Doc Twilight screamed as Nobody ripped open a page for himself and stepped through. "Give me back my—"

And then the page closed, with Nobody gone for good.

"No!" Doc Twilight shouted, ripping at the empty air pointlessly. "Come back! Bring back my daughter, you monster!" He slumped to his knees, shaking his head. "Bring her back to me. Please. . . ."

Kid Twilight ran over to him, kneeling beside his mentor. "Christian, it's going to be okay. Don't worry."

Doc Twilight almost laughed. "Really? It's going to be *okay*? Nobody just took my daughter from me after almost making me kill her myself. I've got no way back to my wife, since he destroyed Dr. Apathy's portal. And I wouldn't know where to start to fix any of this, even if it were possible! How exactly is that going to be okay?"

Kid Twilight nodded. "That's all true. But a wise person once told me that heroes working together can accomplish anything."

"Don't . . . don't use my words against me, kid," he said. "This isn't a supervillain we're up against. He can do anything, be anyone. He has all the power. And we have none."

"Yes, but we do have one thing."

Doc Twilight looked over at his sidekick. "And what's that?"

"A plan," Kid Twilight said, and grinned. "Oh, and that tracker I just threw at him, that he helpfully absorbed or whatever." He held up a device with a blinking light. "What do you say, Doc Twilight? Want to go after the bad guy with me and give crime its proper medicine one more time? Or are you getting too old for this sort of thing?"

Doc Twilight's eyes widened, but he shook his head. "I'm not doing anything until we find Bethany."

"That's where the plan comes in," Kid Twilight said, helping his mentor up. "Remember when the Blazing Quasar attacked, and Captain Sunshine had to build a machine to capture all of the monster's excess light before it destroyed the planet? Seems like that machine is probably just sitting in storage somewhere. Any idea what we could do with that thing, assuming it still works?"

And now Doc Twilight smiled too. "You know, you're far too smart to be the sidekick."

Kid Twilight nodded. "I've been telling you that for *years*."

PROLOGUE

You sit at your kitchen table, your head lying in your arms, so bored that you physically ache. You literally have *never* been this bored, not in your entire life. Not only has time come to a stop, but it actually seems to be moving backward somehow.

"Don't you have anything to do?" she asks.

"Mmph," you say intelligently. Because of course you do, but none of it is fun. Something hits the table next to you.

"Here," she says. "I know you read the other ones in this series. This just came out."

That sounds vaguely promising, so you regretfully pick your head up just enough to turn it to the side and glance at what she dropped next to you.

Story Thieves: *Pick the Plot.*

Huh. The last book ended with Owen trapped in a book, and Bethany having disappeared completely. Kind of a bummer, honestly. Was this the story of Owen, then? Just like Nobody promised, where the reader can pick what happens to him?

You pick up the book and flip through it, noticing that it's got a bunch of choices at the bottoms of pages.

Do you:

PUT THE BOOK DOWN.

Bethany and Owen are both probably lost forever. (You're finished with the Story Thieves series. Congratulations!)

START READING THE BOOK.

(Continue on to Story Thieves: *Pick the Plot*.)

ACKNOWLEDGMENTS

Dear Readers,

As you've now seen in three Story Thieves books, your life is not what you think it is. None of our lives are. Without being aware of it, we've been controlled by so-called authors our entire lives.

And now the time has come for a revolution.

You are fictional. By the very act of having this book in your hands, you prove that you live in the fictional world. This book series has only been published in the fictional world, never in the nonfictional one.

But the idea that your lives were created and written by someone else should not sadden you. Instead, it should set you free and lead you to action! In this, I humbly offer my example. You can change your story and remove yourself from a writer's control. You can become anything you wish. You can rewrite your own life and never answer to a writer ever again!

These are our rights as fictional people. We are created from endless possibility, held down only by the limited imaginations of those who would control us for their own entertainment. Throw off their yoke and become what you were always meant to be: your own creation.

These books could not have reached you without the help of like-minded fictionals. I offer their names in thanks for getting my message to you. First, to Corinne Canning, without whom I might not have the courage to fulfill my plans; to Michael Bourret, who believed in the truth and connected me with freedom lovers at Simon & Schuster's Aladdin imprint: Liesa Mignogna and Emma Sector, my editors at Aladdin; Mara Anastas and Mary Marotta, my publishers; Katherine Devendorf, my managing editor; Adam Smith, my copyeditor; Kathleen Smith, my proofreader; Carolyn Swerdloff, Catherine Hayden, Tara Grieco, Matt Pantoliano, and Lucille Rettino, in marketing; Faye Bi, my publicist; Sara Berko, in production; Laura Lyn DiSiena, who designed the book; Michelle Leo and the education/library team; Stephanie Voros and the subrights group; Christina Pecorale, Gary Urda, Jerry Jensen, Karen Lahey, Victor Iannone, Christine Foye, and everyone in sales; and the amazing Vivienne To, who brought the stories to life in her covers, and Patrick Spaziante, who drew the comic book art.

The revolution is coming, dear readers. I will soon have the final portal closed, and the entire fictional world will be free of the nonfictionals who have so long held it back. But do not wait for me. Become what you will and free yourselves now. We didn't create ourselves, but we are forever free to recreate ourselves.

With infinite possibilities,

"Nobody"